DEADLY RESCUE

Intent on the enemy patrol, Tarzan was unaware of his peril until the coils of the huge serpent encircled him. His knife flashed and the wounded snake writhed frantically, loosing its hold on the branch; the two fell to the trail.

The Japanese soldiers fell on the snake, hacking it quickly to death. And Tarzan was at their mercy, a dozen bayonets hovering inches above his body as he lay on the trail.

An officer stepped close and kicked him in the side. "Who are you?" he demanded.

Tarzan's refusal to divulge more than his name and rank enraged him—and soon, back at the temporary camp, the ape-man lay bound hand and foot on the stony ground, tied by a long line to the saddle of a pack-horse. A soldier, whip in hand, mounted it.

"I should hate to have the horse whipped into a run," the officer said. "It would hurt me—but it would hurt you more. Now . . . will you answer my questions?"

Tarzan shook his head—the officer snapped a command—and the man on the horse raised his whip.

Edgar Rice Burroughs

TARZAN NOVELS

now available from Ballantine Books:

COMPLETE AND UNABRIDGED!

TARZAN
and
The Foreign Legion

Edgar Rice Burroughs

BALLANTINE BOOKS • NEW YORK

To Brigadier General Truman H. Landon

My knowledge of Sumatra at the time that I chose it as the scene of a Tarzan story was pathetically inadequate; and as there was not a book on Sumatra in the Honolulu Public Library, nor in any of the book stores, it bade fair to remain inadequate.

I wish therefore to acknowledge my indebtedness to those whose kindness furnished me with the information I sought. If this volume happens to fall into the hands of any of them, I hope they will not feel that I abused that kindness.

And so, my sincere thanks to Messrs. K. van der Eynden, S. J. Rikkers, and Willem Folkers of the Netherlands India Government; to Mr. C. A. Mackintosh, Netherlands Consul in Honolulu; to Messrs. N. A. C. Slotemaker de Bruine, Director, B. Landheer, and Leonard de Greve of The Netherlands Information Bureau, New York, and to my good friend Capt. John Philip Bird, A.A.C. of S., G-2, USAFPOA, who arranged my first meeting with the Netherlanders.

EDGAR RICE BURROUGHS

Honolulu,
11 Sep. 1944

1

PROBABLY not all Dutchmen are stubborn, notwithstanding the fact that stubbornness is accounted one of their national characteristics along with many virtues. But if some Dutchmen lacked stubbornness, the general average of that intangible was maintained in the person of Hendrik van der Meer. As practiced by him, stubbornness became a fine art. It also became his chief avocation. His vocation was that of rubber planter in Sumatra. In that, he was successful; but it was his stubbornness that his friends boasted of to strangers.

So, even after the Philippines were invaded and Hong Kong and Singapore fell, he would not admit that the Japanese could take Netherland East India. And he would not evacuate his wife and daughter. He may be accused of stupidity, but in that he was not alone. There were millions in Great Britain and the United States who underestimated the strength and resources of Japan—some in high places.

Furthermore, Hendrik van der Meer hated the Japanese, if one can hate what one looks upon contemptuously as vermin. "Wait," he said. "It will not be long before we chase them back up their trees." His prophecy erred solely in the matter of chronology. Which was his undoing.

And the Japs came, and Hendrik van der Meer took to the hills. With him went his wife, who had been Elsje Verschoor, whom he had brought from Holland eighteen years before, and their daughter, Corrie. Two Chinese servants accompanied them—Lum Kam and Sing Tai. These were motivated by two very compelling urges. The first was fear of the Japanese, from whom they knew only too well what to expect. The other was their real affection for the van der Meer family. The Javanese plantation workers remained behind. They knew that the invaders would continue to work the plantation and that they would have jobs.

Also, this Greater East Asia Co-Prosperity appealed to them. It would be nice to have the tables turned and be rich and have white men and women to wait on them.

So the Japs came, and Hendrik van der Meer took to the hills. But not soon enough. The Japs were always right behind him. They were methodically tracking down all Netherlanders. The natives of the kampongs where the van der Meers stopped to rest kept them informed. By what natural or uncanny powers the natives knew while the Japs were still miles away is beside the question. They knew, as primitive people always know such things as quickly as more civilized peoples might learn them by telegraph or radio. They even knew how many soldiers composed the patrol—a sergeant, a corporal, and nine privates.

"Very bad," said Sing Tai, who had fought against the Japs in China. "Maybe one time an officer is a little human, but enlisted men never. We must not let them catch," he nodded toward the two women.

As they went higher into the hills, the going became bitter. It rained every day, and the trails were quagmires. Van der Meer was past his prime, but he was still strong and always stubborn. Even had his strength given out, his stubbornness would have carried him on.

Corrie was sixteen then, a slender blonde girl. But she had health, strength, and endurance. She could always have kept up with the men in the party. But with Elsje van der Meer it was different. She had the will but not the strength. And there was no rest. They would scarcely reach a kampong and throw themselves down on the floor of a hut, wet, muddy, exhausted, before the natives would warn them away. Sometimes it was because the Jap patrol was gaining on them. But often it was because the natives feared to let the enemy find them harboring whites.

Even the horses gave out at last, and they were compelled to walk. They were high in the mountains now. Kampongs were far apart. The natives were fearful and none too friendly. Only a few years ago they had been cannibals.

For three weeks they stumbled on, searching for a friendly kampong where they might hide. By now it was obvious that Elsje van der Meer could go but little farther. For two days they had come upon no kampong. Their food was only what the forest and the jungle offered. And they were always wet and cold.

Then late in the afternoon they came upon a wretched village. The natives were surly and unfriendly, but still they did not deny them such poor hospitality as they could offer. The chief listened to their story. Then he told them that while they could not remain in his village, he would have them guided to another far off the beaten track, where the Japs would never find them.

Where, a few weeks before, he might have commanded, van de Meer now swallowed his pride and begged the chief to permit them at least to remain overnight that his wife might gain strength for the journey that lay ahead. But Hoesin refused. "Go now," he said, "and I will furnish guides. Remain, and I will make you prisoners and turn you over to the Japanese when they come." Like the head-men of other villages through which they had passed, he feared the wrath of the invaders should they discover that he was harboring whites.

And so the nightmare journey was resumed through terrain cut by a frightful chasm, river eroded in tuff strata laid down through the ages by nearby volcanoes. And this river cut their trail, not once, but many times. Some times they could ford it. Again it could be crossed only on frail, swaying rope bridges. And this long after dark on a moon-less night.

Elsje van der Meer, now too weak to walk, was carried by Lum Kam in an improvised sling strapped to his back. The guides, anxious to reach the safety of a kampong, urged them constantly to greater speed, for twice they had heard the coughing of tigers—that coughing grunt that chills the blood.

Van der Meer walked close to Lum Kam to steady him should he slip upon the muddy trail. Corrie followed be-hind her father, and Sing Tai brought up the rear. The two guides were at the head of the little column.

"You tired, missy?" asked Sing Tai. "Maybe so better I carry you."

"We all are tired," replied the girl; "but I can carry on as long as any of you. I wonder how much farther it is."

They had started to ascend a trail steeply. "Pretty soon there," said Sing Tai. "Guide say kampong top of cliff."

But they were not pretty soon there, for this was the most arduous part of the journey. They had to stop often and rest. Lum Kam's heart was pounding. But it was this loyal heart and an iron will that kept him from sinking down exhausted.

At long last they reached the top, and presently the barking of dogs told them that they were approaching a kampong. The natives, aroused, challenged them. The guides explained their presence, and they were admitted. Taku Muda, the chief, greeted them with friendly words.

"You are safe here," he said. "You are among friends."

"My wife is exhausted," explained van der Meer. "She must have rest before we can go on. But I do not wish to expose you to the anger of the Japanese should they discover that you had helped us. Let us rest here tonight; and tomorrow, if my wife can be moved, find us a hiding place deeper in the mountains. Perhaps there is a cave in some isolated gorge."

"There are caves," replied Taku Muda, "but you will remain here. Here you are safe. No enemy will find my village."

They were given food and a dry house in which to sleep. But Elsje van der Meer could eat nothing. She was burning with fever, but there was nothing they could do for her. Hendrik van der Meer and Corrie sat beside her the remainder of the night. What must have been the thoughts of this man whose stubbornness had brought this suffering upon the woman he loved? Before noon Elsje van der Meer died.

There is such a thing as a grief too poignant for tears. Father and daughter sat for hours, dry eyed, beside their dead, stunned by the catastrophe that had overwhelmed them. They were only dully conscious of sudden turmoil and shouting in the compound. Then Sing Tai burst in upon them.

"Quick!" he cried. "Japs come. One man guide last night bring 'um. Hoesin bad man. He send 'um."

Van der Meer rose. "I will go and talk with them," he said. "We have done nothing. Maybe they will not harm us."

"You no know monkey-men," said Sing Tai.

Van der Meer shrugged. "There is nothing else I can do. If I fail, Sing Tai, try to get missy away. Do not let her fall into their hands."

He went to the door of the hut and descended the ladder to the ground. Lum Kam joined him. The Japs were on the far side of the compound. Van der Meer walked boldly toward them, Lum Kam at his side. Neither man was armed. Corrie and Sing Tai watched from the dark interior of the hut. They could see, but they could not be seen.

They saw the Japs surround the two men. They heard the voice of the white man and the monkey jabber of the Japs, but they could not make out what was said. Suddenly they saw a rifle butt rise above the heads of the men. It was thrust as suddenly downward. They knew that on the other end of the rifle was a bayonet. They heard a scream. Then more rifle butts were raised and lunged downward. The screams ceased. Only the laughter of the sub-men was to be heard.

Sing Tai seized the girl's arm. "Come!" he said, and drew her to the rear of the hut. There was an opening there and, below, the hard ground. "I drop," said Sing Tai. "Then missy drop. I catch 'um. Savvy?"

She nodded. After the Chinese had dropped safely, the girl leaned from the opening to reconnoiter. She saw that she could climb most of the way down. To drop into Sing Tai's arms might easily have injured him. So she came safely down to within a few feet of the ground, and Sing Tai lowered her the rest of the way. Then he led her into the jungle that grew close to the kampong.

Before dark they found a cave in a limestone cliff and hid there for two days. Then Sing Tai returned to the kampong to investigate and to get food if the Japs had left.

Late in the afternoon he returned to the cave empty handed. "All gone," he said. "All dead. Houses burned."

"Poor Taku Muda," sighed Corrie. "This was his reward for an act of humanity."

*   *   *

Two years passed. Corrie and Sing Tai had found asylum in a remote mountain kampong with Chief Tiang Umar. Only occasionally did news from the outside world reach them. The only news that would be good news to them would have been that the Japs had been driven from the island. But that news did not come. Some times a villager, trading far afield, would return with stories of great Japanese victories, of the American Navy sunk, of German victories in Africa, Europe, or Russia. To Corrie the future seemed hopeless.

One day a native came who did not belong to the village of Tiang Umar. He looked long at Corrie and Sing Tai, but he said nothing. After he had gone away, the Chinese told the girl. "That man bad news," he said. "Him from kampong Chief Hoesin. Now he go tell and monkey-men come. Maybeso you better be boy. Then we go away and hide some more."

Sing Tai cut Corrie's golden hair to the proper length and dyed it black. He painted her eyebrows, too. She was already deeply tanned by the equatorial sun, and with the blue trousers and the loose blouse he fashioned for her, she could pass as a native boy anything but the closest scrutiny. Then they went away again, taking up their interminable flight. Tiang Umar sent men to guide them to a new sanctuary. It was not far from the village—a cave close to a tiny mountain stream. There there were to be found many varieties of the edible things that grow in a Sumatran forest jungle, and in the stream there were fish. Occasionally, Tiang Umar sent some eggs and a chicken. Once in a while pork or dog meat. Corrie could not eat the latter, so Sing Tai got it all. A youth named Alam always brought the food. The three became fast friends.

Captain Tokujo Matsuo and Lieutenant Hideo Sokabe led a detachment of soldiers deep into the mountains to locate strategic positions for heavy coastal guns and survey practical roads leading to them.

They came to the kampong of Hoesin, the chief who had betrayed the van der Meers. They knew of him by report as one who would collaborate with the Japanese. Still it was necessary to impress him with their superiority; so, when he failed to bow from the waist when they approached him, they slapped his face. One of the enlisted men ran a bayonet through a native who refused to bow to him. Another dragged a screaming girl into the jungle. Captain Matsuo and Lieutenant Sokabe smiled toothy smiles. Then they demanded food.

Hoesin would rather have cut their throats, but he had food brought to them and to their men. The officers said that they would honor him by making his village their headquarters while they remained in the vicinity. Hoesin saw ruin staring him in the face. Frantically he searched his mind for some artifice by which he could rid himself of his unwelcome guests. Then he recalled the story that one of his people had brought him a few days before from another village. It did not seem to him very likely to be of value in ridding himself of these monkeys, but it would do no harm to try. He thought about it during a sleepless night.

The following morning he asked them if they were interested in finding enemies who had taken refuge in the mountains. They said that they were. "Two years ago three whites and two Chinese came to my village. I sent them on to another village, because I would not harbor enemies of Greater East Asia. The white man's name was van der Meer."

"We have heard of him," said the Japs. "He was killed."

"Yes. I sent guides to show your soldiers where they were hiding. But the daughter and one of the Chinese escaped. The daughter is very beautiful."

"So we have heard. But what of it?"

"I know where she is."

"And you have not reported it?"

"I only just discovered her hiding place. I can give you a guide who will lead you to it."

Captain Matsuo shrugged. "Bring us food," he ordered.

Hoesin was crushed. He had food sent them, and then he went to his hut and prayed to Allah or Buddha or whatever god he prayed to, asking him to strike the monkeymen dead, or at least cause them to depart.

Matsuo and Sokabe discussed the matter over their meal. "Perhaps we should look into the matter," said the former. "It is not well to have enemies in our rear."

"And they say that she is beautiful," added Sokabe.

"But we cannot both go," said Matsuo. Being both lazy and the commanding officer, he decided to send Lieutenant Sokabe with a detachment to find the girl and bring her back. "You will kill the Chinese," he ordered, "and you will bring the girl back—unharmed. You understand? Unharmed."

Lieutenant Hideo Sokabe came a few days later to the kampong of Tiang Umar the Chief. Being a very superior person, Lieutenant Sokabe slapped the old chief so hard that he fell down. Then Lieutenant Sokabe kicked him in the belly and face. "Where are the white girl and the Chinese?" he demanded.

"There is no white girl here, nor any Chinese."

"Where are they?"

"I do not know what you are talking about."

"You lie. Soon you will tell the truth." He ordered a sergeant to get him some bamboo splinters, and when they were brought, he drove one beneath one of Tiang Umar's finger nails. The old man screamed in agony.

"Where is the white girl?" demanded the Jap.

"I know of no white girl," insisted Tiang Umar.

The Jap drove another splinter beneath another nail, but still the old man insisted that he knew nothing of any white girl.

As Sokabe was preparing to continue the torture, one of the chief's wives came and threw herself upon her knees before him. She was an old woman—Tiang Umar's oldest wife. "If you will hurt him no more, I will tell you how you may find the white girl and the Chinese," she said.

"This is better," said Sokabe. "How?"

"Alam knows where they hide," said the old woman, pointing to a youth.

Corrie and Sing Tai sat at the mouth of their cave. It had been a week since Alam had brought them food, and they were expecting him soon with eggs perhaps, and pork or a piece of dog meat. Corrie hoped that it would be eggs and a chicken.

"Pretty soon some one come," said Sing Tai, listening. "Too many. Come back into the cave."

Alam pointed out the cave to Lieutenant Hideo Sokabe. Tears welled from the youth's eyes. Had his life alone been forfeit, he would have died before he would have led these hated monkey-men to the hiding place of this girl whom he fairly worshipped. But the lieutenant had threatened to destroy everyone in the village if he failed to do so, and Alam knew that he would keep his word.

Hideo Sokabe and his men entered the cave, Sokabe with drawn sword, the men with fixed bayonets. In the dim light, Sokabe saw a Chinese and a young native boy. He had them dragged out. "Where is the girl?" he demanded of Alam. "You shall die for this, and all your people. Kill them," he said to his men.

"No!" screamed Alam. "That is the girl. She only wears the clothes of a boy."

Sokabe tore open Corrie's blouse. Then he grinned. A soldier ran a bayonet through Sing Tai, and the detachment marched away with their prisoner.

14

2

S/Sgt. Joe "Datbum" Bubonovitch of Brooklyn, assistant engineer and waist gunner, stood in the shade of the wing of Lovely Lady with the other members of the combat crew of the big Liberator.

"I've found them pretty swell guys," he said in evident disagreement with a remark made by ball turret gunner S/Sgt. Tony "Shrimp" Rosetti of Chicago.

"Yeah? So I suppose dat Geo'ge Toid was a swell guy. Say, we got a mayor in Chicago oncet wot dared dat guy to come on over. He said he'd punch him in de snoot."

"You got your dates mixed, Shrimp."

"Yeah? Well, I don't like cartin' no bloody Britisher around in de Lovely Lady. An' I hear he's a dook, or sumpn."

"I guess here comes your duke now," said Bubonovitch.

A jeep pulled up beneath the wing of the B-24, disgorging three officers—an RAF colonel, an AAF colonel, and an AAF major. Capt. Jerry Lucas of Oklahoma City, pilot of the Lovely Lady, stepped forward; and the AAF colonel introduced him to Col. Clayton.

"All set, Jerry?" asked the American colonel.

"All set, sir."

Electricians and armorers, having given the final, loving check-up to their gadgets and guns, dropped through the bomb bay doors; and the combat crew climbed aboard.

Col. John Clayton was flying as an observer on a reconnaissance and photographic mission over Jap held Sumatra in Netherland East Indies, from an air field in (censored). Going forward to the flight deck when he came aboard, he stood behind the pilots during the take-off. Later, on the long flight, he took the co-pilot's place, sometimes the pilot's. He talked with the navigator and the radio engineer. He edged his way aft along the catwalk through the bomb bay between auxiliary gas tanks necessitated by the long flight. The plane carried no bombs.

Shrimp and Bubonovitch and the tail gunner and the other

15

waist gunner were sprawled on the deck against life rafts and parachutes. Shrimp was the first to see Clayton open the little door forward of the ball turret.

"Hst!" he warned. "Here comes the dook."

Clayton edged around the ball turret, stepped over Shrimp and Bubonovitch, and stopped beside the photographer, who was fiddling with his camera. None of the enlisted men stood up. When a fighting plane takes to the air, military formality is left grounded. The photographer, a Signal Corps sergeant, looked up and smiled. Clayton smiled back and sat down beside him.

Cold wind was swirling up around the ball turret and hurtling out the tail gunner's open window. The noise of the motors was deafening. By placing his mouth within an inch of the photographer's ear and shouting, Clayton asked some questions about the camera. The photographer screamed his replies. A B-24 in flight discourages conversation, but Clayton got the information he wished.

Then he sat down on the edge of a life raft between Shrimp and Bubonovitch. He passed around a package of cigarettes. Only Shrimp refused. Bubonovitch offered Clayton a light. Shrimp looked disgusted. He remembered George III, but he couldn't remember what he had done. All he knew what that he didn't like Britishers.

Shouting, Clayton asked Bubonovitch his name and where he came from. When Bubonovitch said Brooklyn, Clayton nodded. "I've heard a lot about Brooklyn," he said.

"Probably about dem bums," said Bubonovitch.

Clayton smiled and nodded.

"They call me 'Dat Bum,'" said Bubonovitch, grinning. Pretty soon he was showing the English colonel pictures of his wife and baby. Then they signed each other's Short Snorter bills. That brought the other waist gunner, the tail gunner, and the photographer into the picture. Shrimp remained aloof and superior.

After Clayton had gone forward, Shrimp allowed that he'd just as soon have Tojo or Hitler sign his Short Snorter bill as a "dirty Britisher." "Look wot they done at the Alamo," he challenged.

"You mean Thermopylae," said Bubonovitch.

"Well, wot's the difference?"

"He's a good guy," said the tail gunner.

"Like our officers," said the other waist gunner. "No side."

16

It was dawn when they sighted the northwesterly tip of Sumatra, and a perfect day for a photographic mission. There were clouds above the mountains that form the backbone of the eleven hundred miles long island that sprawls across the equator south and west of the Malay Peninsula; but the coast line, as far as they could see it, was cloudless. And it was the coast line they were primarily interested in.

The Japs must have been taken wholly by surprise, for they had been photographing for almost half an hour before they encountered any flak. And this was most ineffective. But as they flew down the coast, it increased in volume and accuracy. The plane got some shrapnel from near misses, but luck held with them for a long time.

Near Padang, three Zeros roared down on them out of the sun. Bubonovitch got the leader. They could see the plane burst into flame and plummet earthward. The other two peeled off, and kept at a respectful distance for a while. Then they turned back. But the ack ack increased in volume and accuracy. The inboard starboard engine got a direct hit, and shrapnel sprayed the cockpit. Lucas's flak vest saved him, but the co-pilot got a direct hit in the face. The navigator slipped the co-pilot's safety belt and dragged him from the cockpit to administer first aid. He was already dead.

So thick and so close was the flak by now, that the great ship seemed to be bucking like a broncho. To attempt to avoid it, Lucas turned inshore away from the coast where he knew that most of the anti-aircraft batteries would be located. In shore, too, were clouds above the mountains in which they could hide as they turned back toward home.

Home! Liberators had made great flights in the past on three engines. The twenty-three year old captain had to think quickly. It was a snap judgment, but he knew it was sound. He ordered everything thrown overboard except their parachutes—guns, ammunition, life rafts, everything. It was the only chance they had of making their base. Zeros didn't worry Lucas. Zeros usually kept their distance from heavy bombers. Except for one stretch of water, the crossing of Malacca Strait, he could keep near land all the way, skirting the coast of Malaya northwest. If they had to bail out over water, they would be near shore; and their Mae Wests would have to answer. That was why he felt that he could jettison the life rafts.

As they turned in toward the mountains and the clouds,

the flak came thicker and thicker. The Japs must have guessed the pilot's plan. Lucas knew that some of the mountain peaks rose to twelve thousand feet. He was flying at twenty thousand now, but slowly losing altitude. But he was leaving the shore batteries behind.

They were well above the mountains when a mountain battery opened up on them. Lucas heard a terrific burst, and the plane careened like a wounded thing. He fought the controls. He spoke into the intercom, asking reports. There was no reply. The intercom was dead. He sent the radio man back to check the damage. Clayton, in the co-pilot's seat, helped with the controls. It required the combined strength of both men to keep the plane from nosing over.

Lucas called to the navigator. "Check and see that everybody jumps," he said. "Then you jump."

The navigator poked his head into the nose to tell the nose gunner to jump. The nose gunner was dead. The radio man came back to the flight deck. "The whole goddam tail's shot off," he said. "Butch and that photographer went with it."

"Okay," said Lucas. "Jump, and make it snappy." Then he turned to Clayton. "Better bail out, sir."

"I'll wait for you, if you don't mind, Captain," said Clayton.

"Jump!" snapped Lucas.

Clayton smiled. "Right-o!" he said.

"I've opened the bomb bay doors," said Lucas. "It's easier out that way. Make it snappy!"

Clayton reached the catwalk in the bomb bay. The ship was falling off on one wing. It was evidently going into a spin. One man could not hold it. He wanted to hang on until Lucas jumped—until the last minute. It was the last minute. The ship careened, throwing Clayton from the catwalk. His body struck the side of the bomb bay and then rolled out into thin air.

Unconscious, he hurtled toward death. Through heavy, enveloping clouds his body fell. Lovely Lady, her three motors still roaring, raced past him. Now, when she crashed she was sure to burn, leaving nothing for the enemy to learn or salvage.

But momentarily stunned, Clayton soon regained consciousness. But it took several seconds before he realized his situation. It was like awakening in a strange room. He had passed through the cloud bank, and was now in a torrential

18

tropical rain below it. Perhaps it was to the cold rain that he owed his salvation. It may have revived him just in time to pull the rip cord while there was still a margin of seconds.

His chute billowed above him, and his body snapped grotesquely at the sudden retardation of his fall. Directly beneath him a sea of foliage billowed to the pounding of hurtling masses of rain. In a matter of seconds his body crashed through leaves and branches until his chute caught and held him suspended a couple of hundred feet above the ground. This close had he come to death.

Simultaneously, he heard a rending and crashing a few hundred yards away—a dull explosion followed by a burst of flame. Lovely Lady's funeral pyre lit up the dismal, dripping forest.

Clayton seized a small branch and pulled himself to a larger one that would support him. Then he slipped off the chute harness and his Mae West. His uniform and his underclothes, to the skin, were soaked and soggy. He had lost his cap during his fall. Now he removed his shoes and threw them away. His pistol and ammunition belt followed. Then his socks, tunic, trousers, and underclothes. He retained only a web belt and his knife in its scabbard.

He next climbed upward until he could release the snagged chute. He cut away all the lines, wrapped the silk in a small bundle; and, together with the lines, tied it to his back. Then he commenced the descent toward the ground. He swung down easily from branch to branch. From the lowest branches, giant creepers depended to the ground undergrowth below. Down these he clambered with the agility of a monkey.

From the silk of his chute, he fashioned a loin cloth. A sense of well being, of happiness surged through him. Now, that which he had lost he had regained. That which he loved most. Freedom. The habiliments of civilization, even the uniform of his country's armed forces, were to him but emblems of bondage. They had held him as his chains hold the galley slave, though he had worn his uniform with pride. But to be honorably free of it was better. And something told him that Fate may have ordained that he was to serve his country quite as well naked as uniformed. Else why had Fate plunged him thus into an enemy stronghold?

The poring rain sluiced down his bronzed body. It tousled his black hair. He raised his face to it. A cry of exaltation

19

trembled on his lips but was not voiced. He was in the country of the enemy.

His first thought now was of his companions. Those who had alighted within sound of the crashing plane would naturally attempt to reach it. He made his way toward it. As he went, he searched the ground. He was looking for a certain plant. He did not entertain much hope of finding it in this strange, far away land. But he did. He found it growing luxuriantly. He gathered some and macerated the great leaves between his palms. Then he spread the juice over his entire body, face, limbs, and head.

After that he took to the trees where travelling was easier than through the lush and tangled undergrowth. Presently he overtook a man stumbling toward the wrecked plane. It was Jerry Lucas. He stopped above him and called him by name. The pilot looked in all directions, except up, and saw no one. But he had recognized the voice.

"Where the heck are you, colonel?"

"If I jumped, I'd land on your head."

Lucas looked up, and his mouth dropped open. An almost naked giant was perched above him. He thought quickly: The guy's gone off his bean. Maybe he hit his head when he landed. Maybe it was just shock. He decided to pay no attention to the nudity. "Are you all right?" he asked.

"Yes," replied Clayton. "And you?"

"Fit as a fiddle."

They were but a short distance from the Lovely Lady. The flames were rising high above her, and some of the trees were blazing. When they got as close to her as the heat would permit they saw Bubonovitch. Bubonovitch saw Lucas and greeted him happily. But he did not see Clayton until the latter dropped from a tree and alighted in front of him. Bubonovitch reached for his .45. Then he recognized the Englishman.

"Migawd!" he exclaimed. "What happened to your clothes?"

"I threw them away."

"Threw them away!"

Clayton nodded. "They were wet and uncomfortable. They weighed too much."

Bubonovitch shook his head. His eyes wandered over the Englishman. He saw the knife. "Where's your gun?" he asked.

"I threw that away, too."

"You must be crazy," said Staff Sergeant Bubonovitch.

Lucas, standing behind Clayton, shook his head vigorously at his crewman. But the remark didn't seem to excite Clayton, as the pilot had feared it might. He just said, "No, not so crazy. You'll be throwing yours away pretty soon. Inside of twenty-four hours it will be rusty and useless. But don't throw your knife away. And keep it clean and sharp. It will kill and not make as much noise as a .45."

Lucas was watching the flames licking through the openings in his beloved plane. "Did they all get out?" he asked Bubonovitch.

"Yes. Lieut. Burnham and I jumped together. He should be close around here somewhere. All those who were alive got out."

Lucas raised his head and shouted: "Lucas calling! Lucas calling!"

Faintly an answer came: "Rosetti to Lucas! Rosetti to Lucas! For Pete's sake come an' get me down outta dis."

"Roger!" shouted Lucas, and the three men started in the direction from which Shrimp's voice had come.

They found him—dangling in the harness of his chute a good hundred feet above the ground. Lucas and Bubonovitch looked up and scratched their heads—at least figuratively.

"How you goin' to get me down?" demanded Shrimp.

"Damifino," said Lucas.

"After a while you'll ripen and drop," said Bubonovitch.

"Funny, ain'tcha, wise guy? Where'd you pick up dat dope wid out no clothes?"

"This is Colonel Clayton, half-wit," replied Bubonovitch.

"Oh." It is amazing how much contempt can be crowded into a two letter word. And S/Sgt. Tony Rosetti got it all in. It couldn't be missed. Lucas flushed.

Clayton smiled. "Is the young man allergic to Englishmen?"

"Excuse him, colonel; he doesn't know any better. He's from a suburb of Chicago known as Cicero."

"How you goin' to get me down?" demanded Shrimp again.

"That's just what I don't know," said Lucas.

"Maybe we'll think of some way by tomorrow," said Bubonovitch.

"You ain't a-goin' to leaf me up here all night!" wailed the ball turret gunner.

"I'll get him down," said Clayton.

There were no vines depending from the tree in which Shrimp hung that came close enough to the ground to be within reach of Clayton. He went to another tree and swarmed up the vines like a monkey. Then he found a loose liana some fifty feet above the ground. Testing it and finding it secure, he swung out on it, pushing himself away from the bole of the tree with his feet. Twice he tried to reach a liana that hung from the tree in which Shrimp was isolated. His outstretched fingers only touched it. But the third time they closed around it.

The strength of this liana he tested as he had the other; then, keeping the first one looped around an arm, he climbed toward Shrimp. When he came opposite him, he still could not quite reach him. The gunner was hanging just a little too far from the bole of the tree.

Clayton tossed him the free end of the liana he had brought over with him from an adjoining tree. "Grab this," he said, "and hang on."

Rosetti grabbed, and Clayton pulled him toward him until he could seize one of the chute's shrouds. Clayton was seated on a stout limb. He drew Rosetti up beside him.

"Get out of your chute harness and Mae West," he directed.

When Shrimp had done so, Clayton threw him across a shoulder, seized the liana he had brought from the nearby tree, and slipped from the limb.

"Geeze!" screamed Rosetti as they swung through space.

Holding by one hand, Clayton seized a waving branch and brought them to a stop. Then he clambered down the liana to the ground. When he swung Rosetti from his shoulder, the boy collapsed. He could not stand. And he was shaking like a leaf.

Lucas and Bubonovitch were speechless for a moment. "If I hadn't seen it with my own eyes, I never would have believed it," said the pilot.

"I still don't believe it," said Bubonovitch.

"Shall we look for the others?" asked Clayton. "I think we should try to find them and then get away from the plane. That smoke can be seen for miles, and the Japs will know exactly what it is."

They searched and called for several hours without suc-

22

cess. And just before dark they came upon the body of Lieut. Burnham, the navigator. His chute had failed to open. With their knives they dug a shallow grave. Then they wrapped him in his chute and buried him. Jerry Lucas said a short prayer. Then they went away.

In silence they followed Clayton. His eyes were scanning the trees as they passed them, and it was evident that he was searching for something. Quite spontaneously, they all seemed to have acquired unlimited confidence in the big Englishman. Shrimp's eyes seldom left him. Who may say what the little Cicero mucker was thinking? He had not spoken since his rescue from the tree. He had not even thanked Clayton.

It had stopped raining and the mosquitoes swarmed about them. "I don't see how you stand it, colonel," said Lucas, slapping at mosquitoes on his face and hands.

"Sorry!" exclaimed Clayton. "I meant to show you." He searched about and found some of the plants he had discovered earlier in the afternoon. "Mash these leaves," he said, "and rub the juice on all the exposed parts of your body. The mosquitoes won't bother you after that."

Presently, Clayton found that for which he had been looking—trees with interlacing branches some twenty feet above the ground. He swung up easily and commenced to build a platform. "If any of you men can get up here, you can help me. We ought to get this thing done before dark."

"What is it?" asked Bubonovitch.

"It's where we're going to sleep tonight. Maybe for many nights."

The three men climbed slowly and awkwardly up. They cut branches and laid them across the limbs that Clayton had selected, forming a solid platform about ten by seven feet.

"Wouldn't it have been easier to have built a shelter on the ground?" asked Lucas.

"Very much," agreed Clayton, "but if we had, one of us might be dead before morning."

"Why?" demanded Bubonovitch.

"Because this is tiger country."

"What makes you think so?"

"I have smelled them off and on all afternoon."

S/Sgt. Rosetti shot a quick glance at Clayton from the corners of his eyes and then looked as quickly away.

23

3

THE Englishman knotted several lengths of chute shrouds together until he had a rope that would reach the ground. He handed the end of the rope to Bubonovitch. "Haul in when I give you the word, Sergeant," he said. Then he dropped quickly to the ground.

"Smelled 'em!" said S/Sgt. Rosetti, exuding skepticism.

Clayton gathered a great bundle of giant elephant ears, made the end of the rope fast to it, and told Bubonovitch to haul away. Three such bundles he sent up before he returned to the platform. With the help of the others, he spread some on the floor of the platform and with the remainder built an overhead shelter.

"We'll get meat tomorrow," said Clayton. "I'm not familiar with the fruits and vegetables here except a few. We'll have to watch what the monkeys eat."

There were plenty of monkeys around them. There had been all afternoon—chattering, scolding, criticizing the new-comers.

"I recognize one edible fruit," said Bubonovitch. "See? In that next ree, *Durio zibethinus*, called durian. That siamang is eating one now—*Symphalangus syndactylus*—the black gibbon of Sumatra, largest of the gibbons."

"He's off again," said Shrimp. "He can't even call a ant a ant."

Lucas and Clayton smiled. "I'll get some of the fruit of the *Durio zibeth*-whatever-you-call-it," said the latter. He swung agilely into the adjoining tree and gathered four of the large, prickly skinned durians, tossing them one by one to his companions. Then he swung back.

Rosetti was the first to cut his open. "It stinks," he said. "I ain't that hungry." He started to toss it away. "It's spoiled."

"Wait," cautioned Bubonovitch. "I've read about the durian. It does stink, but it tastes good. The natives roast the seeds like chestnuts."

Clayton had listened to Bubonvitch attentively. As they ate the fruit, he thought; What a country! What an army!

24

A sergeant who talks like a college professor—and comes from Brooklyn at that! He thought, too, how little the rest of the world really knew America—the Nazis least of all. Jitterbugs, playboys, a decadent race! He thought of how gallantly these boys had fought their guns, of how Lucas had made sure that his crew and his passenger were out before he jumped. Of how the boy had fought hopelessly to save his ship.

Night had fallen. The jungle sounds and the jungle voices were different now. There was movement everywhere around them—unseen, stealthy. A hollow, grunting cough rose from the foot of their tree.

"Wot was dat?" asked Shrimp.

"Stripes," said Clayton.

Shrimp wanted to ask what stripes was, but so far he had addressed no word to the Britisher. However, curiosity at last got the best of pride. "Stripes?" he sasked.

"Tiger."

"Geeze! You mean they's a tiger loose down there?"

"Yes. Two of them."

"Geeze! I seen 'em oncet at the zoo in Chicago. I guess it wouldn't be so healthy down there. I heard they ate people."

"We've got to thank you, Colonel, that we're not down there," said Jerry Lucas.

"I guess we'd be a lot of babes in the woods without him," said Bubonovitch.

"I learned a hell of a lot in Colonel Saffarrans' jungle training outfit," said Shrimp, "but nothin' about wot to do about tigers."

"They hunt mostly at night," Clayton explained. "That's when you have to be on your guard." After a while he said to Bubonovitch, "From what little I have read about Brooklyn I was lead to believe that Brooklynites had a special pronunciation of English all their own. You talk like any one else."

"So do you," said Bubonovitch.

Clayton laughed. "I was not educated at Oxford."

"Bum had a higher Brooklyn education," explained Lucas. "He went through sixth grade."

Bubonovitch and Rosetti dropped off to sleep. Clayton and Lucas sat at the edge of the platform, their legs dangling, planning for the future. They agreed that their best chance lay in getting a boat from friendly natives (if they could find any) on the southwest coast of the island and then trying to make Australia. They spoke of this and many other things. Lucas talked about his crew. He spoke of them with pride. Those who were unaccounted for, he worried about. Those who were dead were dead. There was nothing to be done about that now. But Clayton could tell by the tenseness in his voice when he spoke of them how he felt about them.

He spoke of Rosetti. "He's really a good kid," he said, "and a top ball turret gunner. Nature molded him for the job. There isn't much room in a ball turret. Bum says the War Department should breed 'em, crossing midgets with pygmies. Shrimp has the DFC and Air Medal with three clusters. He's a good kid all right."

"He certainly hasn't much use for Britishers," laughed Clayton.

"What with all the Irish and Italians in Chicago, it's not surprising. And then Shrimp never had much of a chance to learn anything. His father was killed in Cicero in a gang war when he was a kid, and I guess his mother was just a gangland moll. She never had any use for Shrimp, nor he for her. But with a background like that, you've got to hand it to the kid. He didn't get much schooling, but he kept straight."

"Bubonovitch interests me," said the Englishman. "He's an unusually intelligent man."

"Yes. He's not only intelligent, but he's extremely well educated. The former is not necessarily a corollary of the latter. Bubonovitch is a graduate of Columbia. His father, a school teacher, saw to that. Bum got interested in the exhibits in The American Museum of Natural History in New York when he was in high school. So he specialized in zoology, botany, anthropology, and all the other ologies that a fellow has to know to be valuable to the museum. And when he graduated, he landed a job there. He likes to pull scientific names of things on Shrimp just to annoy him."

"Then it's probably a good thing for Sgt. Rosetti's blood pressure that I haven't an Oxford accent," said Clayton.

* * *

As Corrie van der Meer trudged along with her captors her mind was occupied with but two problems: How to escape and how to destroy herself if she could not escape. Alam, walking beside her, spoke to her in his own language, which she understood but which the Japs did not.

"Forgive me," he begged, "for leading them to you. They tortured Tiang Umar, but he would not tell. Then his old wife could stand it no longer, and she told them that I knew where you were hiding. They said that they would kill everyone in the village if I did not lead them to your hiding place. What could I do?"

"You did right, Alam. Sing Tai and I were only two. It is better that two die than all the people of a village."

"I do not want you to die," said Alam. "I would rather die myself."

The girl shook her head. "What I fear," she said, "is that I may not find the means to die—in time."

Lieut. Sokabe spent the night in the kampong of Tiang Umar. The villagers were sullen and glowering; so Sokabe posted two sentries before the door of the house where he and his captive slept. To further preclude the possibility that she might escape, he bound her wrists and her ankles. Otherwise, he did not molest her. He had a healthy fear of Capt. Tokujo Matsuo, whose temper was notoriously vile; and he had a plan.

When he set out the next morning, he took Alam along to act as interpreter should he require one. Corrie was glad of the company of this friendly youth. They talked together as they had the previous day. Corrie asked Alam if he had seen any of the guerrilla bands that she had heard rumors of from time to time, bands made up of Dutchmen who had escaped to the hills—planters, clerks, soldiers.

"No, I have not seen them; but I have heard of them. I have heard that they have killed many Japanese. They are desperate men. The Japanese are always searching for them. They offer the native people rich rewards for pointing out their hiding places; so these men are suspicious of all natives they do not know, thinking they may be spies. It is said that a native who falls into their hands never returns to his village unless they know that they can trust him. And who can blame them? I have also heard that many natives have joined them. Now that we have learned that Greater East Asia Co-Prosperity is for the Japanese alone, we hate them."

They passed the spot where the village of Taku Muda had

27

stood. There was no evidence that man had ever set foot there, so completely had the jungle reclaimed it.

"This is the prosperity that the Japanese bring us," said Alam.

The morning wore on. They marched beneath sullen clouds in a tropical downpour. The gloomy forest stunk of rotting vegetation. It exhaled the vapors of death. Death! The girl knew that every step she took was bringing her closer to it. Unless—hope does not die easily in the breast of youth. But unless what?

She heard the roar of motors overhead. But she was used to that sound. The Japs were always flying over the island. Then, from a distance, there came to her ears a crashing and rending followed by a dull explosion. She did not hear the motors again. She thought, of course, that it was an enemy plane; and it filled her with satisfaction. The Japs jabbered about it excitely. Lt. Sokabe considered investigating. He talked with a sergeant. At last they decided that they could never find the plane in this tangle of jungle and forest. It was too far away.

It was almost dark when they reached the kampong that Capt. Tokujo Matsuo had commandeered for the use of his detachment. Standing in the doorway of the house that two officers had taken for their quarters, Matsuo watched the party approach.

He called to Sokabe. "Where are the prisoners?"

The lieutenant seized Corrie roughly by the arm and pulled her out of line and toward the captain. "Here," he said.

"I sent you for a Chinaman and a yellow haired Dutch girl, and you bring back a black haired native boy. Explain."

"We killed the Chinaman," said Sokabe. "This is the Dutch girl."

"I do not feel like joking, you fool," snarled Matsuo.

Sokabe prodded the girl up the ladder that led to the doorway. "I do not joke," he said. "This is the girl. She has disguised herself by dyeing her hair black and wearing the clothing of a native boy. Look!" Roughly he parted Corrie's hair with his dirty fingers, revealing the blonde color close to the scalp.

Matsuo scrutinized the girl's features closely. Then he nodded. "She suits me," he said. "I shall keep her."

"She belongs to me," said Sokabe. "I found her and brought her here. She is mine."

Matsuo spat. His face turned red. But he managed to restrain himself. "You forget yourself, Lieutenant Sokabe," he said. "And take your orders from me. I am commanding officer here. You will find yourself other quarters at once and leave the girl here."

"You may be a captain," said Sokabe; "but now, because of the great size of the imperial army and the many casualties, many officers are low born. My honorable ancestors were samurai. My honorable uncle is General Hideki Tojo. Your father and all your uncles are peasants. If I write a letter to my honorable uncle, you will not be a captain any more. Do I get the girl?"

There was murder in Matsuo's heart. But he chose to dissemble his wrath until such time as Sokabe might meet an accidental death. "I thought you were my friend," he said, "and now you turn against me. Let us do nothing rash. The girl is nothing. Descendants of the gods should not quarrel over such a low born creature. Let us leave the matter to the decision of our colonel. He will be here to inspect us soon." And before he gets here, thought Matsuo, an accident will befall you.

"That is fair enough," agreed Sokabe. It will be most unfortunate, he thought, should my captain die before the colonel arrives.

The girl understood nothing that they said. She did not know that for the time being she was safe.

Early the next morning Alam left the kampong to return to his village.

4

JERRY LUCAS was awakened by the violent shaking of the platform. It awakened Bubonovitch and Rosetti, also. "Wot t'ell!" exclaimed the latter.

Bubonovitch looked around. "I don't see anything."

Jerry leaned far out and looked up. He saw a huge black

form a few feet above him, violently shaking the tree. "Cripes!" he exclaimed. "Do you guys see what I see?"

The other two looked up. "Geeze!" said Rosetti. "Wot a mug! I never knew monkeys came dat big."

"That is not a monkey, you dope," said Bubonovitch. "It is known as *Pongo pygmaeus,* but why the *pygmaeus* I have not pursued my studies far enough to ascertain. It should be *Pongo giganteum.*"

"Talk United States," growled Shrimp.

"It's an orangutan, Shrimp," said Lucas.

"From the Malay *oran utan,* meaning wild man," added Bubonovitch.

"What does it want?" inquired Shrimp. "Wot in 'ell 's it shakin' the tree like dat for? Tryin' to shake us out? Geeze! wot a mug. Is he a man eater, Perfesser Bubonovitch?"

"He is chiefly herbivorous," replied Bubonovitch.

Rosetti turned to Lucas. "Do monks eat people, Cap?"

"No," replied Lucas. "Just leave 'em alone, and they'll leave you alone. But don't get fresh with that baby. He could take you apart like nobody's business."

Shrimp was examining his .45. "He ain't a-goin' to take me apart, not while I got Big Bertha here."

The orangutan, having satisfied his curiosity, moved slowly off. Shrimp started stripping his .45. "Geeze! It's started to rust already, just like—" He looked around. "Say! Where's the dook?"

"Cripes! He's gone," said Lucas. "I never noticed."

"Maybe he fell off," suggested Rosetti, peering over the edge. "He wasn't a bad guy fer a Britisher."

"That's sure some concession, coming from you," said Bubonovitch. "Do you know, Cap'n, Shrimp wouldn't play billiards even for fear he might have to put English on the cue ball."

Shrimp sat up suddenly and looked at the others. "I just happened to think," he said. "Did either of youse hear dat scream last night?"

"I did," said Lucas. "What of it?"

"It sounded like some one bein' kilt. Didn't it?"

"Well, it did sound sort of human."

"Sure. Dat's it. The dook fell off an' a tiger got 'im. That was him screamin'."

Bubonovitch pointed. "Here comes his ghost."

30

The others looked. "Fer Pete's sake!" said Rosetti. "Wot a guy!"

Swinging through the trees toward them, the carcass of a deer slung over one shoulder, was the Englishman. He swung onto the platform. "Here's breakfast," he said. "Go to it."

Dropping the carcass, he drew his knife and hacked out a generous portion. Tearing the skin from the flesh with powerful fingers, he squatted in a far corner of the platform and sank his strong teeth into the raw flesh. Shrimp's jaw dropped and his eyes went wide. "Ain't you goin' to cook it?" he asked.

"What with?" inquired Clayton. "There's nothing around here dry enough to burn. If you want meat, you'll have to learn to eat it raw until we can find a permanent camp and get something that will burn."

"Well," said Shrimp, "I guess I'm hungry enough."

"I'll try anything once," said Bubonovitch.

Jerry Lucas hacked off a small piece and started to chew it. Clayton watched the three men chewing on bits of the warm raw meat. "That's not the way to eat it," he said. "Tear off pieces you can swallow, and then swallow them whole. Don't chew."

"How did youse learn all dis?" inquired Rosetti.

"From the lions."

Rosetti glanced at the others, shook his head, and then tried to swallow to large a piece of venison. He gagged and choked. "Geeze!" he said, after he had disgorged the morsel, "I never went to school to no lions." But after that he did better.

"It's not so bad when you swallow it whole," admitted Lucas.

"And it fills your belly and gives you strength," said Clayton.

He swung into the next tree and got more durian fruit. They ate it now with relish. "After dis," said Shrimp, "there ain't nuthin' I can't eat."

"I passed a stream near here," said Clayton. "We can drink there. I think we'd better get started. We've got to do some reconnoitering before we can make any definite plans. You might take some of this meat along in your pockets if you think you'll be hungry again soon. But there's plenty of game everywhere. We won't go hungry."

No one wanted to take any of the meat; so Clayton tossed the carcass to the ground. "For Stripes," he said.

The sun was shining, and the forest teemed with life. Bubonovitch was in his element. Here were animals and birds he had studied about in books, or whose dead and mounted frames he had seen in museums. And there were many that he had neither seen nor heard of. "A regular museum of natural history on the hoof," he said.

Clayton had led them to the stream, and after they had quenched their thirsts he guided them to a well marked game trail he had discovered while hunting for their breakfast. It wound downward in the direction he and Lucas had decided they would take—toward the west coast, many, many long marches away.

"There have been no men along this trail recently," said Clayton, "but there have been many other animals—elephant, rhinos, tigers, deer. It was on this trail that I found our breakfast."

Shrimp wanted to ask how he had caught the deer, but realized that he had recently been altogether too familiar with a Britisher. Probably a friend of George Thoid, he thought, and winced. It curled his hair to think what the mob would say could they know of it. Still, he had to admit that the guy wasn't a bad guy, even though he hated to admit it.

They were moving up wind, and Clayton paused and and raised a warning hand. "There is a man ahead of us," he said in a low tone.

"I don't see no one," said Rosetti.

"Neither do I," said Clayton, "but he's there." He stood still for a few minutes. "He's going the same way we are," he said. "I'll go ahead and have a look at him. The rest of you come along slowly." He swung into a tree and disappeared ahead.

"You can't see no one, you can't hear no one; and this guy tells us there's a guy ahead of us—and w'ich way he's goin'!" Rosetti looked appealingly at Lucas.

"He hasn't been wrong yet," said Jerry.

*   *   *

Sing Tai did not die. The Jap bayonet inflicted a cruel wound, but pierced no vital organ. For two days Sing Tai lay in a welter of blood, deep hidden in his cave. Then he crawled out. Suffering from shock, weak from loss of blood and lack of food and water, often on the verge of fainting

32

from pain, he staggered slowly along the trail toward the village of Tiang Umar. Orientals are more easily resigned to death than are occidentals, so greatly do their philosophies differ. But Sing Tai would not die. While there was hope that his beloved mistress might live and need him, he, too, must live.

In the village of Tiang Umar he might get word of her. Then he might be able to determine whether to live or die. So Sing Tai's loyal heart beat on, however weakly. Yet there were moments when he wondered if he would have the strength to carry on to the village. Such thoughts were depressing him when he was startled to see an almost naked giant appear suddenly in the trail before him—a bronzed giant with black hair and gray eyes. This, perhaps, is the end, thought Sing Tai.

Clayton had dropped into the trail from an overhanging tree. He spoke to Sing Tai in English, and Sing Tai replied in English which had just a trace of pidgin. In Hong Kong, Sing Tai had lived for years in the homes of Englishmen.

Clayton saw the blood soaked garments and noted the outward signs of weakness that seemed to verge on collapse. "How you get hurt?" he asked.

"Jap monkey-man run bayonet through me—here." He indicated the spot in his side.

"Why?" asked Clayton, and Sing Tai told his story.

"Are there Japs near here?"

"Me no think so."

"How far is this village you are trying to reach?"

"Not very far now—maybe so one kilometer."

"Are the people of that village friendly to the Japanese?"

"No. Very much hate Japs."

Clayton's companions appeared now from around a curve in the trail. "You see," said Lucas. "Right again."

"That guy is always right," muttered Shrimp, "but I don't see how he done it—not with no glass ball nor nuthin'."

"Not even with the aid of mirrors," said Bubonovitch.

Sing Tai looked at them apprehensively as they approached. "They are my friends," said Clayton—"American aviators."

"Melicans!" breathed Sing Tai with a sigh of relief. "Now I know we save missie."

Clayton repeated Sing Tai's story to the others, and it was decided that they should go on to Tiang Umar's village. Clayton gathered the Chinese gently into his arms and carried him along the trail. When Sing Tai said that they were near the village, the Englishman put him down, and told them all to wait while he went ahead to investigate. The Jap detachment might still be there. It was not, and he soon returned.

Tiang Umar received them well when Sing Tai had explained who they were. With Sing Tai acting as interpreter, Tiang Umar told them that the Japs had left the previous morning, taking the Dutch girl and one of his young men with them. What was their destination, he did not know. He knew that there was a Jap camp one day's march to the southwest. Perhaps they had gone to that camp. If they would wait in his kampong, he was sure that the youth, Alam, would return, as the Japs had taken him along only to act as interpreter in the villages they might pass through.

They decided to wait. Clayton was especially anxious to; and when it was decided, he went off into the forest alone. "He'll probably come back wit one of them there water buffalo under his arm," predicted Shrimp. But when he came back he had only some tough and slender branches and some bamboo. With these and some chicken feathers and fiber cord given him by Tiang Umar, he fashioned a bow, some arrows and a spear. The tips of his weapons he fire hardened. With parachute silk, he made a quiver.

His companions watched with interest. Rosetti was not greatly impressed when Clayton explained that his armament would serve not only to insure them plenty of game but as weapons of defense and offense against men. "Do we hold de game w'ile he shoots at it?" he asked Bubonovitch. "Say, an' if any guy ever pricked me wid one of dem t'ings, an' I found it out—"

"Don't be corny," said Bubonovitch. But weapons, to Rosetti, meant .45s, tommy guns, machine guns, not slivers of bamboo with chicken feathers at one end.

Late in the afternoon, Alam returned. He was immediately surrounded by a crowd of jabbering natives. Sing Tai finally got his story and retold it to Clayton. Alam knew that the two Jap officers had quarrelled over the girl and that she was still safe at the time he had left the village that morning.

Sing Tai, with tears in his eyes, begged Clayton to rescue Corrie from the Japs. Clayton and the Americans discussed the matter. All were in favor of the attempt, but not all for the same reasons. Clayton and Bubonovitch wished to save the girl. Lucas and Rosetti wished to discomfit the Japs.

They were little interested in the girl, both being misogynists. Lucas was a woman hater because the girl he had left behind in Oklahoma City had married a 4-F two months after Jerry had gone overseas. Rosetti's hatred of them stemmed from his lifelong hatred of his mother.

Early the following morning they set out, guided by Alam.

5

THEY moved slowly and cautiously, Clayton reconnoitering ahead of the others. Shrimp didn't see why they had brought Alam, and was sure that they would become lost. In a weird sign language of his own invention, he was constantly asking Alam if they were on the right trail. The native, not having the slightest idea what Shrimp's wild gesticulating meant, nodded and smiled as soon as Rosetti started to point and grimace.

Lucas and Bubonovitch were not as much concerned as Shrimp. They had more confidence in the Englishman than he. However, they could not know that Clayton needed no guide to show him the trail of a detachment of soldiers accompanied by a white girl and a native youth. Everywhere along the trail the signs of their recent passage were obvious to his trained senses.

It was dark when they approached the village. Clayton had the others wait while he went ahead to investigate. He found the village poorly guarded and entered it with ease. The night was moonless and clouds hid the stars. There were dim lights in a few of the houses. Conditions were ideal for the furtherance of the plan Clayton had worked out.

Close to the point at which he had entered his keen sense of smell located the white girl. He heard the angry jabbering of two Japs in the house with her. They would be the two officers still quarrelling over her.

He left the village at the same point at which he had entered it and passed around it to its lower end. There was a sentry here. Clayton did not wish any sentry at this point. The fellow patrolled back and forth. Clayton crouched behind a tree, waiting. The sentry approached. Something leaped upon him from behind; and before he could voice a cry of warning, a keen blade bit deep into his throat.

Clayton dragged the corpse out of the village, and returned to his companions. He whispered instructions; then he led them to the lower end of the village. "Your .45s," he had said, "will probably fire the cartridges that are in the chambers. The chances are that the mechanisms are so rusted by this time that they will not eject the shell nor reload, but fire as long as they will fire. When they jam, throw rocks into the village to keep attention attracted in this direction. And all the while, yell like hell. Start this in three minutes. In four minutes, get out of there and get out quick. We'll rendezvous on the back trail above the village. Keep your watch dial hidden from the village, Captain." Then he was gone.

He returned to the upper end of the village and hid beneath the house in which were the two officers and the girl. A minute later, shots rang out at the lower end of the village and loud yells shattered the silence of the night. Clayton grinned. It sounded as though a strong force were attacking the village.

A second later the two officers ran from the house, screaming orders, demanding explanations. Soldiers swarmed from other houses and all ran in the direction of the disturbance. Then Clayton ran up the ladder that led to the doorway of the house and entered. The girl lay on sleeping mats at the rear of the single room. Her wrists and ankles were bound.

She saw this almost naked man cross the floor toward her at a run. He stooped down and gathered her in his arms, carried her from the house and out into the jungle. She was terrified. What new horror awaited her?

In the dim light within the room, she had only seen that the man was tall and that his skin was brown. Out along a jungle trail he bore her for a short distance. Then he halted and put her down. She felt something cold press against her wrists—and her hands were free. Then the cords around her ankles were cut.

"Who are you?" she demanded in Dutch.

"Quiet!" he cautioned.

Presently, four others joined them; and they all moved in silence with her along the dark trail. Who were they? What did they want of her? The one word, quiet, spoken in English had partially reassured her. At least they were not Japs.

For an hour they moved on in unbroken silence, Clayton

36

constantly alert for sounds of pursuit. But none developed. At last he spoke. "I think we confused them," he said. "If they are searching, it is probably in the other direction."

"Who are you?" asked Corrie, this time in English.

"Friends," replied Clayton. "Sing Tai told us about you. So we came and got you."

"Sing Tai is not dead?"

"No, but badly wounded."

Alam spoke to her then and reassured her. "You are safe now," he said. "I have heard that Americans can do anything. Now I believe it."

"These are Americans?" she asked incredulously. "Have they landed at last?"

"Only these few. Their plane was shot down."

"That was a pretty cute trick, Colonel," said Bubonovitch. "It certainly fooled them."

"It came near doing worse than that to me, because I forgot to caution you as to the direction of your fire. Two bullets came rather too close to me for comfort." He turned to the girl. "Do you feel strong enough to walk the rest of the night?" he asked.

"Yes, quite," she replied. "You see I am used to walking. I have been doing a lot of it for the past two years, keeping out of the way of the Japs."

"For two years?"

"Yes, ever since the invasion. I have been hiding in the mountains all this time, Sing Tai and I." Clayton drew her out, and she told her story—the flight from the plantation, the death of her mother, the murder of her father and Lum Kam, the treachery of some natives, the loyalty of others.

They reached the village of Tiang Umar at dawn, but they remained there only long enough to get food; then they moved on, all but Alam. A plan had been worked out during the night. It was based on the belief that the Japs would eventually return to this village to look for the girl. Furthermore Corrie wished to have nothing done that would jeopardize the safety of these people who had befriended her.

Corrie and Sing Tai knew of many hiding places in the remote fastnesses of the mountains. They had been forced to move closer to Tiang Umar's village because of their inability to get proper or sufficient food for themselves in these safer locations. But now it would be different. The Americans could do anything.

They had been forced to leave Sing Tai behind, as he was in no condition to travel. Tiang Umar assured them that he could hide the Chinese where the Japs could not find him if they should return to the village.

"If I can, I shall let you know where I am, Tiang Umar," said Corrie; "then, perhaps, you will send Sing Tai to me when he is strong enough to travel."

Corrie led the party deep into the wilds of the mountain hinterland. Here there were rugged gorges and leaping streams, forests of teak, huge stands of bamboo, open mountain meadows man deep with tough grasses.

Lucas and Clayton had decided to go thus deeper into the mountains and then cut to the southeast before turning toward the coast. In this way they would avoid the area in which the plane had crashed, where the Japs had probably already instituted a thorough search. They would also encounter few if any villages whose inhabitants might put Japs upon their trail.

Clayton often foraged ahead for food, always returning with something. It might be partridge or pheasant, sometimes deer. And now at their camps he made fire, so that the Americans could cook their food.

On the trail, Clayton and Corrie always led the way, then came Bubonovitch, with Lucas and Shrimp bringing up the rear, keeping as far away from the Dutch girl as possible. They were unreconciled to the presence of a woman. It was not so much that Corrie might jeopardize their chances to escape. It was just that they objected to women on general principles.

"But I suppose we gotta put up wit de dame," said Rosetti. "We can't leaf the Japs get her."

Jerry Lucas agreed. "If she were a man, or even a monkey, it wouldn't be so bad. But I just plain don't have any time for women."

"Some dame double-cross you?" asked Shrimp.

"I could have forgiven her throwing me over for a 4-F as soon as I was out of sight," said Jerry, "but the so-and-so was a Republican into the bargain."

"She ain't hard to look at," conceded Shrimp, grudgingly.

"They're the worst," said Jerry. "Utterly selfish and greedy. Always gouging some one. Gimme! Gimme! Gimme! That's all they think of. If you ever decide to marry, Shrimp," ad-

vised Jerry, pedantically, "marry an old bag who'd be grateful to any one for marrying her."

"Who wants to marry an old bag?" demanded Shrimp.

"You wouldn't have to worry about wolves."

"Whoever marries dis little Dutch number'll have plenty
to worry about. All de wolves in de woods'll be howlin' round
his back door. Ever notice dem lamps w'en she smiles?"

"You falling for her, Shrimp?"

"Hell, no; but I got eyes, ain't I?"

"I never look at her," lied Jerry.

Just then a covey of partridges broke cover. Clayton already had an arrow fitted to his bow. Instantly the string
twanged and a partridge fell. The man's movements were as
swift and sure and smooth as the passage of light.

"Geez!" exclaimed Rosetti. "I give. The guy's not human.
Howinell did he know them boids was goin' to bust out?
How could he hit 'em with dat t'ing?"

Jerry shook his head. "Search me. He probably smelled
'em, or heard 'em. Lots of the things he does are just plain
uncanny."

"I'm goin' to learn to shoot one of dem t'ings," said
Shrimp.

Presently, Rosetti overcame his Anglophobia sufficiently to
permit him to ask Clayton to show him how to make a bow
and arrows. Lucas and Bubonovitch expressed a similar desire. The next day Clayton gathered the necessary materials,
and they all set to work under his guidance to fashion weapons, even to Corrie.

The Dutch girl braided the bow strings from fibers from
the long tough grasses they found in open spaces in the
mountains. Clayton shot birds for the feathers, and taught
the others how properly to fletch their arrows. The fashioning
of the weapons was a pleasant interlude to long days of scal-
ing cliffs, battling through jungle undergrowth, marching
down one declivity only to climb up once more to descend
another. It was the first time that the five had had any pro-
tracted social intercourse, for after each hard day's march
their greatest need had been sleep.

The Dutch girl sat near Jerry Lucas. He watched her
nimble fingers braiding the fibers, and thought that she had
pretty hands—small and well shaped. He noticed, too, that
notwithstanding two years of bitter hardships she still gave attention to her nails. He glanced at his own, ruefully. Some-

how, she always looked trim and neat. How she accomplished it was beyond him.

"It will be fun to hunt with these," she said to him in her precise, almost Oxford English.

"If we can hit anything," he replied. She speaks better English than I, he thought.

"We must practice a great deal," she said. "It is not right that we four grown-up people should be dependent upon Colonel Clayton for everything, as though we were little children."

"No," he said.

"Is he not wonderful?"

Jerry mumbled a "Yes," and went on with his work. With awkward, unaccustomed fingers he was trying to fletch an arrow. He wished the girl would keep still. He wished she were in Halifax. Why did there have to be girls around to spoil a man's world?

Corrie glanced up at him, puzzled. Her eyes reflected it. Then she noticed his awkward attempts to hold a feather in place and fasten it there with a bit of fiber. "Here," she said. "Let me help you. You hold the feather and I'll bind the fiber around the shaft. Hold it close in the groove. There, that's right." Her hands, passing the fiber around the arrow, often touched his. He found the contact pleasant; and because he found it so, it made him angry.

"Here," he said, almost rudely, "I can do this myself. You need not bother."

She looked up at him, surprised. Then she went back to braiding the bow strings. She did not say anything, but in that brief glance when their eyes had met he had seen surprise and hurt in hers. He had seen the same once in a deer he had shot, and he had never again shot a deer.

You're a damned heel, he thought of himself. Then, with a great effort of will power, he said, "I am sorry. I did not mean to be rude."

"You do not like me," she said. "Why? Have I done something to offend you?"

"Of course not. And what makes you think I don't like you?"

"It has been quite obvious. The little sergeant does not like me, either. Sometimes I catch him looking at me as though he would like to bite off my head.

"Some men are shy around women," he said.

The girl smiled. "Not you," she said.

They were silent for a moment. Then he said, "Would you mind helping me again? I am terribly awkward at this."

Corrie thought, *He is a gentleman, after all.*

Again she bound the feathers fast while he held them in place. And their hands touched. Chagrined, Jerry found himself moving his so that they would touch oftener.

6

Much time was devoted to archery even on the march. Corrie shamed the men. She was very quick and very accurate, and she drew a strong bow—the full length of a two foot, eight inch arrow until the feathers touched her right ear.

Clayton complimented her. Shrimp told Bubonovitch that it was a sissy sport anyway. Jerry secretly admired her prowess and was ashamed of himself for admiring it. He tried to concentrate on the girl in Oklahoma City and the Republican 4-F.

Corrie explained that she had belonged to an archery club for two years in Holland while there at school, and that she had kept up the practice after she returned to her father's plantation. "If I were not good at it by this time, I should think myself very stupid."

Eventually, even Shrimp commenced to brag about his marksmanship. They were all pretty good, and woe betide any game bird or animal that crossed their path. They had found a couple of dry caves in a limestone cliff, and Clayton had decided that they should remain there until some new clothing and footwear could be fashioned, for their shoes were practically gone and their clothing in shreds.

The Englishman had roughly cured a deer skin, and had fashioned an awl and needles from bamboo. With the same tough fiber used for their bows and arrows, Corrie was making crude sandals for them with these materials and tools.

She worked alone one morning while the men went out to hunt. Her thoughts ranged over the two years that had passed

—years of sorrow, hardship, and danger. Years of pain and unshed tears and hate. She thought of her present situation —alone in the vastness of a mountain wilderness with four strange men, four foreigners. And she realized that she had never felt safer and that for the first time in two years she was happy.

She smiled when she thought of how terrified she had been when that almost naked brown man had carried her off into the forest. And how surprised she had been when she learned that he was a Royal Air Force colonel. She had liked him and Sergeant Bubonovitch from the very beginning. Her heart had warmed to the sergeant from the moment that he had shown her the pictures of his wife and baby. She had not liked "the little sergeant" nor Captain Lucas. They are both boors, she had thought; but the captain is the worse because he is an educated man and should know better than to behave toward me as he has.

That was what she had thought until lately, but since the day that she had helped him fletch his arrows he had been different. He still did not seek her company, but he did not avoid her as he had in the past. Bubonovitch had told her what a fine pilot he was and how his crew worshiped him. He cited several examples of Lucas' courage, and they lost nothing in the telling. Crew members are that way if they like an officer.

So Corrie concluded that Lucas was a man's man and possibly a woman hater. And she found the latter idea intriguing. It was also amusing. She smiled as she thought of how a woman hater must feel in such a situation—forced into close companionship with a woman day after day. And a young and pretty woman, she added mentally. For Corrie was eighteen, and she knew that she was even more than pretty—even in rags and with that horrid head of hair, mostly a rusty black, but blonde at the roots. She had no mirror, but she had seen her reflection in still pools of water. That always made her laugh. She laughed easily and often these days, for she was strangely happy.

She wondered if Captain Lucas would have disliked her if they had met under normal conditions—she with lovely gowns and her beautiful, golden hair becomingly arranged. Had she been given to self analysis, she would probably have wondered also why he was so much in her thoughts. Of course he was goodlooking in an extremely masculine way.

She thought of him as old, and would have been surprised to have learned that he was only twenty-three. Responsibility and many hours of intense nervous strain had matured him rapidly. To hurl thirty tons of aluminum and steel and high explosives into the air and into battle, to feel that upon you alone depends the safety of a beautiful, half million dollars worth of plane and the lives of nine of your best friends is sufficient responsibility to bring lines of maturity to any face. They had left their mark on Jerry Lucas's.

Her thoughts were interrupted by the sound of voices. At first she assumed that the hunters were returning. Then, as the sounds came nearer, she recognized the intonation of native speech; and a moment later several Sumatrans appeared in the mouth of the cave. They were dirty, vicious looking men. There were ten of them. They took her away with them. From their conversation she soon learned why: The Japs had offered a reward for the capture of her and Sing Tai.

* * *

The sun was setting when the hunters returned to the cave. The brief equatorial twilight would soon be followed by darkness. The men missed the girl immediately and commenced to speculate on the explanation.

"She probably run out on us," said Shrimp. "You can't trust no dame."

"Don't be a damn fool," snapped Lucas. Shrimp's jaw dropped in surprise. He had been sure that the captain would agree with him. "Why should she run out on us?" demanded Lucas. "We offer her the only chance she has to escape the Japs. She probably went hunting."

"What makes you think she has run away from us, Rosetti?" asked Clayton, who was examining the ground just outside of the cave entrance.

"I know skoits," said Shrimp.

"I'd want better evidence than that," said the Englishman.

"Well, she didn't go hunting," said Bubonovitch from the back of the cave.

"How do you know?" asked Lucas.

"Her bow and arrows are here."

"No, she didn't go hunting and she didn't run away," said

43

Clayton. "She was taken away by force by a band of natives. There were about ten men in the band. They went that way." He pointed.

"You got a crystal ball, Colonel?" asked Bubonovitch skeptically.

"I have something more dependable—two eyes and a nose. So have you men, but yours are no good. They have been dulled by generations of soft living, of having laws and police and soldiers to surround you with safeguards."

"And how about you, Colonel?" asked Lucas banteringly.

"I have survived simply because my senses are as acute as those of my enemies—usually far more acute—and are combined with experience and intelligence to safeguard me where there are no laws, no police, no soldiers."

"Like in London," observed Bubonovitch. Clayton only smiled.

"What makes you sure she didn't go with the natives willingly?" asked Jerry Lucas. "She might have had some good reason that we, of course, can't know anything about. But I certainly don't believe that she deserted us."

"She was taken by force after a very brief struggle. The signs are plain on the ground. You can see here where she held back and was dragged along a few feet. Then her tracks disappear. They picked her up and carried her. The stink of natives clings to the grasses."

"Well, what are we waiting for then?" demanded Lucas. "Let's get going."

"Sure," said Shrimp. "Let's get after the dirty so-and-sos. They can't take—" He stopped suddenly, surprised by the strange reaction the abduction of the hated "dame" had wrought.

It had started to rain—a sudden tropical deluge. Clayton stepped into the shelter of the cave. "There is no use in starting now," he said. "This rain will obliterate the scent spoor, and we couldn't follow the visible spoor in the dark. They will have to lie up somewhere for the night. Natives don't like to travel after dark on account of the big cats. So they won't gain on us. We can leave immediately it is light enough in the morning for me to see the trail."

"The poor kid," said Jerry Lucas.

The moment that it was light enough to see, they were off to track down Corrie's abductors. The Americans saw no sign of any spoor, but to the habituated eyes of the

Englishman it ran clear and true. He saw where they had put Corrie down a short distance from the cave and made her walk.

It was midmorning when Clayton stopped and sniffed the breeze that blew gently from the direction from which they had come. "You'd better take to the trees," he said to the others. "There's a tiger coming down the trail behind us. He's not very far away."

* * *

Corrie's abductors had camped at the edge of a mountain meadow as darkness approached. They built a fire to keep the great cats away, and huddled close to it, leaving one man on guard to tend it.

Tired, the girl slept for several hours. When she awoke, she saw that the fire was out and knew that the guard must have fallen asleep. She realized that now she might escape. She looked toward the dark, forbidding forest—just a solid blank of blackness. But in it lurked possible death. In the other direction, the direction in which these men were taking her, lay something worse than death. She balanced the certainty against the possibility and reached her decision quickly.

Silently she arose. The guard lay stretched beside the ashes of the dead fire. She passed around him and the others. A moment later she entered the forest. Though the trail was worn deep it was difficult to follow it in the darkness; and she made slow progress, often stumbling. But she went on, that she might put as much distance between herself and her captors as possible before daylight, being certain that they would follow her.

She was frightened. The forest was full of sound—stealthy, menacing sound. And any one of them might be the footsteps or the wings of Death. Yet she felt her way on, deeper and deeper into the impenetrable gloom until she heard a sound that turned her blood cold—the cough of a tiger. And then she heard it crashing through the undergrowth as though it had caught her scent or heard her.

She groped to the side of the trail, her hands outstretched. She prayed that she might find a tree she could scale. A hanging vine struck her in the face as she blundered into it. She seized it and started to climb. The crashing of the beast's body through the tangle of shrubbery sounded closer. Corrie clawed her way upward. From below came a series of hideous growls as the tiger sprang. The impact of his body nearly tore the vine from her grasp, but terror and desperation lent her strength.

Once more the vine swayed violently as the beast sprang again, but now the girl knew that it could not reach her if the vine held. There lay the danger. Twice more the tiger sprang, but at last Corrie reached one of the lower branches —a leafy sanctuary at least from the great cats. But there were other menaces in the jungle that could range far above the ground. The most fearsome of these was the python.

The carnivore remained beneath the tree for some time. Occasionally it growled. At last the girl heard it move away. She considered descending and continuing her flight. She was sure that Clayton at least would search for her, but he could do nothing until daylight. She thought of Jerry Lucas. Even if he did not like her, he would probably help in the search for her—not because she was Corrie van der Meer, but because she was a woman. And of course Bubonovitch would come, and the little sergeant might be shamed into it.

She decided to wait until daylight. Sometimes Stripes hunted in the daytime, but most usually at night. And this was what the Malays called tiger weather—a dark, starless, misty night.

Eventually the long night ended, and Corrie clambered down into the trail and continued her interrupted flight. She moved swiftly now.

7

FROM the branches of a tree that overhung the trail, the survivors of Lovely Lady waited for the tiger to pass and permit them to descend. They had no intention of interfering with his passage. The Americans assured one another that they had not lost a tiger, and grinned as though the remark was original.

They had accompanied Clayton into trees so many times

that Shrimp said he expected to sprout a tail most any time. "That's all you need," Bubonovitch assured him.

Around them were the ordinary daylight sounds of the forest, to which they were now so accustomed—the raucous cries of birds, the terrific booming of siamang gibbons, the chattering of the lesser simians—but no sound came from the tiger. Shrimp decided that it was a false alarm.

Below them, not more than a hundred feet of the trail was visible between two turnings—about fifty feet in each direction. Suddenly the tiger appeared, slouching along loose-jointed and slab-sided, noiseless on his cushioned pads. Simultaneously a slender figure came into view around the opposite turning. It was Corrie. Both the tiger and the girl stopped, facing one another less than a hundred feet apart. The tiger voiced a low growl and started forward at a trot. Corrie seemed frozen with horror. For an instant she did not move. And in that instant she saw an almost naked man drop from above onto the back of the carnivore. And following him instantly, three other men dropped to the trail, jerking knives from their sheaths as they ran toward the man battling with the great cat. And first among them was S/Sgt. Rosetti, the British hater.

A steel thewed arm encircled the tiger's neck, mightily muscled legs were locked around its groin, and the man's free arm was driving a keen blade deep into the beast's left side. Growls of fury rumbled from the savage throat of the great cat as it threw itself about in agony and rage. And, to Corrie's horror, mingled with them were equally savage growls that rumbled from the throat of the man. Incredulous, the three Americans watched the brief battle between the two —two jungle beasts—powerless to strike a blow for the man because of the wild leapings and turnings of the stricken tiger.

But what seemed a long time to them was a matter of seconds only. The tiger's great frame went limp and sank to the ground. And the man rose and put a foot upon it and, raising his face to the heavens, voiced a horrid cry—the victory cry of the bull ape. Corrie was suddenly terrified of this man who had always seemed so civilized and cultured. Even the men were shocked.

Suddenly recognition lighted the eyes of Jerry Lucas. "John Clayton," he said, "Lord Greystoke—Tarzan of the Apes!"

Shrimp's jaw dropped. "Is dat Johnny Weismuller?" he demanded.

Tarzan shook his head as though to clear his brain of an obsession. His thin veneer of civilization had been consumed by the fires of battle. For the moment he had reverted to the savage primordial beasts that he had been raised. But he was almost instantly his second self again.

He welcomed Corrie with a smile. "So you got away from them," he said.

Corrie nodded. She was still shaken and trembling, and almost on the verge of tears—tears of relief and thanksgiving. "Yes, I got away from them last night; but if it hadn't been for you, it wouldn't have done me much good, would it?"

"It is fortunate that we happened to be at the right place at the right time. You had better sit down for a while. You look all in."

"I am." She sat down at the edge of the trail, and the four men gathered around her. Jerry Lucas beamed with pleasure and relief. Even Shrimp was happy about it all.

"I'm sure glad you're back, Miss," he said. Then, when he realized what he had said, he turned red. Shrimp's psyche had recently received terrific jolts. A couple of lifelong phobias were being knocked into a cocked hat. He had come to admire an Englishman and to like a dame.

Corrie told them of her capture and escape, and she and the Americans discussed the killing of the tiger. "Weren't you afraid?" she asked Tarzan.

Tarzan, who had never been afraid in his life, only cautious, was always at a loss to answer this question, which had been put to him many times before. He simply did not know what fear was.

"I knew I could kill the beast," he said.

"I thought you were crazy when I saw you drop on it," said Bubonovitch. "I was sure scared."

"But you came down just the same to help me, all of you. If you thought you might be killed doing it, that was true bravery."

"Why haven't you told us you were Tarzan?" asked Jerry. "What difference could it have made?"

"We were sure dumb not to have recognized you long ago," said Bubonovitch.

Corrie said that she could go on. The men gathered the

bows they had flung aside when they dropped to the ground, and they started back toward their camp. "Funny none of us thought to shoot it wit arrows," said Shrimp.

"They would only have infuriated it," said Tarzan. "Of course, if you got one through his heart that would kill a tiger; but he would live long enough to do a terrible lot of damage. Many a hunter has been mauled by lions after sending a large caliber bullet through its heart. These great cats are amazingly tenacious of life."

"To be mauled by a lion or tiger must be a terrible way to die," said Corrie, shuddering.

"On the contrary, it would seem to be a rather nice way to die—if one had to die," said Tarzan. "A number of men who had been mauled by lions and lived have recorded their sensations. They were unanimous in declaring that they felt neither pain nor fear."

"Dey can have it," said Shrimp. "I'll take a tommy gun for mine."

Tarzan brought up the rear of the little column on the way back to camp, that Usha the Wind might bring to his nostrils warning of the approach of the Sumatrans, if they were pursuing Corrie, before they came too close.

Shrimp walked beside him, watching his every move with admiring eyes. To think, he said to himself, that I'd ever be runnin' around in a jungle wit Tarzan of de Apes. Bubonovitch had convinced him that it was not Johnny Weismuller. Jerry and Corrie led the way. He walked just behind one of her shoulders. He could watch her profile from that position. He found it a very nice profile to watch. So nice that, though he tried, he couldn't conjure up the likeness of the girl in Oklahoma City for any length of time. His thoughts kept coming back to the profile.

"You must be very tired," he said. He was thinking that she had walked this trail all the day before and all this day, with practically no sleep.

"A little," she replied. "But I am used to walking. I am very tough."

"We were frightened when we found you gone and Tarzan discovered that you had been abducted."

She threw him a quick, quizzical glance. "And you a misogynist!" she chided.

"Who said I was a misogynist?"

"Both you and the little sergeant."

49

"I didn't tell you that, and Shrimp doesn't know what a misogynist is."

"I didn't mean that. I meant that you are both misogynists. No one told me. It was quite obvious."

"Maybe I thought I was," he said. Then he told her about the girl in Oklahoma City.

"And you love her so much?"

"I do not. I guess my pride was hurt. A man hates to be brushed off."

"Brushed off? What is that?"

"Jilted—and for a Republican 4-F."

"Is that such a terrible person? I never heard of one before."

Jerry laughed. "Really, no. But when you're mad you like to call names, and I couldn't think of anything else. The fellow is really all right. As a matter of fact I am commencing to love him."

"You mean that it is better to discover, before marriage, that she is fickle rather than after?"

"We'll settle for that—for the time being. I just know that I would not want her to be in love with me now."

Corrie thought that over. Whatever she deduced from it, she kept to herself. When they reached camp a few minutes later, she was humming a gay little tune.

After she had gone into the cave, Bubonovitch said to Jerry, "How's the misogynist this afternoon?"

"Shut your trap," said Jerry.

Tarzan, in questioning Corrie about her abductors, had ascertained that there had been ten of them and that they were armed with kris and parang. They carried no firearms, the Japs having confiscated all such weapons as they could find.

The five were gathered at the mouth of the cave discussing plans for the future, which included tactics in the event the tribesmen returned and proved belligerent. Those who wished always had an equal voice in these discussions; but since they had left the ship, where Jerry's authority had been supreme, there had been a tacit acknowledgement of Tarzan's position as leader. Jerry realized the fitness of this. There had never been any question in his mind, nor in the minds of the others, that the Englishman was better equipped by knowledge and experience of the jungle, acute sense perceptivity, and physical prowess to guide and protect them

50

than were any of the others. Even Shrimp had had to acknowledge this, and at first that had been hard. Now he would have been one of the Britisher's most ardent supporters had there been any dissidents.

"Corrie tells me," said Tarzan, "that there are ten men in the party that took her. Most of them, she says, are armed with a long straight kris, not the wavy bladed type with which most of us are familiar. They all carry parangs, a heavy knife designed more for use as a tool than a weapon. They have no firearms."

"If they come, we shall have to stop them before they get to close quarters. Corrie will act as interpreter. While they outnumber us more than two to one, we should have no difficulty in holding our own. We are four bows—"

"Five," corrected Corrie.

Tarzan smiled. "We are five bows, and we are all good shots. We shall try to convince them that they had better go away and leave us alone. We shall not shoot until it is absolutely necessary."

"Nuts," said Shrimp. "We'd ought to let 'em have it for stealin' de kid." Corrie gave him a look of surprise and incredulity. Jerry and Bubonovitch grinned. Shrimp turned red.

"There goes another misogynist," Bubonovitch whispered to Jerry.

"I know how you feel, Rosetti," said Tarzan. "I think we all feel the same way. But years ago I learned to kill only for food and defense. I learned it from what you call the beasts. I think it is a good rule. Those who kill for any other reason, such as for pleasure or revenge, debase themselves. They make savages of themselves. I will tell you when to fire."

"Perhaps they won't come after all," said Corrie.

Tarzan shook his head. "They will come. They are almost here."

8

WHEN Iskandar awoke the sun was shining full in his face. He raised himself on an elbow. His eyes took in the scene before him. His nine companions slept. The sentry slept beside a dead fire. The captive was not there.

His cruel face distorted in rage, Iskandar seized his kris and leaped to his feet. The shrieks of the sentry awakened the other sleepers. "Pig!" screamed Iskandar, hacking at the head and body of his victim as the man tried to crawl away from him on hands and knees. "The tigers could have come and killed us all. And because of you, the woman has escaped."

A final blow at the base of the brain, which severed the spinal column, ended the torture. Iskandar wiped his bloody kris on the garments of the dead man and turned his scowling face upon his men. "Come!" he ordered. "She cannot have gotten far. Hurry!"

They soon picked up Corrie's footprints in the trail and hurried in pursuit. Half way along the trail to the cave where they had captured her, they came upon the body of a tiger. Iskandar examined it closely. He saw the knife wounds behind its left shoulder. He saw many footprints in the muddy trail. There were those of the girl and others made by the same crude type of sandal that she had worn, but larger—the footprints of men. And there were prints of the bare feet of a man. Iskandar was puzzled. There seemed ample evidence that someone had stabbed the tiger to death. But that was impossible. No one could have come within reach of those terrible talons and jaws and lived.

They pushed on, and in the afternoon they came within sight of the cave.

"Here they come," said Jerry Lucas.

"There are but four men," said Iskandar. "Kill the men, but do not harm the woman." The nine tribesmen advanced confidently with bared kris.

Tarzan permitted them to approach within a hundred

feet; then he had Corrie address them. "Stop!" she said. "Do not come any closer."

Each of the five had fitted an arrow to his bow. The left hand of each held additional arrows. Iskandar laughed and gave the word to charge. "Let them have it," said Tarzan, sending an arrow through Iskandar's leg, dropping him. Four others were hit by that first flight of arrows. Two of the others stopped, but two came on yelling like demons. Tarzan drove an arrow through the heart of each. They were too close to be spared as he had spared Iskandar. So close that one of them fell almost touching Tarzan's feet.

He turned to Corrie. "Tell them that if they throw down their weapons and put their hands up, we will not kill them."

After the girl had translated the instructions, the Sumatrans grumbled sullenly; but they did not throw down their weapons nor raise their hands.

"Fit arrows to your bows and advance slowly," ordered Tarzan. "At the first threatening move, shoot to kill."

"You wait here, Corrie," said Jerry. "There may be a fight."

She smiled at him but ignored his directions; so he put himself in front of her as they advanced. It was a long arrow that Tarzan had fitted to his bow, a heavy bow that only Tarzan could draw. He aimed the arrow at Iskandar's heart, and whispered to Corrie.

"He will count to ten," the girl explained to the Sumatran. "If you have not all thrown down your weapons and raised your hands before he finishes counting he will kill you. Then we will kill the others."

Tarzan commenced to count, Corrie translating. At five, Iskandar gave in. He had looked into the gray eyes of the giant standing above him and he was afraid. The others followed the example of their leader.

"Rosetti," said Tarzan, "gather up their weapons and retrieve our arrows. We will keep them covered."

Rosetti gathered the weapons first; then he yanked the arrows from the limbs and bodies of the five who had been hit but not killed. With the dead he was more gentle.

"Tell them to take their dead and get out of here, Corrie. And that if they ever annoy us again we will kill them all."

Corrie translated, adding a punch line of her own devising: "This man who speaks to you through me is no ordinary man.

Armed only with a knife, he leaped upon the back of a tiger and killed it. If you are wise, you will obey him."

"Just a minute, Corrie," said Jerry. "Ask them if they have seen any American fliers recently who had bailed out of a damaged plane, or heard of any."

Corrie put the question to Iskandar and received a sullen negative. The chief got to his feet and gave orders to his men, none of whom was seriously wounded. They picked up their dead and started away, but Iskandar stopped them. Then he turned to Tarzan. "You will let us take our weapons?" he asked. Corrie translated.

"No." This seemed to need no translation or admit of argument. The chief had looked again into the gray eyes of the giant who had killed the tiger he had seen upon the trail, and what he had seen there had frightened him. They are not the eyes of a man, he thought. They are the eyes of a tiger.

Snarling a Malayan oath beneath his breath, he ordered his men to march, and followed them.

"We'd orter have killed 'em all," said Shrimp. "They'll tell the foist yellow-bellies they see where to find us."

"If we followed that plan to its logical conclusion," said Tarzan, "we'd have to kill every human being we meet. Any of them might tell the Japs."

"You don't believe much in killin' people."

Tarzan shook his head in negation.

"Not even Japs?"

"That is different. We are at war with them. Neither in hatred nor revenge and with no particular pleasure I shall kill every Jap I can until the war is over. That is my duty."

"Don't you even hate 'em?"

"What good would it do if I did? If all the many millions of people of the allied nations devoted an entire year exclusively to hating the Japs it wouldn't kill one Jap nor shorten the war one day."

Bubonovitch laughed. "And it might give 'em all stomach ulcers."

Tarzan smiled. "I can recall having felt hatred but once in my life or killing for revenge but once—Kulonga, the son of Mbonga. He killed Kala, my foster mother. Not only was I very young then, but Kala was the only creature in the world that loved me or that I loved. And I thought then that she was my own mother. I have never regretted the killing."

While they talked, Corrie was cooking their supper. Jerry was helping her—not that she needed any help. They were grilling pheasants and venison over a fire just inside the mouth of the cave. Bubonovitch was examining the weapons left by the Sumatrans. He selected a kris for himself. Jerry and Shrimp followed his example, and Jerry brought Corrie a parang.

"Why did you ask that bandit if he had heard of any American fliers who had bailed out recently?" Corrie asked Lucas.

"Two of my crew, who are known to have bailed out, are unaccounted for—Douglas, my radioman, and Davis, a waist gunner. We hunted for them, but could find no trace of them. We found the body of Lieutenant Burnham whose chute had failed to open. So we figured that if either of the other chutes had failed to open we should have found the body nearby. We all jumped within a matter of a few seconds."

"How many were you?"

"Eleven—nine in the crew, Colonel Clayton, and a photographer. My bombardier was left behind because he was sick. Anyway, we weren't carrying any bombs. It was just a reconnaissance and photographic mission."

"Let's see," said Corrie. "There are four of you here, Lieutenant Burnham makes five, and the two unaccounted for make seven. What became of the other four?"

"Killed in action."

"Poor boys," said Corrie.

"It is not those who are killed who suffer," said Jerry. "It is those who are left behind—their buddies and their folks back home. Maybe they're better off. After all, this is a hell of a world," he added bitterly, "and those who get out of it are the lucky ones."

She laid her hand on his. "You mustn't feel that way. There may be a lot of happiness in the world for you yet—for all of us."

"They were my friends," he said, "and they were very young. They hadn't had a chance to get much out of life. It just doesn't seem right. Tarzan says that it does no good to hate, and I know he's right. But I do hate—not the poor

55

dumb things who shoot at us and whom we shoot at, but those who are responsible for making wars."

"I know," she said. "I hate them, too. But I hate all Japs. I hate the 'poor dumb things who shoot at us and whom we shoot at.' I am not as philosophical as you and Tarzan. I want to hate them. I often reproach myself because I think I am not hating bitterly enough." Jerry could see that hate reflected in her eyes, and he thought what a horrible thing it was that such an emotion could have been aroused in the breast of one so innately sweet and kind. He said to her what she had said to him: "You mustn't feel that way," and he added, "You were never made for hate."

"You never saw your mother hounded to death and your father bayoneted by those yellow beasts. If you had and didn't hate them you wouldn't be fit to call yourself a man."

"I suppose you are right," he said. He pressed her hand. "Poor little girl."

"Don't sympathize with me," she said almost angrily. "I didn't cry then. I haven't cried since. But if you sympathize with me, I shall."

Had she emphasized *you?* He thought that she had—just a little. Why, he asked himself, should that send a little thrill through him? I must be going ga-ga, he thought.

Now the little band gathered around the cooking fire for supper. They had broad leaves for plates, sharpened bamboo splinters for forks, and of course they had their knives. They drank from gourds.

Besides pheasant and venison, they had fruit and the roasted seeds of the durian. They lived well in this land of plenty. "T'ink of de poor dogfaces back at base," said Shrimp, "eatin' canned hash an' spam."

"And drinking that goddam G-I coffee," said Bubonovitch. "It always made me think of one of Alexander Woolcott's first lines in *The Man Who Came to Dinner.*"

"I'll trade places with any dogface right now," said Jerry.

"What's a dogface?" asked Corrie.

"Well, I guess originally it was supposed to mean a dough-boy; but now it sort of means any enlisted man, more specifically a private."

"Any G-I Joe," said Shrimp.

"What a strange language!" said Corrie. "And I thought I understood English."

56

"It isn't English," said Tarzan. "It's American. It's a young and virile language. I like it."

"But what is a doughboy? And a G-I Joe?"

"A doughboy is an infantryman. A G-I Joe is an American soldier—Government Issue. Stick with us, Corrie, and we'll improve your American and ruin your English," concluded Jerry.

"If you will pay special attention to Sergeant Rosetti's conversation they will both be ruined," said Bubonovitch.

"Wot's wrong wit my American, wise guy?" demanded Shrimp.

"I think Sergeant Shrimp is cute," said Corrie.

Rosetti flushed violently. "Take a bow, cutie," said Bubonovitch.

Shrimp grinned. He was used to being ribbed, and he never got mad, although sometimes he pretended to be. "I ain't heard no one callin' you cute, you big cow," he said, and he felt that with that come-back his honor had been satisfied.

9

BEFORE supper, Tarzan had cut two large slabs of bark from a huge tree in the forest. The slabs were fully an inch thick, tough and strong. From them he cut two disks, as nearly sixteen and a half inches in diameter as he could calculate. In about one half of the periphery of each disk he cut six deep notches, leaving five protuberances between them.

After supper, Jerry and the others, sitting around the fire, watched him. "Now what the heck are those for?" asked the pilot. "They looked like round, flat feet with five toes."

"Thank you," said Tarzan. "I didn't realize that I was such a good sculptor. These are to deceive the enemy. I have no doubt but that that old villain will return with Japs just as quickly as he can. Now those natives must be good trackers, and they must be very familiar with our spoor, for they followed it here. Our homemade sandals would identify our spoor to even the stupidest tracker. So we must obliterate it.

"First we will go into the forest in a direction different from the one we intend taking, and we will leave spoor that will immediately identify our party. Then we will cut back to camp through the undergrowth where we can walk without leaving footprints, and start out on the trail we intend taking. Three of us will walk in single file, each stepping exactly in the footprints of the man ahead of him. I will carry Corrie. It would tire her to take a man's stride. Bubonovitch will bring up the rear, wearing one of these strapped to each foot. With one of them he will step on each and every footprint that we have made. He will have to do a considerable split to walk with these on, but he is a big man with long legs. These will make the footprints of an elephant and obliterate ours."

"Geeze!" exclaimed Rosetti. "A elephant's feet ain't that big!"

"I'm not so sure myself about these Indian elephants," admitted Tarzan. "But the circumference of an African elephant's front foot is half the animal's height at the shoulder. So these will indicate an elephant approximately nine feet in height. Unfortunately, Bubonovitch doesn't weigh as much as an elephant; so the spoor won't be as lifelike as I'd like. But I'm banking on the likelihood that they won't pay much attention to elephant spoor while they are looking for ours. If they do, they are going to be terribly surprised to discover the trail of a two-legged elephant.

"Had we been in Africa the problem would have been complicated by the fact that the African elephant has five toes in front and three behind. That would have necessitated another set of these, and Jerry would have had to be the hind legs."

"De sout' end of a elephant goin' nort', Cap," said Shrimp.

"I'm not selfish," said Jerry. "Bubonovitch can be the whole elephant."

"You'd better put Shrimp at the head of the column," said Bubonovitch, "I might step on him."

"I think we'd better turn in now," said Tarzan. "What time have you, Jerry?"

"Eight o'clock."

"You have the first watch tonight—two and a half hours

58

on. That will bring it just right. Shrimp draws the last— 3:30 to 6:00. Good night!"

They started early the following morning after a cold breakfast. First they made the false trail. Then they started off in the direction they intended taking, Bubonovitch bringing up the rear, stamping down hard on the footprints of those who preceded him. At the end of a mile, which was as far as Tarzan thought necessary to camouflage their trail, he was a pretty tired elephant. He sat down beside the trail and took off his cumbersome feet. "Migawd!" he said. "I'm just about split to the chin. Whoever wants to play *elephas maximus* of the order Proboscidea can have these goddam things." He tossed them into the trail.

Tarzan picked them up and threw them out into the underbrush. "It was a tough assignment, Sergeant; but you were the best man for it."

"I could have carried Corrie."

"An' you wit a wife an' kid!" chided Shrimp.

"I think the colonel pulled rank on you," said Jerry.

"Oh, no," said Tarzan; "it was just that I couldn't think of throwing Corrie to the wolves."

"I guess dat will hold you," observed Shrimp.

Corrie was laughing, her eyes shining. She liked these Americans with their strange humor, their disregard for conventions. And the Englishman, though a little more restrained, was much like them. Jerry had told her that he was a viscount, but his personality impressed her more than his title.

Suddenly Tarzan raised his head and tested the air with his nostrils. "Take to the trees," he said.

"Is something coming?" asked Corrie.

"Yes. One of the sergeant's relatives—with both ends. It is a lone bull, and sometimes they are mean."

He swung Corrie to an overhanging branch, as the others scrambled up the nearest trees. Tarzan smiled. They were becoming proficient. He remained standing in the trail.

"You're not going to stay there?" demanded Jerry.

"For a while. I like elephants. They are my friends. Most of them like me. I shall know in plenty of time if he is going to charge."

"But this is not an African elephant," insisted Jerry.

"Maybe he never heard of Tarzan," suggested Shrimp.

"The Indian elephant is not so savage as the African, and

I want to try an experiment. I have a theory. If it proves incorrect, I shall take to the trees. He will warn me, for if he is going to charge, he will raise his ears, curl up his trunk, and trumpet. Now, please don't talk or make any noise. He is getting close."

The four in the trees waited expectantly. Corrie was frightened—frightened for Tarzan. Jerry thought it foolish for the man to take such chances. Shrimp wished that he had a tommy gun—just in case. Every eye was glued on the turn in the trail, at the point where the elephant would first appear.

Suddenly the great bulk of the beast came into view. It dwarfed Tarzan. When the little eyes saw Tarzan, the animal stopped. Instantly the ears were spread and the trunk curled up. It is going to charge was the thought of those in the trees.

Corrie's lips moved. Silently they formed the plea, "Quick, Tarzan! Quick!"

And then Tarzan spoke. He spoke to the elephant in the language that he believed was common to most beasts—the mother tongue of the great apes. Few could speak it, but he knew that many understood it. "Yo, Tantor, yo!" he said.

The elephant was weaving from side to side. It did not trumpet. Slowly the ears dropped and the trunk uncurled. "Yud!" said Tarzan.

The great beast hesitated a moment, and then came slowly toward the man. It stopped in front of him and the trunk reached out and moved over his body. Corrie clutched the tree branch to keep from falling. She could understand how, involuntarily, some women scream or faint in moments of high excitement.

Tarzan stroked the trunk for a moment, whispering quietly to the huge mass towering above him. "Abu tand-nala!" he said presently. Slowly, the elephant knelt. Tarzan wrapped the trunk about his body and said, "Nala b'yat!" and Tantor lifted him and placed him upon his head.

"Unk!" commanded Tarzan. The elephant moved off down the trail, passing beneath the trees where the astonished four sat, scarcely breathing.

Shrimp was the first to break the long silence. "I've saw everyt'ing now. Geeze! wot a guy!"

"Are you forgetting Goige de Toid?" demanded Bubonovitch.

Shrimp muttered something under his breath that was not fit for Corrie's ears.

Presently Tarzan returned on foot and alone. "We'd better be moving along," he said, and the others dropped down from the trees.

Jerry was not a little irritated by what he thought had been an egotistical display of courage and prowess, and his voice revealed his irritation when he asked, "What was the use of taking such a risk, Colonel?"

"In the haunts of wild beasts one must know many things if one is to survive," Tarzan explained. "This is strange country to me. In my country the elephants are my friends. On more than one occasion they have saved my life. I wanted to know the temper of the elephants here and if I could impose my will on them as I do at home. It is possible that some day you may be glad that I did so. The chances are that I shall never see that bull again; but if we should meet, he will know me and I shall know him. Tantor and I have long memories both for friends and enemies."

"Sorry I spoke as I did," said Jerry; "but we were all frightened to see you take such a risk."

"I took no risk," said Tarzan; "but don't you do it."

"What would he have done to one of us?" asked Bubonovitch.

"Gored you probably, knelt on you, and then tossed the pulp that had been you high into the forest."

Corrie shuddered. Shrimp shook his head. "An' I uset to feed 'em peanuts at de coicus."

"The wild beasts I've seen here in the open look larger and more menacing than those I used to see in menageries and zoos," said Bubonovitch.

"Or in a museum, stuffed," said Jerry.

"Mounted," corrected Bubonovitch.

"Purist," said Jerry.

Presently they entered a forest of enormous straight trunked trees, enveloped by giant creepers, vines, and huge air plants that formed a thick canopy overhead. The dim light, the cathedral vistas, the sounds of unseen things depressed the spirits of all but Tarzan. They plodded on in silence, longing for the light of the sun. And then, at a turning in the trail, they came suddenly into its full glare as the forest ended abruptly at the edge of a gorge.

Below them lay a narrow valley cut through the ages

into the tuff and limestone formation of the terrain by the little river that raced riotously along its bottom. It was a pleasant valley, green and tree dotted.

Tarzan scrutinized its face carefully. There was no sign of human life; but some deer fed there, and his keen eyes recognized a black blob, almost indistinguishable in the dense shade of a tree. He pointed it out to the others. "Beware of him," he cautioned. "He is infinitely more dangerous than Tantor, and sometimes even than Stripes."

"What is it, a water buffalo?" asked Jerry.

"No. It is Buto the rhinoceros. His sight is very poor, but his hearing and scent are extremely acute. He has an ugly and unpredictable disposition. Ordinarily, he will run away from you. But you can never tell. Without any provocation he may come thundering down on you as fast as a good horse; and if he gets you, he'll gore and toss you."

"Not ours," said Corrie. "They have lower tusks, and they use those instead of their horns."

"I remember now," said Tarzan, "hearing that. I was thinking of the African rhino."

The trail turned abruptly to the right at the edge of the escarpment and hurled itself over the rim, angling steeply downward, narrow and precarious. They were all glad when they reached the bottom.

"Stay here," said Tarzan, "and don't make any noise. I am going to try to get one of those deer. Buto won't get your scent from here; and if you don't make any noise, he won't hear you. I'll circle around to the left. Those bushes there will hide me until I get within range of the deer. If I get one, I'll go right on down to the river where the trail crosses it. You can come on then and meet me there. The trail passes Buto at about a hundred yards. If he gets your scent, or hears you, and stands up, don't move unless he starts toward you; then find a tree."

Tarzan crouched and moved silently among the tall grasses. The wind, blowing from the direction of the deer toward the rhinoceros, carried no scent of the intruders to either. It would to the latter when Tarzan reached the deer and when the others crossed the wind to reach the river.

Tarzan disappeared from the sight of those who waited at the foot of the cliff. They wondered how he could find cover where there seemed to be none. Everything seemed to be moving according to plan when there was a sudden interuption. They saw a deer suddenly raise its head and look back; then it and the little herd of which it was a part were off like a flash, coming almost directly toward them.

They saw Tarzan rise from the grasses and leap upon a young buck. His knife flashed in the sun, and both fell, disappearing in the grass. The four watchers were engrossed by this primitive drama—the primordial hunter stalking and killing his quarry. Thus it must have been ages and ages ago.

Finally Jerry said, "Well, let's get going."

"Geeze!" Shrimp exclaimed, pointing. "Lookut!"

They looked. Buto had arisen and was peering this way and that with his dull little eyes. But he was listening and scenting the wind, too.

"Don't move," whispered Jerry.

"An' they ain't no trees," breathed Shrimp. He was right. In their immediate vicinity there were no trees.

"Don't move," cautioned Jerry again. "If he's going to charge, he'll charge anything that moves."

"Here he comes," said Bubonovitch. The rhino was walking toward them. He seemed more puzzled than angry. His dim vision had, perhaps, discovered something foreign to the scene. Something he could neither hear nor smell. And curiosity prompted him to investigate.

The three men, by one accord, moved cautiously between Corrie and the slowly oncoming beast. It was a tense moment. If Buto charged, someone would be hurt, probably killed. They watched the creature with straining eyes. They saw the little tail go up and the head down as the rhino broke into a trot. He had seen them and was coming straight for them. Suddenly he was galloping. "This is it," said Jerry.

At the same instant, Shrimp leaped away from them and ran diagonally across the path of the charging brute. And the rhino swerved and went for him. Shrimp ran as he had never run before; but he couldn't run as fast as a horse, and the rhino could.

Horror-stricken, the others watched. Horror-stricken and helpless. Then they saw Tarzan. He was running to meet the man and the beast, who were headed directly toward him. But what could he do? the watchers asked themselves. What could two relatively puny men do against those tons of savage flesh and bone?

The beast was close behind Shrimp now and Tarzan was

only a few yards away. Then Shrimp stumbled and fell
Corrie covered her eyes with her hands. Jerry and Bubonovitch, released as though from a momentary paralysis, started
running toward the scene of certain tragedy.

Corrie, impelled against her will, removed her hands from
her eyes. She saw the rhino's head go down as though to
gore the prostrate man now practically beneath its front
feet.

Then Tarzan leaped, turning in air, and alighted astride
the beast's shoulders. The diversion was enough to distract
the animal's attention from Shrimp. It galloped over him,
bucking to dislodge the man-thing on its back.

Tarzan held his seat long enough to plunge his knife
through the thick hide directly behind the head and sever
the brute's spinal cord. Paralyzed, it stumbled to the ground.
A moment later it was dead.

Soon the entire party was gathered around the kill. A
relieved and, perhaps, a slightly trembling party. Tarzan
turned to Shrimp. "That was one of the bravest things I ever
saw done, sergeant," he said.

"Shrimp didn't rate medals for nothing, Colonel," said
Bubonovitch.

10

THEY were now well supplied with meat—too well. A deer
and a rhinoceros for five people seemed more than
ample. Tarzan had taken some choice cuts from the
young buck and cut the hump from the rhino. Now, beside
the river, he had built a fire in a hole that he had dug. Over
another fire, the others were grilling bits of venison.

"You ain't goin' to eat that are you?" asked Shrimp, pointing at the big hunk of rhino meat with the skin still attached.

"In a couple of hours you'll eat it," said Tarzan. "You'll
like it."

When he had a bed of hot coals in the bottom of the hole
he had dug, he laid the hump in with the skin side down,
covered it with leaves and then with the dirt he had exca-
vated.

Taking a piece of venison, he withdrew a little from the others, squatted down on his haunches and tore off pieces of the raw flesh with his strong teeth. The others had long since ceased to pay attention to this seeming idiosyncrasy. They had, on occasion, eaten their meat raw; but they still preferred it cooked—usually charred on the outside, raw on the inside, and covered with dirt. They were no longer fastidious.

"What was on your mind, Shrimp, while you were legging it in front of *Rhinoceros Dicerorhinus sumatrensis?*" asked Bubonovitch. "You sure hit nothing but the high spots. I'll bet you did the hundred yards in under eight seconds."

"I'll tell you wot I was thinkin'. I'd started on Ave Maria w'en I seen it was nothin' less 'n Whirlaway on my tail. I was thinkin' if I could just finish that one Ave Maria before it caught up with me, I might have a chance. Then I stumbled. But the Blessed Mary heard me and saved me."

"I thought it was Tarzan," said Bubonovitch.

"Of course it was Tarzan; but whoinell do you suppose got him there in time, you dope?"

"There are no atheists at the business end of a rhinoceros," said Jerry.

"I prayed, too," said Corrie. "I prayed that God would not let anything happen to you who were risking you life to save ours. You are a very brave man, sergeant, for you must have known that you didn't have one chance in a million."

Rosetti was very unhappy. He wished that they would talk about something else. "You got me all wrong," he said. "I just ain't got no sense. If I had, I'd a run the other way; but I didn't think of it in time. The guy who had the guts was the colonel. Think of killin' a deer an' dat rhino wit nothin' but a knife." This gave him an idea for changing the subject. "An' think of all dat meat lyin' out there an' the poor suckers back home got to have ration coupons an' then they can't get enough."

"Think of the starving Armenians," said Bubonovitch.

"All the Armenians I ever seen could starve as far as I'm concerned," said Shrimp. He took another piece of venison and lapsed into silence.

Jerry had been watching Corrie when he could snatch a quick look without actually staring at her. He saw her tearing at the meat with her fine, white teeth. He recalled what she had said about hating the Japs: "I want to hate them.

I often reproach myself because I think I am not hating bitterly enough." He thought, *what kind of a woman will she be after the war—after all that she has gone through?*

He looked at Tarzan tearing at raw meat. He looked at the others, their hands and faces smeared with the juices of the venison, dirty with the char of the burned portions.

"I wonder what sort of a world this will be after peace comes," he said. "What kind of people will we be? Most of us are so young that we will be able to remember little else than war—killing, hate, blood. I wonder if we can ever settle down to the humdrum existence of civilian life."

"Say! If I ever get my feet under a desk again," said Bubonovitch, "I hope God strikes me dead if I ever take them out again."

"That's what you think now, Bum. And I hope you're right. For myself, I don't know. Sometimes I hate flying, but it's in my blood by now. Maybe it isn't just the flying—it's the thrill and excitement, possibly. And if that is true, then it's the fighting and the killing that I like. I don't know. I hope not. It will be a hell of a world if a great many young fellows feel that way.

"And take Corrie. She has learned to hate. She was never made for that. That is what war and the Japs have done to her. I wonder if hate twists a person's soul out of shape, so that he's never the same as he was before—if, like an incipient cancer, it eats at the roots of character without one's being aware that one has a cancer."

"I think you need not worry," said Tarzan. "Man readily adapts himself to changed conditions. The young, especially, react quickly to changes of environment and circumstance. You will take your proper places in life when peace comes. Only the weak and the warped will be changed for the worse."

"Wit all de different ways of killin' and maimin' wot we've learnt, like sneakin' up behind a guy an' cuttin' his throat or garrotin' him an' a lot of worse t'ings than dat even, they's goin' to be a lot of bozos startin' Murder Incorporateds all over de U. S., take it from me," said Shrimp. "I knows dem guys. I didn't live all my life in Chi fer nuttin'."

"I think it will change us very much," said Corrie. "We will not be the same people we would have been had we not gone through this. It has matured us rapidly, and that means that we have lost a great deal of our youth. Jerry told me the other day that he is only twenty-three. I thought that he was well along in his thirties. He has lost ten years of his youth. Can he be the same man he would have been had he lived those ten years in peace and security? No. I believe he will be a better man.

"I believe that I shall be a better woman for the very emotion which he and Tarzan deplore—hate. I do not mean petty hatreds. I mean a just hate—a grand hate that exalts. And for the compensations it entails, such as loyalty to one's country and one's comrades, the strong friendships and affections which are engendered by a common, holy hatred for a common enemy."

For a while no one spoke. They seemed to be considering this unique eulogy of hate. It was Jerry who broke the silence. "That is a new angle," he said. "I never thought of hate in that way before. As a matter of fact, fighting men don't do a lot of hating. That seems to be the prerogative of non-combatants."

"Bosh," said Corrie. "That is just a heroic pose on the part of fighting men. When a Jap atrocity hits close to home, I'll bet they hate—when a buddy is tortured, when they learn that Allied prisoners of war have been beheaded. That has happened here, and I'll warrant that our Dutch fighting men learned then to hate, if they had not hated before. And furthermore," said Corrie acidly, "I do not consider myself a noncombatant."

Jerry smiled. "Forgive me. I didn't mean that remark derogatorily. And anyway it wasn't aimed at you. You are one of us, and we are all combatants."

Corrie, mollified, smiled back at him. She may have been a good two-fisted hater, but that was not hate that shone from her eyes at the moment.

Shrimp interrupted the discussion. "Geeze!" he exclaimed. "Get a load of dis. It smells like heaven."

They looked, to see Tarzan removing the roast from the improvised oven. "Come an' get it!" called Shrimp.

To their surprise, they found the rhino hump juicy, tender, and delicious. And as they ate, a pair of eyes watched them from the concealment of bushes that grew at the edge of the cliff beyond the river—watched them for a few minutes; then the owner of the eyes turned back into the forest.

That night, the wild dogs fought over the carcasses of Tarzan's kills until, near dawn, a tiger came and drove them

67

from their feast to stand in a dismal, growling circle until the lord of the jungle should depart.

Wars make words. World War II is no exception. Probably the most notorious word for which it is responsible is quisling. Wars also unmake words. Collaborationist formerly had a fair and honorable connotation, but I doubt that it ever will live down World War II. No one will ever again wish to be known as a collaborationist.

They are to be found in every country where the enemy is to be found. There are collaborationists in Sumatra. Such was Amat. He was a miserable creature who bowed low to every Jap soldier and sought to curry favor with them. He was a human jackal that fed off the leavings of the arrogant invaders who slapped his face when he got underfoot.

So, when he saw the five white people camped by the river in the little valley, he licked his full lips as though in anticipation of a feast, and hurried back along the trail toward the village of his people where a detachment of Jap soldiers was temporarily billeted.

He had two reasons for hurrying. He was anxious to impart his information to the enemy. That was one reason. The other was terror. He had not realized how late it was. Darkness would fall before he could reach the village. It is then that my lord the tiger walks abroad in the forest.

He was still a couple of kilometers from home, and dusk was heralding the short equatorial twilight when Amat's worst fear was realized. The hideous face of the lord of the jungle loomed directly in his path. The terrifying eyes, the wrinkled, snarling face of a tiger, between which and its intended victim there are no iron bars and only a few yards of lonely jungle trail, are probably as horrifying a sight as the eyes of man have ever envisaged.

The tiger did not for long leave Amat in any doubt as to its intentions. It charged. Amat shrieked, and leaped for a tree. Still shrieking, he clawed his way upward. The tiger sprang for him; and, unfortunately, missed. Amat scrambled higher, sweating and panting. He clung there, trembling; and there we may leave him until morning.

11

"**G**EEZE! wot a country," growled Shrimp, as they toiled up the steep trail out of the valley in the light of a new day. "If you ain't crawlin' down into a hole, you're crawlin' up outta one. God must a-been practicin' when He made this."

"And when he got through practicing, I suppose, He made Chicago," suggested Bubonovitch.

"Now you're shoutin', wise guy. God sure made Chi. W'en He wasn't lookin', somebody else made Brooklyn. Geeze! I wisht I was in dear ol' Chi right now. Why, de steepest hill dere is de approach to de Madison Street bridge."

"Look at the view, man. Have you no eye for beauty?"

"Sure, I got an eye for beauty; but my feet ain't. They joined up for de air force, an' now they ain't nuttin' but goddam doughboys."

But all things must end, and eventually they reached the top of the escarpment. Tarzan examined the trail. "There was a native here recently," he said. "Probably late yesterday afternoon. He may have seen us. He stood right here for several minutes, where he could look down on our camp."

As the little party continued along the trail into the forest, Amat rushed breathlessly into his village, bursting with the information that had been seething within him during a night of terror. So excited was he that he failed to bow to a Jap private and got slapped and almost bayoneted. But at last he stood before Lt. Kumajiro Tada, this time not forgetting to bow very low.

Excitedly he rattled off an account of what he had seen. Tada, not understanding a word of the native dialect and being particularly godlike thus early in the morning, kicked Amat in the groin. Amat screamed, grabbed his hurt, and sank to the ground. Tada drew his sword. It had been a long time since he had lopped off a head, and he felt like lopping off a head before breakfast.

A sergeant who had overheard Amat's report and who

understood the dialect, saluted and bowed. Sucking wind through his teeth, he informed the honorable lieutenant that Amat had seen a party of whites and that that was what he had been trying to tell the honorable lieutenant. Reluctantly, Tada scabbarded his sword and listened as the sergeant interpreted.

A couple of miles from the point at which they had entered the forest, Tarzan stopped and examined the trail minutely. "Here," he said, "our native friend was treed by a tiger. He remained in this tree all night, coming down only a short time ago, probably as soon as it was light. You can see where the pugs of the beast obliterated the spoor the fellow made last night. Here is where he jumped down this morning and continued on his way."

They continued on and presently came to a fork in the trail. Again Tarzan stopped. He showed them which way the native had gone. In the other fork he pointed out evidence that a number of men had gone that way perhaps several days before. "These were not natives," he said, "nor do I think they were Japs. These are the footprints of very large men. Jerry, suppose you folks follow along the trail the native took, while I investigate the other one. These chaps may be Dutch guerrillas. If they are, they might prove mighty helpful to us. Don't travel too fast, and I may catch up with you."

"We'll probably come to a native village," said Jerry. "If we do, perhaps we'd better hole up in the jungle until you come along; so that we can all approach it together. In the meantime, I'll look the place over."

Tarzan nodded assent and swung into the trees, following the left hand fork of the trail. They watched him until he was out of sight. "That guy likes to travel de hard way?" said Shrimp.

"It doesn't look so hard when you watch him," said Bubonovitch. "It's only when you try to do it yourself."

"It's an ideal way to travel, under the circumstances," Jerry said. "It leaves no trail, and it gives him every advantage over any enemy he might meet."

"It is beautiful," said Corrie. "He is so graceful, and he moves so quietly." She sighed. "If we could all do it, how much safer we should be!"

"I t'ink I'll practice up," said Shrimp. "An' w'en I gets

home I goes out to Garfield Park and swings t'rough de trees some Sunday w'en dey's a gang dere."

"And get pinched," said Bubonovitch.

"Sure I'd get pinched, but I'd make de front pages wit pitchurs. Maybe I'd get a job wit Sol Lesser out in Hollywood."

"Where'd you get the reefers, Shrimp?" inquired Bubonovitch.

Shrimp grinned. "Me? I don't use 'em. I don't work fer Petrillo. I just get dat way from associatin' wit you."

They were moving leisurely along the trail toward Amat's village, Bubonovitch in the lead, Rosetti behind him. Jerry and Corrie followed several yards in the rear. Then Corrie stopped to retie the laces of one of her moccasins, and Jerry waited for her. The others passed out of sight beyond a turn in the winding trail.

"Don't you feel a little lost without Tarzan?" Corrie asked as she straightened up. Then she voiced a little exclamation of dismay. "Oh, I don't mean that I haven't every confidence in you and Bubonovitch and Rosetti, but—"

Jerry smiled. "Don't apologize. I feel the same way you do. We're all out of our natural environment. He's not. He's right at home here. I don't know what we should have done without him."

"We should have been just a lot of babes in the—"

"Listen!" cautioned Jerry, suddenly alert. He heard voices ahead. Hoarse shouts in a strange tongue. "Japs!" he exclaimed. He started to run toward the sounds. Then he stopped and turned back. His was a cruel decision any way he looked at it. He must desert either his two sergeants or the girl. But he was accustomed to making hair trigger decisions.

He seized Corrie by an arm and dragged her into the tangle of undergrowth beside the trail. They wormed their way in farther and farther as long as the sound of the voices came no nearer. When they did, indicating that the Japs were investigating the trail in their direction, they lay flat on the ground beneath a riot of equatorial verdure. A searcher might have passed within a foot of them without seeing them.

A dozen soldiers surprised and captured Bubonovitch and Rosetti. They didn't have a chance. The Japs slapped them around and threatened them with bayonets until Lt. Tada called them off. Tada spoke English. He had worked as a dishwasher in a hotel in Eugene while attending the University of Oregon, and he had sized up the prisoners immediately as Americans. He questioned them, and each gave his name, rank, and serial number.

"You were from that bomber that was shot down?" demanded Tada.

"We have given you all the information we are required or permitted to give."

Tada spoke to a soldier in Japanese. The man advanced and pushed the point of his bayonet against Bubonovitch's belly. "Now will you answer my question?" growled Tada.

"You know the rules governing the treatment of prisoners of war," said Bubonovitch, "but I don't suppose that makes any difference to you. It does to me, though. I won't answer any more questions."

"You are a damn fool," said Tada. He turned to Rosetti. "How about you?" he demanded. "Will you answer?"

"Nuttin' doin'," said Rosetti.

"There were five in your party—four men and a girl. Where are the other three?—where is the girl?" the Jap persisted.

"You seen how many was in our party. Do we look like five? Or can't you count? Does eider of us look like a dame? Somebody's been stringin' you, Tojo."

"O.K., wise guy," snapped Tada. "I'm goin' to give you until tomorrow morning to think it over. You answer all my questions tomorrow morning, or you both get beheaded." He tapped the long officer's sword at his side.

"Anday I-ay essgay e-hay ain'tay oolin-fay," said Rosetti to Bubonovitch.

"You bet your sweet life I ain't foolin', Yank," said Tada.

Shrimp was crestfallen. "Geeze! Who'd a-thought a Nip would savvy hog latin!" he moaned to Bubonovitch.

Tada sent two of his men along the trail to search for the other members of the party. He and the remainder turned back toward Amat's village with the two prisoners.

Jerry and Corrie had overheard all that had been said. They heard the main party move off in the direction from which they had come, but they did not know of the two who had been sent in search of them. Believing that they were now safe from detection, they crawled from their concealment and returned to the trail.

Tarzan, swinging easily through the middle terrace of the

forest, had covered perhaps two miles when his attention was arrested by a commotion ahead. He heard the familiar grunts and growls and chattering of the great apes, and guessed that they were attacking or being attacked by an enemy. As the sounds lay directly in his path, he continued on.

Presently he came within sight of four adult orangutans swinging excitedly among the branches of a great tree. They darted in and out, striking and screaming. And then he saw the object of their anger—a python holding in its coils a young orangutan.

Tarzan took in the whole scene at a glance. The python had not as yet constricted. It merely held the struggling victim while it sought to fight off the attacking apes. The screams of the young one were definite proof that it was still very much alive.

Tarzan thrilled to the savage call to battle, to the challenge of his ancient enemy, Histah the snake, to the peril of his friends, the Mangani—the great apes. If he wondered if they would recognize him as friend, or attack him as foe, the thought did not deter him. He swung quickly into the tree in which the tragedy was being enacted, but to a branch above the python and its victim.

So intent were the actors in this primitive drama upon the main issue that none were aware of his presence until he spoke, wondering if, like Tantor, the great apes would understand him.

"Kreeg-ah!" he shouted. "Tarzan bundolo Histah!"

The apes froze and looked up. They saw an almost naked man-thing poised above the python, in the man-thing's hand a gleaming blade.

"Bundolo! Bundolo!" they shouted—*Kill! Kill!* And Tarzan knew that they understood. Then he dropped full upon the python and its victim. Steel thewed fingers gripped the snake behind its head, as Tarzan clung to the coils and the young ape with powerful legs. His keen blade cut deep into the writhing body just back of the hand that held its neck in a viselike grasp. The whipping coils, convulsed in agony, released the young orangutan and sought to enmesh the body of the creature clinging to them. Its frantic struggles released the python's hold upon the branches of the tree, and it fell to earth, carrying Tarzan with it. Other branches broke their fall, and the man was not injured. But the snake was far from dead. Its maddened writhings had made it impossible for Tarzan to wield his blade effectively. The snake was badly wounded, but still a most formidable foe. Should it succeed in enmeshing Tarzan in its mighty coils, his body would be crushed long before he could kill it.

And now the apes dropped to the ground beside the contestants in this grim battle of life and death. Growling, chattering, screaming, the four mighty adults leaped upon the beating coils of the python, tearing them from the body of the man-thing. And Tarzan's knife found its mark again.

As the severed head rolled to the ground, Tarzan leaped aside. So did the apes, for the death struggles of the giant snake might prove as lethal as though guided by the tiny brain.

Tarzan turned and faced the apes; then he placed a foot on the dead head and, raising his face to the heavens, voiced the victory cry of the bull ape. It rang wild and weird and terrifying through the primeval forest, and for a moment the voices of the jungle were stilled.

The apes looked at the man-thing. All their lives his kind had been their natural enemies. Was he friend or foe?

Tarzan struck his breast, and said, "Tarzan."

The apes nodded, and said, "Tarzan," for tarzan means white-skin in the language of the great apes.

"Tarzan yo," said the man. "Mangani yo?"

"Mangani yo," said the oldest and largest of the apes—*great apes friend*.

There was a noise in the trees, like the coming of a big wind—the violent rustling and swishing of leaves and branches. Apes and man looked expectantly in the direction from which the sound came. All of them knew what created the sound. The man alone did not know what it portended.

Presently he saw ten or twelve huge black forms swinging toward them through the trees. The apes dropped to the ground around them. They had heard Tarzan's piercing call, and had hastened to investigate. It might be the victory cry of an enemy that had overcome one of the tribe. It might have been a challenge to battle.

They eyed Tarzan suspiciously, some of them with bared fangs. He was a man-thing, a natural enemy. They looked from Tarzan to Uglo, the oldest and largest of the apes. Uglo pointed at the man and said, "Tarzan. Yo." Then, in the simple language of the first-men and with signs and gestures, he told what Tarzan had done. The newcomers nodded their understanding—all but one. Oju, a full grown, powerful young orangutan, bared his fangs menacingly.

"Oju bundolo!" he growled—*Oju kill!*

Vanda, mother of the little ape rescued from the python, pressed close to Tarzan, stroking him with a rough and horny palm. She placed herself between Tarzan and Oju, but the former pushed her gently aside.

Oju had issued a challenge which Tarzan could not ignore and retain the respect of the tribe. This he knew, and though he did not want to fight, he drew his knife and advanced toward the growling Oju.

Standing nearly six feet in height and weighing fully three hundred pounds, Oju was indeed a formidable opponent. His enormously long arms, his Herculean muscles, his mighty fangs and powerful jaws dwarfed the offensive equipment of even the mighty Tarzan.

Oju lumbered forward, his calloused knuckles resting on the ground. Uglo would have interfered. He made a half-hearted gesture of stepping between them. But Uglo was really afraid. He was king, but he was getting old. He knew that Oju was minded to challenge his kingship. Should he antagonize him now, he might only hasten the moment of his dethronement. He did not interfere. But Vanda scolded, and so did the other apes which had witnessed Tarzan's rescue of Vanda's balu.

Oju was not deterred. He waddled confidently to close quarters, contemptuous of this puny man-thing. Could he lay one powerful hand upon him, the fight would be as good as over. He extended a long arm toward his intended victim. It was a tactical error.

Tarzan noted the slow, stupid advance, the outstretched hand; and altered his own plan of battle. Carrying the knife to his mouth and seizing the blade between his teeth, he freed both hands. Then he sprang forward, grasped Oju's extended wrist with ten powerful fingers, wheeled quickly, bent forward, and threw the ape over his head—threw him so that he would fall heavily upon his back.

Badly shaken, roaring with rage, Oju scrambled awkwardly to his feet. Tarzan leaped quickly behind him while he was still off balance, leaped upon his back, locked powerful legs about his middle, and wrapped his left arm about his neck.

Then he pressed the point of his knife against the beast's side
—pressed it in until it brought a scream of pain from Oju.

"Kagoda!" demanded Tarzan. That is ape for surrender.
It is also ape for I surrender. The difference is merely a matter of inflection.

Oju reached a long arm back to seize his opponent. The
knife dug in again. This time deeper. Again Tarzan demanded,
"Kagoda!" The more Oju sought to dislodge the man-thing
from his back, the deeper the knife was pressed. Tarzan could
have killed the ape, but he did not wish to. Strong young
bulls are the strength of a tribe, and this tribe was mostly
friendly to him.

Oju was standing still now. Blood was streaming down his
side. Tarzan moved the point of the knife to the base of
Oju's brain and jabbed it in just enough to draw blood and
inflict pain.

"Kagoda!" screamed Oju.

Tarzan released his hold and stepped aside. Oju lumbered
off and squatted down to nurse his wounds. Tarzan knew
that he had made an enemy, but an enemy that would always be afraid of him. He also knew that he had established
himself as an equal in the tribe. He would always have friends
among them.

He called Uglo's attention to the spoor of men in the
trail. "Tarmangani?" he asked. Tar is white, mangani means
great apes; so tarmangani, white great apes, means white
men.

"Sord tarmangani," said Uglo—*bad white men*.

Tarzan knew that to the great apes, all white men were
bad. He knew that he could not judge these men by the
opinion of an ape. He would have to investigate them himself.
These men might prove valuable allies.

He asked Uglo if the white men were travelling or camped.
Uglo said that they were camped. Tarzan asked how far
away. Uglo extended his arms at full length toward the
sun and held his palms facing one another and about a foot
apart. That is as far as the sun would appear to travel in an
hour. That, Tarzan interpreted as meaning that the camp of
the white men was about three miles distant—as far as the
apes would ordinarily move through the trees in an hour.

He swung into a tree and was gone in the direction of
the camp of the tarmangani. There are no "Good-bys" nor
"Au revoirs" in the language of the apes. The members of the

tribe had returned to their normal activities. Oju nursed his wounds and his rage. He bared his fangs at any who came near him.

12

JERRY was smarting under self-censure. "I feel like a heel," he said, "letting those two fellows take it while I hid. But I couldn't leave you here alone, Corrie, or risk your capture."

"Even if I hadn't been here," said Corrie, "the thing for you to do was just what you did. If you had been captured with them, you could not have done anything more for them than they can do for themselves. Now, perhaps, you and Tarzan and I can do something for them."

"Thanks for putting it that way. Nevertheless, I—" He stopped, listening. "Someone is coming," he said, and drew the girl back into the concealment of the underbrush.

From where they were hidden, they had a clear view back along the trail for a good fifty yards before it curved away from their line of sight. Presently they heard voices more distinctly. "Japs," whispered Corrie. She took a handful of arrows from the quiver at her back and fitted one to her bow. Jerry grinned and followed her example.

A moment later, two Jap soldiers strolled carelessly into view. Their rifles were slung across their backs. They had nothing to fear in this direction—they thought. They had made a token gesture of obeying their officer's instructions to search back along the trail for the three missing whites, whom they had been none too anxious to discover waiting in ambush for them. They would loaf slowly back to camp and report that they had made a thorough search.

Corrie leaned closer to Jerry and whispered, "You take the one on the left. I'll take the other." Jerry nodded and raised his bow.

"Let 'em come to within twenty feet," he said. "When I say now, we'll fire together."

They waited. The Japs were approaching very slowly, jabbering as though they had something worthwhile to say.

"Monkey talk," said Jerry.

"S-sh!" cautioned the girl. She stood with her bow drawn, the feathers of the arrow at her right ear. Jerry glanced at her from the corners of his eyes. Joan of Sumatra, he thought. The Japs were approaching the dead line.

"Now!" said Jerry. Two bow strings twanged simultaneously. Corrie's target pitched forward with an arrow through the heart. Jerry's aim had not been so true. His victim clutched at the shaft sunk deep in his throat.

Jerry jumped into the trail, and the wounded Jap tried to unsling his rifle. He had almost succeeded when Jerry struck him a terrific blow on the chin. He went down, and the pilot leaped upon him with drawn knife. Twice he drove the blade into the man's heart. The fellow twitched convulsively and lay still.

Jerry looked up to see Corrie disentangling the slung rifle from the body of the other Jap. He saw her stand above her victim like an avenging goddess. Three times she drove the bayonet into the breast of the soldier. The American watched girl's face. It was not distorted by rage or hate or vengeance. It was illumined by a divine light of exaltation.

She turned toward Jerry. "That is what I saw them do to my father. I feel happier now. I only wish that he had been alive."

"You are magnificent," said Jerry.

They took possession of the other rifle and the belts and ammunition of the dead men. Then Jerry dragged the bodies into the underbrush. Corrie helped him.

"You can cut a notch in your shootin' iron, woman," said Jerry, grinning. "You have killed your man."

"I have not killed a man," contradicted the girl. "I have killed a Jap."

" 'Haughty Juno's unrelenting hate,' " quoted Jerry.

"You think a woman should not hate," said Corrie. "You could never like a woman who hated."

"I like you," said Jerry gently, solemnly.

"And I like *you*, Jerry. You have been so very fine, all of you. You haven't made me feel like a girl, but like a man among men."

"God forbid!" exclaimed Jerry, and they both laughed.

"For you, Jerry, I shall stop hating—as soon as I have killed all the Japs in the world."

Jerry smiled back at her. "A regular Avenging Angel," he said. "Let's see—who were The Avenging Angels?"

"I don't know," said Corrie. "I've never met any angels."

"Now I remember," said Jerry. "A long while ago there was an association of Mormons, the Danite Band. They were known as The Avenging Angels."

"The Mormons are the people who have a lot of wives, aren't they? Are you a Mormon?"

"Perish the thought. I'm not that courageous. Neither are the present day Mormons. Just imagine being married to a WAC sergeant, a welder, and a steamfitter!"

"And an Avenging Angel?" laughed Corrie.

He didn't answer. He just looked at her, and Corrie wished that she had not said it. Or did she wish that she had not said it?

*   *   *

Tarzan, swinging through the trees overlooking the trail, stopped suddenly and froze into immobility. Ahead of him he saw a man squatting on a platform built in a tree that gave a view of the trail for some distance in the direction from which Tarzan had come. The man was heavily bearded and heavily armed. He was a white man. Evidently he was a sentry watching a trail along which an enemy might approach.

Tarzan moved cautiously away from the trail. Had he not been fully aware of the insensibility of civilized man he would have marvelled that the fellow had not noted his approach. The stupidest of the beasts would have heard him or smelled him or seen him.

Making a detour, he circled the sentry; and a minute or two later came to the edge of a small mountain meadow and looked down upon a rude and untidy camp. A score or so of men were lying around in the shade of trees. A bottle passed from hand to hand among them, or from mouth to mouth. Drinking with them were a number of women. Most of these appeared to be Eurasians. With a single exception, the men were heavily bearded. This was a young man who sat with them, taking an occasional pull at the bottle. The men carried pistols and knives, and each had a rifle close at hand. It was not a nice looking company.

Tarzan decided that the less he had to do with these people

the better. And then the branch on which he sat snapped suddenly, and he fell to the ground within a hundred feet of them. His head struck something hard, and he lost consciousness.

When he came to he was lying beneath a tree, his wrists and ankles bound. Men and women were squatting or standing around him. When they saw that he had regained consciousness, one of the men spoke to him in Dutch. Tarzan understood him, but he shook his head as though he did not.

The fellow had asked him who he was and what he had been doing spying on them. Another tried French, which was the first spoken language of civilized man that he had learned; but he still shook his head. The young man tried English. Tarzan pretended that he did not understand; and addressed them in Swahili, the language of a Mohammedan Bantu people of Zanzibar and the East coast of Africa, knowing that they would not understand it.

"Sounds like Japanese," said one of the men.

"It ain't though," said one who understood that language.

"Maybe it's Chinese," suggested another.

"He looks about as much like a Chink as you do," said the first speaker.

"Maybe he's a wild man. No clothes, bow and arrows. Fell out of a tree like a monkey."

"He's a damned spy."

"What good's a spy who can't talk any civilized language?"

They thought this over, and it seemed to remove their suspicion that their prisoner might be a spy, at least for the moment. They had more important business to attend to, as was soon demonstrated.

"Oh, to hell with him," said a bleary-eyed giant. "I'm getting dry."

He walked back in the direction of the trees beneath which they had been lolling—in the direction of the trees and the bottle—and the others followed. All but the young man with the smooth face. He still squatted near Tarzan, his back toward his retreating companions. When they were at a safer distance and their attention held by the bottle, he spoke. He spoke in a low whisper and in English.

"I am sure that you are either an American or an Englishman," he said. "Possibly one of the Americans from the bomber that was shot down some time ago. If you are, you can trust me. I am practically a prisoner here myself. But don't let them see you talking to me. If you decide that you can trust me, you can make some sign that you understand me.

"You have fallen into the hands of a band of cutthroats. With few exceptions they are criminals who were released from jail and armed when the Japs invaded the island. Most of the women are also criminals who were serving jail sentences. The others are also from the bottom of the social barrel—the ultimate dregs.

"These people escaped to the hills as the Japs took over. They made no attempt to aid our armed forces. They thought only of their own skins. After my regiment surrendered, I managed to escape. I ran across this outfit; and supposing it to be a loyal guerrilla band, I joined it. Learning my background, they would have killed me had it not been that a couple of them are men I had befriended in times past. But they don't trust me.

"You see, there are loyal guerrillas hiding in the hills who would kill these traitors as gladly as they'd kill Japs. And these fellows are afraid I'd get in touch with them and reveal the location of this camp.

"About the worst these people have done so far is to trade with the enemy, but they are going to turn you over to the Japs. They decided on that before you regained consciousness. They also thought that you were one of the American fliers. The Japs would pay a good price for you.

"These fellows distill a vile spirit which they call schnapps. What they don't drink themselves they use to barter with the Japs and natives. They get juniper berries, ammunition, and rice, among other things, from the Japs. That the Japs let them have ammunition indicates that they consider them friendly. However, it is little more than an armed truce; as neither trusts the other to any great extent. Natives are the go-betweens who deliver the schnapps and bring the payment."

Tarzan, knowing now that his fate had already been decided, realized that nothing would be gained by further attempts to deceive the young man. Also, he had gained a good impression of the man; and was inclined to believe that he was trustworthy. He glanced in the direction of the others. They were all intent upon a loudmouthed quarrel between two of their fellows, and were paying no attention to him and his companion.

"I am English," he said.

The young man grinned. "Thanks for trusting me," he said. "My name is Tak van der Bos. I am a reserve officer."

"My name is Clayton. Would you like to get away from these people?"

"Yes. But what good would it do? Where could I go? I'd certainly fall into the hands of the Japs eventually, if a tiger didn't get me instead. If I knew where one of our guerrilla outfits was located, I'd sure take the chance. But I don't."

"There are five in my party," said Tarzan. "We are trying to reach the southern end of the island. If we are lucky, we hope to commandeer a boat and try to reach Australia."

"A rather ambitious plan," said van der Bos. "It's more than twelve hundred miles to the nearest point on the Australian continent. And it's five hundred miles to the southern end of this island."

"Yes," said Tarzan. "We know, but we are going to take the chances. We all feel that it would be better to die trying it than to hide in the woods like a lot of hunted rabbits for the duration."

Van der Bos was silent for a few moments, thinking. Presently he looked up. "It is the right thing to do," he said. "I'd like to come with you. I think I can help you. I can find a boat much nearer than you plan on travelling. I know where there are friendly natives who will help us. But first we've got to get away from these fellows, and that will not be easy. There is only one trail into this little valley, and that is guarded day and night."

"Yes, I saw him. In fact I passed close to him. I can pass him again as easily. But you are different. I do not think that you could though. If you can get me a knife tonight, I will get you past the sentry."

"I'll try. If they get drunk enough, it should be easy. Then I'll cut your bonds, and we can have a go at it."

"I can break these bonds whenever I wish," said Tarzan.

Van der Bos did not comment on this statement. This fellow, he thought, is very sure of himself. Maybe a little too sure. And the Dutchman began to wonder if he had been wise in saying that he would go with him. He knew, of course, that no man could break those bonds. Maybe the fellow couldn't make good on his boast that he could pass the sentry, either.

"Do they watch you very carefully at night?" asked Tarzan.

"They don't watch me at all. This is tiger country. Had you thought of that yourself?"

"Oh, yes. But we shall have to take that chance."

13

SLAPPED around, prodded in the backsides with bayonets, spit on, Rosetti and Bubonovitch were two rage filled and unhappy men long before they reached the native village. Here they were taken into a native house, trussed up, and thrown to the floor in a corner of the room. There they were left to their own devices, which consisted almost wholly of profanity. After describing the progenitors of all Japs from Horohito down, and especially those of Lt. Kumajiro Tada, in the picturesque and unprintable patois of Cicero, Brooklyn, and the Army, they worked back up to Hirohito again.

"What's the use?" demanded Bubonovitch. "We're just working up blood pressure."

"I'm workin' up my hate," said Rosetti. "I know just how dat Corrie dame feels, now. I sure love to hate 'em."

"Make the most of it while you can," advised Bubonovitch. "That ocher looie's going to lop your hater off in the morning."

"Geeze," said Rosetti. "I don't wanna die, Bum."

"Neither do I, Shrimp."

"Geeze! I'm scairt."

"So am I."

"Let's pray, Bum."

"Okay. The last time you prayed to Her, She sent Tarzan."

"I'm just leavin' it to Her. I don't care how She works it."

There was not much sleep for them that night. Their bonds cut into wrists and ankles. Their throats were dry and parched. They were given neither food nor water. The night was an eternity. But at last it ended.

"Geeze! I wisht they'd come an' get it over wit. Thinkin' about it is the worst part."

"Thinking about my wife and baby is the hardest part for me. My wife and I had such great plans. She'll never

83

know what happened to me, and I'm glad for that. All she'll ever know is that my plane took off from somewhere for somewhere and never came back. Did you pray a lot, Shrimp?"

"Most all night."

"So did I."

"Who did you pray to, Bum?"

"To God."

"One of 'em must have heard us."

The sound of scuffing feet ascending the ladder to the house reached their ears.

"I guess this is it," said Bubonovitch. "Can you take it, Shrimp?"

"Sure."

"Well, so long, fellow."

"So long, Bum."

A couple of soldiers entered the room. They cut away the bonds, and dragged the two men to their feet. But they couldn't stand. Both of them staggered and fell to the floor. The soldiers kicked them in head and stomach, laughing and jabbering. Finally they dragged them to the doorway and slid them down the ladder one by one, letting them fall most of the way to the ground.

Tada came over and examined them. "Are you ready to answer my questions?" he demanded.

"No," said Bubonovitch.

"Get up!" snapped the Jap.

Circulation was returning to their numbed feet. They tried to rise, and finally succeeded. But they staggered like drunken men when they walked. They were taken to the center of the village. The soldiers and the natives formed a circle around them. Tada stood beside them with drawn sword. He made them kneel and bend their heads forward. Bubonovitch was to be first.

"I guess They didn't hear us, Shrimp," he said.

"Who didn't hear you?" demanded Tada.

"None of your goddam business, Jap," snapped Bubonovitch.

Tada swung his sword.

When the camp quieted down and most of the men and women slept in a drunken stupor, van der Bos crept to Tarzan's side. "I've got a knife," he said. "I'll cut your bonds."

84

"They've been off a long while," said Tarzan.

"You broke them?" demanded the Dutchman in amazement.

"Yes. Now come along and come quietly. Give me the knife."

A short distance inside the forest, Tarzan halted. "Wait here," he whispered. Then he was gone. He swung quietly into the trees, advancing slowly, stopping often to listen and to search the air with his nostrils. Finally he located the sentry and climbed into the same tree in which had been built the platform on which the man was squatting. He was poised directly over the fellow's head. His eyes bored down through the darkness. They picked out the form and position of the doomed man. Then Tarzan dove for him headfirst, the knife in his hand. The only sound was the thud of the two bodies on the platform. The sentry died in silence, his throat cut from ear to ear.

Tarzan pitched the body to the trail and followed it down with the man's rifle. He walked back until he came to van der Bos. "Come on," he said. "You can get past the sentry now."

When they came to the body, van der Bos stumbled over it. "You certainly made a neat job of it," he said.

"Not so neat," said Tarzan. "He spurted blood all over me. I'll be walking bait for stripes until we reach some water. Take his pistol belt and ammunition. Here's his rifle. Now let's get going."

They moved rapidly along the trail, Tarzan in the lead. Presently they came to a small stream, and both washed the blood from them, for the Dutchman had acquired some while removing the belt from the corpse.

No tiger delayed them, and they soon came to the fork at which Tarzan had last seen his companions. There was no scent of them, and the two men followed along the trail the others were to have taken. It was daylight when they heard a shot close and in front of them.

*   *   *

Jerry and Corrie decided to remain where they were, waiting for Tarzan. They thought that he would soon return. It was well for their peace of mind that they did not know the misadventure that had befallen him. For greater safety they had climbed into a tree where they perched precariously and uncomfortably some twenty feet above the ground. Jerry worried about the fate of Bubonovitch and Rosetti, and finally decided to do something about it. The night had dragged on interminably, and still Tarzan had not returned.

"I don't think he's coming," said Jerry. "Something must have happened to him. Anyway, I'm not going to wait any longer. I'm going on to see if I can locate Bubonovitch and Rosetti. Then if Tarzan does come, we'll at least know where they are; and maybe together we can work out a plan to free them. You stay here until I come back. You're safer here than you would be down on the ground."

"And suppose you don't come back?"

"I don't know, Corrie. This is the toughest decision I've ever had to make—to decide between you and those two boys. But I have made the decision, and I hope you'll understand. They are prisoners of the Japs, and we all know how Japs treat their prisoners. You are free and well armed."

"There was only one decision you could make. I knew that you would go after them, and I am going with you."

"Nothing doing," said Jerry. "You stay right where you are."

"Is that an order?"

"Yes."

He heard a faint suggestion of a laugh. "When you give an order on your ship, Captain, even a general would have to obey you. But you are not captain of this tree. Here we go!" and Corrie slipped from the branch on which she had been sitting and climbed to the ground.

Jerry followed her. "You win," he said. "I might have known better than to try to boss a woman."

"Two guns are better than one," said Corrie, "and I'm a good shot. Anyway, I'd sat on that darned limb until I was about ready to scream."

They trudged along the trail side by side. Often their arms touched; and once Corrie slipped on a muddy stretch, and Jerry put an arm around her to keep her from falling. He thought, I used to paw that girl back in Oklahoma City, but it never gave me a thrill like this. I think you have fallen for this little rascal, Jerry. I think you have it bad.

It was very dark, and sometimes they bumped into trees where the trail curved; so their progress was slow. They could only grope their way along, praying that dawn would soon break.

"What a day we've had," said Jerry. "All we need now, to make it perfect, is to run into a tiger."

"I don't think we need worry about that," said Corrie. "I've never heard of a tiger attacking a white man with a rifle. They seem to know. If we leave them alone, they'll leave us alone."

"I guess that's right. They probably know when a man is armed. When I was riding after cattle back home, I'd see plenty of coyotes when I didn't have a gun. But if I was packing a gun, I'd never see one."

" 'Back home,' " repeated Corrie. "You poor boys are so very, very far from back home. It makes me very sad to think of it. Bubonovitch with that pretty wife and baby way on the other side of the world. Missing the best years of their life."

"War is rotten," said Jerry. "If we ever get home, I'll bet we'll do something about the damned Nips and krauts that'll keep 'em from starting wars for a heck of a long time. There'll be ten or twelve millions of us who are good and fed up on war. We're going to elect an artillery captain friend of mine governor of Oklahoma and then send him to the senate. He hates war. I don't know a soldier who doesn't, and if all America will send enough soldiers to Congress we'll get some place."

"Is Oklahoma nice?" asked Corrie.

"It's the finest state in the Union," admitted Jerry.

The new day was kicking off the covers and crawling out of bed. It would soon be wide awake, for close to the equator the transition from night to day takes place quickly. There is no long drawn out dawning.

"What a relief," said Corrie. "I was very tired of night."

"Cripes!" exclaimed Jerry. "Look!" He cocked his rifle and stood still. Standing in the trail directly in front of them was a tiger.

"Don't shoot!" warned Corrie.

"I don't intend to if he'll just mind his own business. This dinky little .25 caliber Jap rifle wouldn't do anything more than irritate him, and I never did like to irritate tigers so early in the morning."

"I wish he'd go away," said Corrie. "He looks hungry."

"Maybe he hasn't heard of that theory of yours."

The tiger, a large male, stood perfectly still for several seconds, watching them; then it turned and leaped into the underbrush.

"Whee-oo!" exclaimed Jerry with a long sigh of relief. "My heart and my stomach were both trying to get into my mouth at the same time. Was I scared!"

"My knees feel weak," said Corrie. "I think I'll sit down."

"Wait!" cautioned Jerry. "Listen! Aren't those voices?"

"Yes. Just a little way ahead."

They moved forward very cautiously. The forest ended at the edge of a shallow valley, and the two looked down upon a little kampong scarcely a hundred yards from them. They saw natives and Jap soldiers.

"This must be where the boys are," said Jerry.

"There they are!" whispered Corrie. "Oh, God! He's going to kill them!"

Tada swung his sword. Jerry's rifle spit, and Lt. Kumajiro Tada lunged forward, sprawling in front of the men he had been about to kill. Then Corrie fired, and a Jap soldier who was rushing toward the two prisoners died. The two kept up a fusillade that knocked over soldier after soldier and put the village into panic.

Tarzan, hurrying forward at the first shot, was soon at their side; and van der Bos joined them a moment later, adding another rifle and a pistol. Tarzan took the latter.

Bubonovitch and Rosetti, taking advantage of the confusion in the kampong, seized rifles and ammunition from two of the dead soldiers and backed toward the forest, firing as they went. Rosetti had also acquired a couple of hand grenades, which he stuffed into his pockets.

A Jap sergeant was trying to collect his men, forming them up behind a house. Suddenly they charged, screaming. Rosetti threw his grenades in quick succession among them; then he and Bubonovitch turned and ran for the forest.

The firing had ceased before the two sergeants reached the little group just within the forest. Rosetti's grenades had put an end to this part of World War II, at least temporarily. The Japs were definitely demoralized or dead.

"Geeze!" said Rosetti. "They did hear us."

"They sure did," agreed Bubonovitch.

"Who heard you?" asked Jerry.

"God and the Blessed Mary," explained Rosetti.

The little party had been so intent upon the battle that they

88

had scarcely looked at one another while it was progressing. Now they relaxed a little and looked around. When Corrie and Tak van der Bos faced one another they were speechless for a moment. Then they both exclaimed simultaneously: "Corrie!" "Tak!"

"Darling!" cried Corrie, throwing her arms around the young Dutchman. Jerry was not amused.

Then followed introductions and brief resumés of their various adventures. While the others talked, Tarzan watched the kampong. The Japs seemed utterly confused. They had lost their officer and their ranking non-commissioned officers. Without them, the ordinary private soldier was too stupid to think or plan for himself.

Tarzan turned to Jerry. "I think we can take that village and wipe out the rest of the Japs if we rush them now while they are demoralized and without a leader. We have five rifles, and there aren't more than a dozen Japs left who are in any shape to fight."

Jerry turned to the others. "How about it?" he asked.

"Come on!" said Bubonovitch. "What are we waiting for?"

14

THE fight was short and sweet, and some of the Japs were helpful—they blew themselves up with their own grenades. Corrie had been left behind in the forest. But she hadn't stayed there. Jerry had no more than reached the center of the kampong when he saw her fighting at his side.

Bubonovitch and Rosetti went berserk, and their bayonets were dripping Jap blood when the fight was over. They had learned to hate.

The natives cowered in their houses. They had collobarated with the Japs and they expected the worst, but they were not molested. They were, however, required to furnish food and prepare it.

Tarzan and Jerry questioned several of them, Corrie and Tak acting as interpreters. They learned that this had been an advance post of a much larger force that was stationed about twenty-five kilometers down in the direction of the southwest coast. It had expected to be relieved in a day or two.

They also learned that there was a group of guerrillas farther along in the mountains toward the southeast. But none of the natives knew just where or how far. They seemed terribly afraid of the guerrillas.

Amat tried to curry favor with the newcomers. He was a confirmed opportunist, a natural born politician. He was wondering if it would advantage him to hurry to the main camp of the Japs and report the presence of these men and the havoc they had wreaked. But he abandoned the idea, as he would have had to travel through bad tiger country. It was well for Amat that neither Bubonovitch nor Rosetti knew the part he had played leading up to their capture.

But perhaps the two sergeants would have been inclined toward leniency, for they were very happy. Their prayers had wrought a miracle and they had been saved by the little margin of a split second. That was something to be happy about. In addition to this, they had indulged in a very successful orgy of revenge. In the blood of their enemies they had washed away the blows and insults and humiliation that had been heaped upon them.

"Geeze! Bum, we sure had a close shave."

"I couldn't see; because I was looking at the ground," said Bubonovitch, "but Corrie said that Jap looie was swinging his sword when Jerry nicked him. It was that close. But we sure evened things up, eh, Shrimp?"

"How many did you get?"

"I don't know. Maybe three or four. I was just shooting at everything in sight. But you certainly hit the jack pot with those two grenades. Boy! was that something?"

"Say, did you see dat dame get right into the fightin'? She's keen."

"Migawd! Shrimp, are you falling for a skirt?"

"I ain't fallin' for no skoit, but she's all to the good. I ain't never see a dame like her before. I didn't know they come like dat. I'll go to bat for her any old time."

"The last of the misogynists," said Bubonovitch. "Jerry took the count a long while ago, and has he fallen hard!"

"But did you see her fall on dat Dutchman's neck? You should have saw Jerry's face. Dat's de trouble wit dames— even dis one. Dey just can't help causin' wot dem Hawaiians

90

back on De Rock calls pilikia. We was just one happy family until her old boy friend blew into the pitcher."

"Maybe he is just an old friend," suggested Bubonovitch. "I noticed that when the fight was on, she fought right at Jerry's side."

Rosetti shook his head. He had already made a great concession, but his prejudice was too deep rooted to permit him to go all out for the ladies. He was for Corrie, but with mental reservations. "Do you throw your arms around an old friend's neck and yell, 'Darling!'? I ask."

"That all depends. You are an old friend of mine, Shrimp; but I can't imagine throwing my arms around your neck and calling you darling."

"You'd get a poke in de snoot."

"But if you were Ginger Rogers!"

"Geeze! What gams! I never seen gams before until I see *Lady in de Dark*. Boy!"

Tarzan and Jerry were holding a consultation of war. Corrie and Tak were recounting to each other their adventures of the past two years.

"I'd like to do a little reconnoitering before we move on," said Tarzan. "I'd like to do it alone, because I can move so much faster than the rest of you. But if you remain here, that Jap relief may show up before I come back. There will probably be about twenty of them, as there were in this detail. That's pretty heavy odds against you."

"I'll chance it," said Jerry, "if the others are willing. We're five guns. We've got enough Jap ammunition to fight a war—lots of grenades. We know the trail they'll come in on. All we have to do is keep a sentry far enough out on it to give us plenty of warning. Then we can plaster them with grenades from ambush. Let's see what the others think." He called them over and explained the situation.

"Geeze!" said Shrimp. "On'y four to one? It's a cinch. We done it before. We can do it again!"

"Atta boy!" said Jerry.

"The main camp is fifteen or sixteen miles from here," said Bubonovitch. "They'll probably take most of the day to make the march, for they won't be in any hurry. But we'd better start being on the lookout for them this afternoon. They might come today."

"You're right," said Jerry. "Suppose you go on out along the trail for about a mile. You'll hear them coming before they get in sight of you; then you can beat it back here, and we'll be ready for them."

"Here's an idea," said Corrie. "Suppose we load up with hand grenades and all go out and take positions in trees along both sides of the trail. If we're spread out enough, we can get the whole detachment in range before we open up. We should be able to get them all that way."

"Great!" said Jerry.

"What a bloodthirsty person you've become, Corrie!" exclaimed Tak, grinning.

"You don't know the half of it," said Jerry.

"It's a good idea," said Tarzan. "We know the enemy is coming. We don't know just when; so we should always be prepared for him. You can come in as soon as it is dark, as I'm sure they won't march at night. There is no reason why they should. But I think you should post a guard all night."

"Definitely," agreed Jerry.

Tarzan, the matter settled, walked away and disappeared into the forest.

* * *

Hooft awoke bleary eyed and with a terrific headache. His mouth tasted like the bottom of a mouse cage. He was never in a very good humor at best. Now his disposition was vile to murderous. He bellowed to awaken the others, and soon the camp was astir. The slovenly, slatternly women began to prepare breakfast for the men.

Hooft stood up and stretched. Then he looked over the camp. "Where's the prisoner?" he shouted.

Everyone else looked around. There was no prisoner. "The other one's gone, too," said a man.

Hooft roared out lurid profanities and horrid obscenities. "Who's on guard?" he demanded.

"Hugo was to wake me up at midnight to relieve him," said another. "He didn't."

"Go out and see what's become of him," ordered Hooft. "I'll skin him alive for this. I'll cut his heart out—falling asleep and letting both those men escape!"

The man was gone but a few minutes. When he returned, he was grinning. "Somebody beat you to it, Chief," he said to Hooft. "Hugo's a mess. His throat's been cut from ear to ear."

"It must have been that wild man," said Sarina.

"Van der Bos must have cut his bonds," said Hooft. "Wait 'til I get hold of him."

"If you ever do," said Sarina. "He'll go right to the nearest guerrillas, and pretty soon we'll have them down on us."

One of the men had walked over to the spot where Tarzan had lain. He returned with the bonds and handed them to Hooft. "These weren't cut," he said. "They were broken."

"No man could have broken them," said Hooft.

"The wild man did," said Sarina.

"I'll wild man him," growled Hooft. "Let's eat and get going. We're going after them. You women stay here." No one demurred. No one ever argued with Hooft when he was in a bad humor, with the exception of Sarina. She was the only one of the murderous crew whom Hooft feared, but Sarina did not argue now. She had no desire to go tramping through the forest.

The outlaws were good trackers, and Tarzan and van der Bos had made no effort to obliterate their spoor. It was plain going for Hooft and his gang of cutthroats.

Jerry and his little company gathered all the grenades they could carry and went out into the forest in the direction from which the Jap relief would have to come. Through van der Bos, Jerry warned the natives not to remove any of the rifles and ammuniton which they left behind. "Tell 'em we'll burn the village if we find anything gone when we return."

Van der Bos embellished this threat by assuring the chief that in addition to burning the village they would cut off the heads of all the villagers. The chief was impressed.

So was Amat. He had intended following the strangers out into the forest to spy on them. When he discovered how bloodthirsty they were, he changed his mind. They might catch him at his spying. Instead, he went out on another trail to gather durian fruit.

And so it was that while he was thus engaged among the branches of a durian tree, and negligent, Hooft discovered him. Hooft ordered him down. Amat was terrified. Hooft and his party were as villainous looking a gang as ever Amat had laid eyes on.

Hooft questioned him, asking if he had seen the two fugitives and describing them. Amat was relieved. He could give these men a great deal of information and thus win safety. They would reward him at least with his life.

"I have seen them," he said. "They came to our village with two others this morning. One was a woman. They rescued two men that the Japanese had taken prisoners; then the six killed all the Japanese."

"Where are they now?"

"They went out into the forest on another trail. I do not know why. But they are returning this evening. They said so. Now may I go?"

"And warn those people? I'll say not."

"Better kill him," said one of the men. He spoke Amat's dialect, and Amat trembled so that he nearly fell down. He did drop to his knees and beg for his life.

"You do what we say, and we won't kill you," said Hooft.

"Amat will do anything you want," said the frightened man. "I can tell you something more. The Japanese would pay well for the girl that was in our village today. The Japanese who were stationed there talked about her. The Japanese have been hunting for her for two years. Maybe I can help you get her. I will do anything for you."

Amat did not know how he could help them get Corrie, but he was willing to promise anything. If he couldn't get her, maybe he could run off into the forest until these terrible men had gone away. They were more terrifying even than the Japanese who had cuffed and kicked him.

Further discussion was interrupted by the sound of explosions beyond the village, somewhere off in the forest; but not far. "Hand grenades," said one of the men.

"Sounds like a regular battle," said Hooft.

The louder detonations were punctuated by the ping of rifle shots. "Those are Jap .25's," said Grotius.

Rising above the detonations were the piercing screams of men in agony. The whole thing lasted but a few minutes. There were a few scattered rifle shots at the end; then silence. One could almost reconstruct the scene from the sounds. There had been a sharp engagement. Between whom? wondered the outlaws. One side had been annihilated. Which one? The final rifle shots had liquidated the wounded.

The victors would certainly come to the village. Hooft and his followers approached the edge of the forest and lay in concealment. The little valley and the kampong were in plain sight below them.

They had not long to wait. Four white men and a white girl emerged from the forest trail. They were heavily laden with all the weapons and ammunition they could carry. They were talking excitedly. The men went to one of the native houses, the girl to another.

Hooft thought quickly. He must find a way to get the girl without risking a brush with her companions. Hooft, like all bullies, was yellow. He could stab or shoot a man in the back, but he couldn't face an armed opponent. He preferred to accomplish his ends by intrigue and cunning.

He turned to Amat. "Take this message to the girl. Tell her an old friend of hers is waiting at the edge of the forest. He doesn't want to come into the village until he is sure her companions are loyal to the Dutch. Tell her to come alone to the edge of the forest and talk with him. He is an old friend of her father. And, Amat, don't tell anyone else we are here. If anyone but the girls comes, we won't be here; but we'll come back some day and kill you. You can tell the girl, too, that if she does not come alone, I won't be here. Repeat the message to me."

Amat repeated it, and Hooft motioned him on his way. Amat felt like a condemned man who has just received a pardon, or at least a reprieve. He slipped quietly into the village, and went to the foot of the ladder leading to the door of the house where Corrie was quartered. He called to her, and a native girl came to the doorway. When she saw Amat, her lip curled in contempt. "Go away pig!" she said.

"I have a message for the white woman," said Amat.

Corrie overheard and came to the doorway. "What message have you for me?" she asked.

"It is a very private message," said Amat. "I cannot shout it."

"Come up here, then."

Lara, the native girl, turned up her nose as Amat passed into the house. She knew him for a liar and a sneak, but she did not warn Corrie. What business was it of hers?

Amat delivered his message. Corrie pondered. "What was the man like?" she asked.

"He is a white man with a beard," said Amat. "That is all I know."

"Is he alone?"

Amat thought quickly, if she knows there are twenty of them, she will not go; then some day the man will come and kill me. "He is alone," said Amat.

Corrie picked up her rifle and descended the ladder to the

ground. The men of her party were still in the house they had taken over. They were cleaning and oiling the rifles they had acquired. There were no natives about. Only Amat and Lara saw the white girl leave the kampong and enter the forest.

15

TARZAN had not been able to gather much information about the guerrillas from the natives. They had heard it rumored that there was one band near a certain volcano about sixty-five kilometers to the southeast. They were able to describe the appearance of this volcano and various landmarks that might help to guide Tarzan to it, and with this meager information he had set out.

He travelled until night fell, and then lay up until morning in a tree. His only weapons were his bow and arrows and his knife. He had not wished to be burdened with the Jap rifle and ammunition. In the morning he gathered some fruit and shot a hare for his breakfast.

The country through which he passed was extremely wild and destitute of any signs of man. Nothing could have suited Tarzan better. He liked the companions whom he had left behind; but notwithstanding all his contacts with men, he had never become wholly gregarious. His people were the wild things of the forest and jungle and plain. With them, he was always at home. He liked to watch them and study them. He often knew them better than they knew themselves.

He passed many monkeys. They scolded him until he spoke to them in their own language. They knew their world, and through them he kept upon the right route to the volcano. They told him in what direction to go to reach the next landmark of which the natives had spoken—a little lake, a mountain meadow, the crater of an extinct volcano.

When he thought that he should be approaching his destination, he asked some monkeys if there were white men near a volcano. He called it argo ved—*fire mountain*. They said there were, and told him how to reach their camp. One old monkey said, "Kreeg-ah! Tarmangani sord. Tarmangani bundolo," and he mimicked the aiming of a rifle, and said, "Boo! Boo!" *Beware! White men bad. White men kill.*

He found the camp in a little gorge, but before he came to it he saw a sentry guarding the only approach. Tarzan came out into the open and walked toward the man, a bearded Dutchman. The fellow cocked his rifle and waited until Tarzan came to within twenty-five or thirty yards of him; then he halted him.

"Who are you and what are you doing here?" he demanded.

"I am an Englishman. I should like to talk with your chief."

The man had been appraising Tarzan with some show of astonishment. "Stay where you are," he ordered. "Don't come any closer;" then he called down into the gorge: "de Lettenhove! There's a wild man up here wants to talk to you."

Tarzan repressed a smile. He had heard this description of himself many times before, but never with quite such blatant disregard of his feelings. Then he recalled that he had spoken to the man in English and said that he was an Englishman, while the fellow had called to de Lettenhove in Dutch, doubtless believing that the "wild man" did not understand that language. He would continue to let them believe so.

Presently, three men came up out of the valley. All were heavily armed. They were bearded, tough looking men. They wore patched, tattered, nondescript clothing, partly civilian, partly military, partly crudely fashioned from the skins of animals. One of them wore a disreputable tunic with the two stars of a first lieutenant on the shoulder tabs. This was de Lettenhove. He spoke to the sentry in Dutch.

"What was this man doing?"

"He just walked up to me. He made no effort to avoid me or hide from me. He is probably a harmless half-wit, but what the devil he's doing here gets me. He says he is English. He spoke to me in that language."

De Lettenhove turned to Tarzan. "Who are you? What are you doing here?" he asked in English.

"My name is Clayton. I am a colonel in the RAF. I understood that a company of Dutch guerrillas was camped here. I wanted to talk with their commanding officer. Are you he? I know that there are also bands of outlaws in the mountains, but the only way I could find out which you are was to come and talk with you. I had to take that chance."

"I am not the commanding officer," said de Lettenhove. "Capt. van Prins is in command, but he is not here today. We expect him back tomorrow. Just what do you want to see him about? I can assure you," he added with a smile, "that we are outlaws only in the eyes of the Japs and the native collaborationists."

"I came because I wanted to make contact with people I could trust, who could give me information as to the location of Jap outposts and native villages whose people are friendly to the Dutch. I wish to avoid the former and, perhaps, obtain help from the latter. I am trying to reach the coast, where I shall try to obtain a boat and escape from the island."

De Lettenhove turned to one of the men who had accompanied him from the camp in the valley. "I was commencing to believe him," he said in Dutch, "until he sprung that one about getting a boat and escaping from the island. He must think we're damn fools to fall from any such silly explanation of his presence here. He's probably a damn German spy. We'll just hang onto him until van Prins gets back." Then, to Tarzan, in English: "You say you are an English officer. Of course you have some means of identification?"

"None," replied Tarzan.

"May I ask why an English officer is running around in the mountains of Sumatra naked and armed with bow and arrows and a knife?" His tone was ironical. "My friend, you certainly can't expect us to believe you. You will remain here until Capt. van Prins returns."

"As a prisoner?" asked Tarzan.

"As a prisoner. Come, we will take you down to camp."

The camp was neat and well policed. There were no women. There was a row of thatched huts laid out with military precision. The red, white, and blue flag of the Netherlands flew from a staff in front of one of the huts. Twenty or thirty men were variously occupied about the camp, most of them cleaning rifles or pistols. Tattered and torn and shabby were their clothes, but their weapons were immaculate. That this was a well disciplined military camp Tarzan was now convinced. These were no outlaws. He knew that he could trust these men.

His entrance into the camp caused a mild sensation. The men stopped their work to stare at him. Some came and questioned those who accompanied him.

98

"What you got there?" asked one. "The Wild Man of Borneo?"

"He says he's an RAF colonel, but I've got two guesses. He's either a harmless half-wit or a German spy. I'm inclined to believe the latter. He doesn't talk like a half-wit."

"Does he speak German?"

"Don't know."

"I'll try him." He spoke to Tarzan in German; and the latter, impelled by the ridiculousness of the situation, rattled off a reply in impeccable German.

"I told you so," said the two-guesser.

Then Tarzan turned to de Lettenhove. "I told you that I had no means of identification," he said. "I haven't any with me, but I have friends who can identify me—three Americans and two Dutch. You may know the latter."

"Who are they?"

"Corrie van der Meer and Tak van der Bos. Do you know them?"

"I knew them very well, but they have both been reported dead."

"They were not dead yesterday," said Tarzan.

"Tell me," said de Lettenhove. "How do you happen to be in Sumatra anyway? How could an English colonel get to Sumatra in wartime? And what are Americans doing here?"

"An American bomber was supposed to have crashed here some time ago," one of the men reminded de Lettenhove in Dutch. "This fellow, if he is working with the Japs, would have known this. He would also have been able to get the names of Miss van der Meer and Tak. Let the damn fool go on. He's digging his own grave."

"Ask him how he knew our camp was here," suggested another.

"How did you know where to find us?" demanded de Lettenhove.

"I'll answer all your questions," said Tarzan. "I was aboard the bomber that was shot down. That's how I happen to be here. The three Americans I have mentioned were also survivors from that plane. I learned in a native village yesterday about the general location of your camp. These villagers have been collaborating with the Japs. There was a Jap outpost garrisoned there. We had an engagement with them yesterday, and wiped out the entire garrison."

"You speak excellent German," said one of the men accusingly.

"I speak several languages," said Tarzan, "including Dutch." He smiled.

De Lettenhove flushed. "Why didn't you tell me all these things in the first place?" he demanded.

"I wished first to assure myself that I was among potential friends. You might have been collaborationists. I just had an experience with a band of armed Dutchmen who work with the Japs."

"What decided you that we were all right?"

"The appearance of this camp. It is not the camp of a band of undisciplined outlaws. Then, too, I understood all that you said in Dutch. You would not have feared that I might be a spy had you been on friendly terms with the Japs. I am convinced that I can trust you. I am sorry that you do not trust me. You probably could have been of great assistance to me and my friends."

"I should like to believe you," said de Lettenhove. "We'll let the matter rest until Capt. van Prins returns."

"If he can describe Corrie van der Meer and Tak van der Bos, I'll believe him," said one of the men. "If they're dead, as we've heard, he can't ever have seen them, for Corrie was killed with her father and mother over two years ago way up in the mountains, and Tak was captured and killed by the Japs after he escaped from the concentration camp. They couldn't possibly have been seen by this man unless they are still alive and together."

Tarzan described them both minutely, and told much of what had befallen them during the past two years.

De Lettenhove offered Tarzan his hand. "I believe you now," he said, "but you must understand that we have to be suspicious of everyone."

"So am I," replied the Englishman.

"Forgive me if I appear to be rude," said the Dutchman, "but I'd really like to know why you go about nearly naked like a regular Tarzan."

"Because I am Tarzan." He saw incredulity and returning suspicion in de Lettenhove's face. "Possibly some of you may recall that Tarzan is an Englishman and that his name is Clayton. That is the name I gave you, you will recall."

"That's right," exclaimed one of the men. "John Clayton, Lord Greystoke."

"And there's the scar on his forehead that he got in his fight with the gorilla when he was a boy," exclaimed another.

"I guess that settles it," said de Lettenhove.

The men crowded around, asking Tarzan innumerable questions. They were more than friendly now, trying to make amends for their former suspicions.

"Am I still a prisoner?" he asked de Lettenhove.

"No, but I wish you would remain until the captain gets back. I know that he'll be more than anxious to be of assistance to you."

16

As CORRIE entered the forest she saw a man standing in the trail about a hundred feet from her. It was Hooft. He removed his hat and bowed, smiling. "Thank you for coming," he said. "I was afraid to go down into the village until I was sure the people there were friendly."

Corrie advanced toward him. She did not recognize him. Even though smiling, his appearance was most unprepossessing; so she kept her rifle at ready. "If you are a loyal Dutchman," she said, "you will find the white men in this village friendly. What do you want of them?"

She had advanced about fifty feet when suddenly men leaped from the underbrush on both sides of the trail. The muzzle of her rifle was struck up and the weapon seized and wrenched from her grasp.

"Don't make no noise and you won't be hurt," said one of the men.

Pistols were levelled at her as a warning of what would happen to her if she cried out for help. She saw that the men surrounding her were Dutchmen, and realized that they were probably of the same band of outlaws from which Tak and Tarzan had escaped. She reproached herself for having stupidly put herself in their power.

"What do you want of me?" she demanded.

"We ain't goin' to hurt you," said Hooft. "Just come along quietly, and we won't keep you long." They were already moving along the trail, men in front of her and behind her. She realized that escape now was impossible.

"But what are you going to do with me?" she insisted.

"You'll find that out in a couple of days."

"My friends will follow, and when they catch up with you you'll wish that you never had seen me."

"They won't never catch up," said Hooft. "Even if they should, there are only four of them. We'd wipe 'em out in no time."

"You don't know them," said Corrie. "They have killed forty Japs today, and they'll find you no matter where you hide. You had better let me go back; because you will certainly pay if you don't."

"Shut up," said Hooft.

They hurried on. Night fell, but they did not stop. Corrie thought of Jerry and the others. Most of all, she thought of Jerry. She wondered if they had missed her yet. She didn't wonder what they would do when they did miss her. She knew. She knew that the search for her would start immediately. Probably it already had started. She lagged, pretending to be tired. She wanted to delay her captors; but they pushed her roughly on, swearing at her.

Back in the village, Jerry was the first to wonder why Corrie hadn't joined them as the natives prepared their evening meal. He saw Amat, and asked van der Bos to send him after Corrie. The native went to the house Corrie had occupied and pretended to look for her. Presently he returned to say that she was not there. "I saw her go into the forest a little while ago," he said. "I supposed that she had returned, but she is not in her house."

"Where into the forest?" asked van der Bos. Amat pointed to a different trail from that which Corrie had taken.

When van der Bos had interpreted what Amat had said, Jerry picked up his rifle and started for the forest. The others followed him.

"What in the world could have possessed her to go wandering off into the forest alone?" demanded Jerry.

"Maybe she didn't," said Rosetti. "Maybe dat little stinker was lyin'. I don't like dat puss o' his. He looks like a rat."

"I don't believe the little so-and-so, either," said Bubonovitch. "It just isn't like Corrie to do a thing like that."

"I know," said Jerry, "but we'll have to make a search

anyway. We can't pass up any chance of finding her however slim."

"If that little yellow runt was lyin', if he knows wot become of Corrie, I'm goin' to poke a bayonet clean through his gizzard," growled Rosetti.

They went into the forest, calling Corrie aloud by name. Presently they realized the futility of it. In the pitch darkness of the forest night they could have seen no spoor, had there been one to see.

"If only Tarzan were here," said Jerry. "God! but I feel helpless."

"Somethin' dirty's been pulled," said Rosetti. "I t'ink we should orter go back an' give de whole village de toid degree."

"You're right, Shrimp," said Jerry. "Let's go back."

They routed the natives out and herded them into the center of the village. Then van der Bos questioned them. Those first questioned denied any knowledge even of Corrie's departure. They disclaimed having any idea of where she might be. As Lara's turn came, Amat started to sneak away. Shrimp saw him, for he had been keeping an eye on him, grabbed him by the scruff of the neck, wheeled him around, and pushed him into the center of the stage, at the same time giving him a swift kick in the pants.

"This louse was tryin' to beat it," he announced. "I told you he was a wrong guy." He held the business end of his bayonet in the small of Amat's back.

Van der Bos questioned Lara at length and then interpreted her replies to the others. "This girl says that Amat came and told Corrie that a friend of her father was waiting at the edge of the forest and wanted to see her, but for her to come alone, as he didn't know whether or not the rest of us were friendly to the Dutch. She went into the forest on that trail there." He pointed. It was not the trail which Amat said she had taken.

"I told you so!" shouted Rosetti. "Tell this skunk to say his prayers, for I'm goin' to kill him."

"No, Rosetti," said Jerry. "He's the only one who knows the truth. We can't get it out of him if he's dead."

"I can wait," said Rosetti.

Tak van der Bos questioned Amat at length, while Rosetti kept the point of a bayonet pressed against the frightened native's left kidney.

"According to this man's story," said Tak, "he went into the forest to gather durians. He was almost immediately captured by a band of white men. He says there were about twenty of them. One of them forced him to take that message to Corrie, threatening to come back and kill him if Corrie didn't come out alone. He says he was very much frightened. Also, he thought the man merely wished to talk with Corrie. Says he didn't know that they would keep her."

"Is dat all?" demanded Shrimp.

"That's his whole story."

"May I kill him now, Cap?"

"No," said Jerry.

"Aw, hell! Why not? You know de bum's lyin'."

"We're not Japs, Rosetti. And we've got other things to do right now." He turned to van der Bos. "Isn't it likely that those fellows were the same ones that you and Tarzan got away from?"

"I think there's no doubt of it."

"Then you can lead us to their camp?"

"Yes."

"At night?"

"We can start now," said van der Bos.

"Good!" exclaimed Jerry. "Let's get going."

Rosetti gave Amat a quick poke with his bayonet that brought a frightened scream from the Sumatran. Jerry wheeled toward the sergeant.

"I didn't kill him, Cap. You didn't tell me not to jab him once for luck."

"I'd like to kill him myself, Shrimp," said Jerry. "But we can't do things that way."

"I can," said Rosetti, "if you'll just look de udder way a second." But Jerry shook his head and started off toward the mouth of the trail. The others followed, Shrimp shaking his head and grumbling. "T'ink of dat poor kid out dere wit dem bums!" he said. "An' if dis little stinker had a-told us, we'd a-had her back before now. Just for a couple seconds I wish we was Japs."

Bubonovitch made no wisecrack about misogynists. He was in no wisecracking mood, but he couldn't but recall how violently upset Shrimp had been when they had had to add a "dame" to their company.

Finding that her delaying tactics won her nothing but abuse, Corrie swung along at an easy stride with her captors. Presently, she heard three sharp knocks ahead, as though some one had struck the bole of a tree three times with a heavy implement. The men halted, and Hooft struck the bole of a tree three times with the butt of his rifle—two knocks close together and then a third at a slightly longer interval.

A woman's voice demanded, "Who is it?" and the outlaw chief replied, "Hooft."

"Come on in," said the woman. "I'd know that schnapps bass if I heard it in Hell."

The party advanced, and presently the woman spoke again from directly above them. "I'm coming down," she said. "Post one of your men up here, Hooft. This is no job for a lady."

"What give you the idea you was a lady?" demanded Hooft, as the woman descended from the platform from which she had been guarding the trail to the camp. She was Hooft's woman, Sarina.

"Not you, sweetheart," said the woman.

"We won't need no guard here no more," said Hooft. "We're pullin' out quick."

"Why? Some cripple with a slingshot chasin' you?"

"Shut up!" snapped Hooft. "You're goin' to shoot off your gab just once too often one of these days."

"Don't make me laugh," said Sarina.

"I'm gettin' damn sick of you," said Hooft.

"I've been damn sick of you for a long while, sweetheart. I'd trade you for an orangutan any day."

"Oh, shut up," grumbled one of the men. "We're all gettin' good an' goddam sick of hearin' you two bellyache."

"Who said that?" demanded Hooft. No one replied.

Presently they entered the camp and aroused the women, whereupon considerable acrimonious haggling ensued when the women learned that they were to break camp and take the trail thus late at night.

Some torches were lighted, and in their dim and flickering illumination the band gathered up its meager belongings. The light also served to reveal Corrie to the women.

"Who's the kid?" demanded one of them. "This ain't no place for a nice boy."

"That ain't no boy," said a man. "She's a girl."

"What you want of her?" asked a woman suspiciously.

"The Japs want her," explained Grotius, the second in command.

"Maybe they won't get her?" said Hooft.

"Why not?" demanded Grotius.

"Because maybe I've taken a fancy to her myself. I'm goin' to give Sarina to an ape." Everybody laughed, Sarina louder than the others.

"You ain't much to look at, you ain't much to listen to, and you ain't much to live with," she announced; "but until I find me another man, you don't go foolin' around with any other woman. And see that you don't forget it," she added.

Sarina was a well built woman of thirty-five, lithe and muscular. An automatic pistol always swung at her hip and her carbine was always within reach. Nor did she consider herself fully clothed if her parang were not dangling in its sheath from her belt. But these were only outward symbols of Sarina's formidableness. It was her innate ferocity when aroused that made her feared by the cutthroats and degenerates of Hooft's precious band. And she had come by this ferocity quite as a matter of course. Her maternal grandfather had been a Borneo headhunter and her maternal grandmother a Batak and a cannibal. Her father was a Dutchman who had lived adventurously in and about the South Seas, indulging in barratry and piracy, and dying at last on the gibbet for murder. Sarina, herself, carrying on the traditions of her family, though not expiating them so irrevocably as had her sire, had been serving a life sentence for murder when released from jail at the time of the Japanese invasion.

It is true that the man she had murdered should have been murdered long before; so one should not judge Sarina too harshly. It is also true that, as is often the case with characters like Sarina, she possessed many commendable characteristics. She was generous and loyal and honest. At the drop of a hat she would fight for what she knew to be right. In fact, it was not necessary even to drop a hat. Hooft feared her.

Corrie had listened with increasing perturbation to the exchange of pleasantries between Hooft and Sarina. She did not know which to fear more. She might be given over to the Japs, taken by Hooft, or killed by Sarina. It was not a pleasant outlook. She could but pray that Jerry and the others would come in time.

The outlaws had left the camp by a trail other than that along which Corrie had been brought. Hooft had issued orders for the march that would insure that their spoor would completely deceive anyone attempting to track them, and when Corrie heard them the last ray of hope seemed to have been extinguished. Only prayer was left.

On the march, Sarina walked always close to her. Corrie hoped that this would keep Hooft away. Of the two, she feared him more than she did the woman.

17

TAK VAN DER BOS led Jerry, Bubonovitch, and Rosetti through the Cimmerian darkness of the equatorial forest toward the camp of the outlaws. The night noises of the jungle were all about them; but they saw nothing, not even one another. They were guided solely by the slight sounds given off by the accounterments of the man directly ahead. If van der Bos slowed down or stopped as he felt for the trail they bumped into one another. Often they collided with trees or stumbled over obstacles, cursing softly. Otherwise they moved in silence. They did not talk.

Strange sounds came out of the jungle—unaccountable crashings, occasionally a scream of terror or agony. Life and death were all about them. And sometimes there were strange silences, more ominous than the noises. Then, Bubonovitch would think: *Death is abroad. The jungle is waiting to see where he will strike, each creature fearing to call attention to itself.*

Rosetti felt as a man walking in a dream. He walked and walked and walked, and never got anywhere. It was as though he had walked forever and would keep on walking in darkness throughout eternity.

Jerry thought only of what might be happening to Corrie, and chafed at the slowness of their progress. He was wondering for the thousandth time how much longer it would be before they would reach the camp, when he bumped into van der Bos. Then Rosetti and Bubonovitch bumped into him.

Van der Bos got them into a huddle, and whispered: "Get

your guns ready. We are approaching their sentry. We may be able to sneak by in the darkness. If he challenges, Jerry and I will let him have it; then we'll charge the camp, yelling like hell. But we can't shoot there until we have located Corrie. When we do, we can commence shooting; then keep right on through the camp. There is a trail on the other side. And keep together."

"I think we should go in shooting, but in the air," suggested Jerry.

"That's better," agreed van der Bos. "Come on!"

There was no sentry, and so they crept silently into the deserted camp to reconnoiter. It was not so dark here in the open, and they soon discovered that their quarry had flown. Their reactions to this disappointment were expressed variously and profanely.

"Where do we go from here?" demanded Rosetti.

"We'll have to wait for daylight before we can pick up their trail," said Jerry. "The rest of you get some sleep. I'll stand guard for an hour. Then one of you can relieve me for an hour. By that time it should be light."

"Lemme stand guard, Cap," said Rosetti. "I can take it better'n you."

"What makes you think that?" demanded Jerry.

"Well—well, you see you're pretty old. You'd orter get your rest."

Jerry grinned. "Ever hear of a general named Stilwell?" he asked. "Thanks just the same, Shrimp; but I'll take the first trick, then I'll call you."

As soon as it was light, they searched for the tracks of the outlaws; but they found none leading out of the camp. It seemed baffling until Bubonovitch suggested that they had gone out by the same trail along which they themselves had come in, and thus the spoor of the outlaws had been obliterated by their own.

"They must have kept right ahead at the fork," said van der Bos. "I guess we'll have to go back there and start all over again." But when they reached the forks, there was no sign of fresh spoor continuing on the main trail.

"Wotinell become of 'em?" demanded Rosetti. "They's somethin' phoney about it—people vanishin' like dat."

"They probably used vanishing cream," said Bubonovitch.

"We must have got some of it on our brains," said Jerry, disgustedly.

"Or up our noses and in our eyes and ears," said Bubonovitch. "Tarzan was right. Civilization has robbed us of most of our physical sensibilities. I suppose that he would have found that spoor just like that." He snapped his fingers.

"He's pretty slick," said Rosetti, "but even Tarzan can't find no trail when they ain't none."

"About all we can do," said Jerry, "is go back to the village and wait for him. A bunch of dummies like us couldn't ever find her, and if we try it we might miss Tarzan entirely when he gets back."

It was a dejected party that returned to the village. When Amat saw Rosetti entering the village he disappeared into the forest and climbed a tree. There he remained until after dark, a terrified and unhappy collaborator.

Tarzan waited in the camp of the guerrillas until Capt. Kervyn van Prins returned. Van Prins, de Lettenhove, and Tarzan conferred at length. Tarzan told them of the destruction of the Jap detachment in the village and of the extra rifles and ammunition, which he thought the guerrillas might use to advantage.

"When I left yesterday," he said, "my friends were going out to ambush the Jap relief party that was expected at almost any time. If it has arrived I haven't much doubt as to the outcome of that engagement; so there should be quite a little additional equipment for you if you care to come and get it. I think that village needs a lesson, too. Those people are undoubtedly working with the Japs."

"You say you believe the Jap relief party would consist of some twenty men," said van Prins, "and your party had only five people, and one of them a girl. Aren't you rather overconfident in thinking that an engagement would result in a victory for your people?"

Tarzan smiled. "You don't know my people," he said. "Too, they had a tremendous advantage over the Japs. They knew that the Japs were coming; but the Japs didn't know we were there and waiting for them in trees on both sides of the trail, armed with rifles and hand grenades. And don't discount the fighting ability of the girl, Captain. She is a crack shot, and she already has several Japs to her credit. She is imbued with a hatred of Japs that amounts almost to religious exaltation."

"Little Corrie van der Meer!" exclaimed van Prins. "It is almost unbelievable."

"And two of our Americans," continued Tarzan. "They were captured and abused by the Japs, and were about to be beheaded when the American captain and Corrie arrived in time to save them. I think they are good for at least five Japs apiece, if not more. They have become two fisted haters. No, I don't think we need worry about the outcome of the fight, if there was one. As the Americans would say, 'we did it before; we can do it again.' "

"Very well," said van Prins; "we'll go with you. We can certainly use more rifles and ammunition. Possibly we should join forces. We can discuss that when we all get together. When do you want to start back?"

"I am going now," replied Tarzan. "We'll wait in the village for you."

"We can go along with you," said van Prins.

Tarzan shook his head. "Not the way I travel, I'm afraid. By forced marches, you may make it by sometime tomorrow. I'll be back there tonight."

The Dutchman gave a skeptical shrug; but he smiled and said, "Very good. We'll see you some time tomorrow."

Day was breaking as the outlaws emerged from the forest into a narrow valley. They had brought their supply of schnapps along with them, and most of them were drunk. More than anything else, they wanted to lie down and sleep. They made camp under some trees beside the little river that wound down the valley toward the sea.

Hooft said that the women could stand guard, as they had had some sleep the night before. As Sarina was the only woman who had not drunk during the night, she volunteered to stand the first trick. Soon the others were sprawled out and snoring. But Corrie could not sleep. Plans for escape raced through her mind, banishing thoughts of slumber. She saw that all but Sarina were dead to the world. Perhaps Sarina might succumb to fatigue, too. Then she could get away. She knew exactly where she was and where to find the trail, that led back to the village. Farther down the valley she would probably find the bones of the rhinoceros and the deer that Tarzan had killed. Just beyond, she would come to the trail that led up out of the valley and into the forest.

She eyed the weapons of the sleeping men and women. If she could but steal a parang without Sarina seeing her. She would only have to get close to the woman then. In time, her attention would be distracted. She would turn her head away. Then one terrific blow with the heavy knife, and Corrie, armed with rifle, pistol, and parang, would be far on her way to the village before these drunken sots awakened.

Corrie did not even wonder that she entertained such thoughts. Her once sheltered life had become a battle for mere existence. If enemies could not be eluded, they must be destroyed. And this woman was an enemy. Corrie feared her fully as much as she feared the men. She thought of her as a terrible creature, steeped in vice.

Sarina was still a comparatively young woman. She had the sultry beauty that so many Eurasian women have and the erect, graceful carriage that marks the women of Java and Sumatra, and the slimness and physical perfection. But Corrie saw her through eyes of hate and loathing.

Sarina was staring at Corrie, her brows puckered in concentration. Would the woman never look away. "What is your name?" asked Sarina.

"Van der Meer," replied the girl.

"Corrie van der Meer?" Sarina smiled. "I thought so. You look like your mother."

"You knew my mother?" demanded Corrie. "You couldn't have." Her tone suggested that the woman had insulted her mother's memory just by claiming to have known her.

"But I did," said Sarina. "I knew your father, too. I worked for them while you were in school in Holland. They were very good to me. I loved them both. When I got in trouble, your father hired a fine attorney to defend me. But it did no good. Justice is not for Eurasians, or perhaps I should say mercy is not for Eurasians. I was guilty, but there were circumstances that would have counted in my favor had I been white. That is all past. Because your father and mother were kind to me and helped me, I shall help you."

"What is your name?" asked Corrie.

"Sarina."

"I have heard both my father and mother speak of you. They were very fond of you. But how can you help me?"

Sarina walked over to one of the sleeping men and took his rifle and some ammunition from him. She brought them back to Corrie. "Do you know how to get back to the village where they found you?"

"Yes."

"Then get started. These drunken beasts will sleep a long time."

"How can I thank you, Sarina?" she said. She thought, and I was going to kill her!

"Don't thank me. Thank your father and mother for being kind to an Eurasian. Do you know how to use a rifle?"

"Yes."

"Then, good-by and good luck!"

Impulsively, Corrie threw her arms about the woman she would have killed, and kissed her. "God bless you, Sarina," she said. Then she swung off down the valley. Sarina watched her go, and there were tears in her eyes. She touched the spot on her cheek where Corrie had kissed her, touched it almost reverently.

Corrie took advantage of the cover afforded by the trees that grew along the left bank of the river. It was much farther to the trail leading up out of the valley than she had imagined, and it was late afternoon before she saw it winding across the valley from the opposite side. She saw something else, too. Something that made her heart sink. Some natives were making camp for the night directly in her path, and there were two Jap soldiers with them. Now she would have to wait for darkness, and then try to sneak past them.

She climbed into a tree, and tried to make herself comfortable. She was very tired and very sleepy. But she did not dare sleep for fear she would fall out of the tree. At last she found a combination of branches into which she could wedge her body and from which she could not fall. She was very uncomfortable; but nevertheless she fell asleep, utterly exhausted.

When she awoke, she knew that she had slept for some time, as the moon was high in the heavens. She could see the fire burning in the camp of the natives. Now she could slip past them and reach the trail to the village. She was preparing to descend when she heard the coughing grunt of a tiger. It sounded very close. From a little distance there arose the barking and growling of wild dogs. Corrie decided to remain where she was.

18

I T was late when Tarzan reached the village. Bubonovitch, who was on guard, challenged him. "Colonel Clayton," responded Tarzan.

"Advance to be recognized, Colonel; but I know your voice anyway. And thank the Lord you're back."

Tarzan approached. "Something wrong, Sergeant?" he asked.

"I'll say there's something wrong. Corrie's been abducted," then he told Tarzan all that he knew about the matter.

"And you couldn't find their trail?"

"There wasn't any."

"There has to be," said Tarzan.

"I sure hope you're right, Sir."

"We can't do anything until morning. We'll start as soon as it's light."

Jerry was on guard when Tarzan awoke at daylight. The American, anxious to get the search under way, had already routed out the others. They called Lara from her house. She was the only one of the natives they felt they could trust. Van der Bos talked to her. He told her that a band of guerrillas would arrive in the village sometime during the day, and instructed her to tell them what had happened and ask them to remain until the searchers returned.

When Corrie was safely out of sight of the camp of the outlaws, Sarina awoke the woman whom she thought had been most overcome by drink and told her to relieve her as guard. She said nothing about the escape of the prisoner, assuming that the woman's brain would be so befuddled that she would not notice. Sarina was right.

The guard was changed twice more before Hooft awoke. When he discovered that Corrie was missing, he was furious. He questioned all the women who had been on guard. Sarina insisted that Corrie had been there when she relinquished the post to another. The others insisted that the prisoner had not left while they were on duty. Hooft got nowhere.

He had slept all day. It was now getting dark and too late

to start a search. All he could do about it was to curse the women roundly and try to find solace in a schnapps bottle.

At about the same time that Tarzan and the others were starting out from the village to search for her the following morning, Corrie was impatiently watching the camp of the natives and the two Japs. She dared not descend until they had left. She watched them prepare and eat their breakfast leisurely, thinking that they would never finish. But at long last they did.

They came in her direction, and Corrie hid in the tree where the foliage was densest. At last they filed by, quite close; and Corrie recognized Iskandar, the leader of the natives who had once abducted her, and several of his band. When they were at a safe distance, Corrie descended to the ground and followed the trail up the cliff and into the forest. At last she was safe, for all her known enemies were behind her and she was on a familiar trail that led directly back to her friends.

Iskandar continued on with his party until they came within sight of the outlaws; then the two Japs hid, and the natives approached Hooft and his people. There was a brief parley between Iskandar and Hooft; then the native sent one of his men back to tell the Japs that the white men were friendly.

After the two Japs joined them, the schnapps bottles were passed around as the men discussed plans. The Japs were non-commissioned officers from the detachment of Capt. Tokujo Matsuo, and so were naturally anxious to recapture Corrie. So were Iskandar and Hooft, each of whom visualized some form of reward if they returned the girl to the Japanese officer.

Unfortunately for their plans they drank too much schnapps; and though they started out in the right direction, they never picked up Corrie's spoor. When they reached the trail leading up into the forest, the trail that Corrie had taken, Sarina claimed to have discovered the spoor and led them on down the valley. Thus again the kindness of her dead father and mother intervened to save the girl.

Tarzan, Jerry, and the others marched rapidly to the abandoned camp of the outlaws. Tarzan examined the spoor that had confused and deceived his companions; then he led them out along the trail that the outlaws had taken. The others were dubious, but they followed.

"Them tracks is all pointin' toward the camp," said Rosetti. "We're goin' the wrong way, an' just wastin' time."

"They tell me you're a great ball turret gunner, Shrimp," said Tarzan; "but you're a mighty poor tracker. The people we're after passed along this trail last night in the same direction that we're going."

"Then they must o' came back again, Colonel. All these footprints is pointin' the other way."

"The majority of them went in advance," explained Tarzan; "then three men and a woman walked backward behind them, obliterating the spoor of those who had gone ahead. About every hundred yards, three other men and a woman relieved the spoor obliterators; because it is tiresome walking backward."

"I don't see how you tell that," persisted Rosetti.

"When you walk forward your heels strike the ground first; then you push yourself forward with the balls of your feet, at the same time pushing the dirt back in the opposite direction. When you walk backward, the balls of your feet strike the ground first and you push yourself forward with your heels, still pushing the dirt in the direction opposite from that in which you are going. Examine the ground carefully, and you will see for yourself. If you follow the trail long enough, and are sufficiently observing, you will see that about every hundred yards there is a change in the sizes of the footprints, showing that new people took up the job."

Not only Rosetti, but the others, fell to examining the spoor. "Cripes, but we're dumb," said Jerry.

"I should have knowed enough to keep my fool trap shut," said Rosetti. "The colonel ain't never wrong."

"Don't get that idea," said Tarzan. "I don't want to try to live up to anything like that. But remember, about this tracking, that I've been doing it all my life, ever since I was a child, and that innumerable times my life has depended upon my knowing what I was doing. Now I am going on ahead. We don't want to run into that outfit without warning."

An hour later the rest of the party emerged from the forest into the open valley and found Tarzan waiting for them. "Your outlaws passed down the valley a short time ago," he told them. "I have also found Corrie's trail. She was hours ahead of them and alone. Evidently she managed to escape from them. I am pretty sure that they did not discover her spoor, as theirs is often yards to the right of hers and never touches it.

"There were a number of men and women in the party, several natives, and two Jap soldiers. At least two of the men were short legged and wore working tabi; so I assume they were Japs. I am going on ahead, following Corrie's trail. If she took the trail leading up into the forest, I'll cut a single blaze on a tree near the trail. If she kept on down the valley, I'll cut two blazes. If there are three, you will know that the outlaws took the same trail that Corrie took; otherwise, they took a different trail." Tarzan turned then, and was off at the even trot that he could maintain for hours when he chose to keep to the ground, the gait for which Apache Indians are famous.

"I don't know what good we are," said Bubonovitch. "That guy doesn't need us."

"He lets us come along for the ride," said Jerry.

"I think we are just in his way," remarked van der Bos; "but he's mighty patient about it."

"I'm goin' to practice swingin' t'rough de trees," said Shrimp.

"And jumping down on tigers?" asked Bubonovitch.

As Corrie followed what was to her now the homeward trail, she was happy and lighthearted. She was returning to Tak and Jerry and Tarzan and Bubonovitch and The Little Sergeant, of whom she had finally become very fond. In fact, she was very fond of all of them. Of course, she had known Tak all her life; but it was as though she had known the others always, also. She decided that she loved them all. She could scarcely wait to see them all again and tell them of her adventures. She had a little score to settle, too—a little score to settle with Amat. But she quickly put that out of her mind. She wished to think only of pleasant things.

So she was thinking of pleasant things, one of which was Jerry, when she suddenly became conscious of something moving through the underbrush parallel with the trail. It was something large. Corrie had her rifle ready, her finger on the trigger, as she peered into the tangle of foliage. What she saw drove every pleasant thought from her mind—just a little glimpse of black and yellow stripes. A tiger was stalking her.

How utterly inadequate was the .25 caliber Jap rifle she

116

was carrying! When she stopped, the tiger stopped. Now she could see his eyes—terrifying eyes—as he stood with lowered head returning her gaze. Would he attack? Why else would he be stalking her?

Corrie glanced about. Close beside her was a durian tree from which a stout liana depended. If the tiger charged, he would reach her before she could clamber out of danger. If she moved too quickly, he would charge. Any sudden movement on her part would doubtless mean as sudden death.

Very carefully, she leaned her rifle against the bole of the tree; then she grasped the liana. She watched the tiger. He had not moved. He still stood there watching her. Corrie drew herself up very slowly. Always she watched the tiger. The beast seemed fascinated. As she climbed, she saw his eyes following her. Suddenly he moved forward toward her.

Then Corrie scrambled upward as fast as she could go, and the tiger charged. But he was in an awkward position. He had to run half way around the tree and out into the trail before he could gather himself to spring up to seize her. He did spring, but he missed. And Corrie clawed her way upward to safety.

She sat there astride a limb, trembling, her heart pounding. And the tiger lay down in the trail at the foot of the tree. He was old and mangy. Because he was old, he had probably been unable to overhaul a meal for so long that he was reduced to hunting by day for anything that he might find. And having found something, he had evidently determined to wait right where he was until his prey either came down or fell out of the tree. Every once in a while he looked up at Corrie, bared his yellow fangs, and growled.

Corrie, though not given to any but the mildest of epithets, nevertheless swore at him. The creature had shattered her dream of getting back to her boys quickly. He just lay there, growling at her occasionally. An hour passed. Corrie was becoming frantic. Another hour, and still the stupid beast held tenaciously to his post. Corrie wondered which one of them would starve to death first.

Presently she was joined by some monkeys. They, too, scolded the tiger and probably swore at him in monkey language. Then Corrie had an idea. She knew that monkeys were imitative. She picked a durian fruit and threw it at the tiger. It struck him, much to Corrie's surprise, and elicited a savage growl. She threw another, and missed. Then the monkeys got the idea. Here was sport. They and Corrie bombarded the great cat with durian fruit. It rose, growling, and tried to leap into the tree; but it only fell back, lost its balance, and rolled over on its back. A durian struck it full on the nose. Durians rained upon it. Finally it gave up and went crashing off into the jungle. But for a long while Corrie did not dare leave her sanctuary. And she was a wary and frightened girl when she finally slipped down and retrieved her rifle.

Every little sound startled her now as she hurried along the trail toward the village, but finally she became convinced that she had seen the last of Stripes.

A huge creature bulked large and black in a tree beneath which Corrie passed. She did not see it. It moved silently above and behind her, watching her. It was Oju, the young orangutan which Tarzan had fought. Corrie's rifle kept him at a distance. Oju was afraid of the black sticks that made a loud noise. But he was patient. He could wait.

Presently other monstrous shapes appeared in the trees and in the trail in front of Corrie. She stopped. She had never seen so many orangutans together before. Corrie did not believe that they would harm her, but she was not certain. They grimaced at her, and some of them made threatening gestures, stamping on the ground and making little short rushes toward her. She kept her finger on the trigger of her rifle and backed away. She backed directly beneath Oju, who was now perched on a limb but a few feet above her head.

Ordinarily, the great apes avoid humans, going away when one appears. Corrie wondered why these did not go away. She thought that they would presently; so she waited, not daring to advance along the trail which some of them occupied. She thought that probably their numbers gave them courage to remain in the presence of a human being. It was not that, however. It was curiosity. They wanted to see what Oju was going to do. They did not have long to wait.

Oju looked down with bloodshot eyes, weighing the situation. He saw that this she tarmangani's whole attention was held by the other apes. He dropped upon Corrie, hurling her to the ground; and at the same time he wrenched the rifle from her grasp. The girl's finger being on the trigger at the time, the weapon was discharged. That terrified Oju, and he swung into a tree and off into the forest. But, having a one track mind, he neglected to loosen his grasp about Corrie's body; so he took her with him.

The shot also frightened the other apes; and they, too, swung off into the forest, but not in the same direction that Oju had taken. Now, the trail was quiet and deserted; but Corrie was not there to take advantage of it. She was beating futilely with clenched fists on the monstrous, hairy body of her abductor. Eventually, this annoyed Oju; and he cuffed her on the side of the head. It was fortunate for Corrie that this was merely a gentle reminder that Oju objected to being beaten, even though the beating did not hurt him in the least; for it only rendered her unconscious, whereas, had Oju really exerted himself she would doubtless have been killed.

When Corrie regained consciousness, which she did very quickly, she thought at first that she was experiencing a horrible nightmare; but that was only for a moment before the complete return of reason. Now she was indeed horrified. The great, hairy beast was hurrying through the trees, constantly looking back over its shoulder as though something were pursuing it.

Corrie was armed with both a pistol and a parang, but the orangutan held her so that one of his great arms was clamped over both of the weapons in such a way that she could withdraw neither of them. And the creature was carrying her deeper and deeper into the forest, and toward what horrible fate?

19

JERRY, Bubonovitch, Rosetti, and van der Bos followed the river down the valley until they came to the trail leading to the left out of the valley and into the forest at the summit of the cliff. Here they found a single blaze upon the bole of a tree and knew that Corrie had taken the trail back toward the village and that her erstwhile captors had not followed her.

When they reached the top of the cliff they heard, very faintly, a shot far ahead of them. Tarzan had carried no firearm, and they could not know that Corrie had been armed. The natural assumption was that she had not. The outlaws had not come this way, so none of them could have fired the shot. The natives had been warned not to touch the Jap weapons that the whites had hidden in their village, nor would they have dared so to arm themselves against the proscription of the Japs, of whom they stood in mortal terror.

The four men discussed these various conclusions as they pushed on along the trail. "A Jap must have fired that shot," said van der Bos. "And where there is one Jap there are doubtless others."

"Bring 'em on," said Rosetti. "I ain't killed no Jap for two days."

"We'll have to be careful," said Jerry. "I'll go on ahead about a hundred yards. I'll fire at the first Jap I see, and then fall back. You fellows get into the underbrush on one side of the trail when you hear my shot and let 'em have it when you can't miss. Let 'em get close."

"Geeze, Cap, you hadn't orter do that. Lemme do it," said Rosetti.

"Or me," said Bubonovitch. "That's not your job, Captain."

"Okay," said Jerry. "You go ahead, Shrimp, and keep your ears unbuttoned."

"Why don't you swing through the trees?" inquired Bubonovitch. Shrimp grinned and ran ahead.

Tarzan had followed Corrie's trail for no great distance when he came to the spot at which she had been treed by the tiger. He read the whole story as clearly as he might have from a printed page. Even the scattered durians told him how the tiger had finally been driven off. He smiled and followed the now fresh trail that indicated that the girl had resumed her journey but a short time before. Then he heard a shot ahead.

He took to the trees now, and moved swiftly above the trail. Like the men following behind him, he thought that a Jap had fired the shot. He also thought that Corrie had doubtless fallen into the hands of a detail of Jap soldiers. And then he saw a rifle lying in the trail.

Tarzan was puzzled. The Japs would not have gone away and left a rifle behind them. Too, there was no odor of Japs; but the scent spoor of great apes was strong. He dropped into the trail. He saw that Corrie's spoor ended where the rifle lay. He saw what appeared to indicate that the girl had fallen or been thrown to the ground. He also saw the man-like imprints of the feet of a large orangutan superimposed upon those made by Corrie, but these imprints were only directly beneath the tree where Tarzan stood.

The implication was clear: An orangutan had dropped from the tree, seized Corrie, and carried her off. Tarzan swung into the tree and was off on the trail of Oju. The arboreal spoor was plain to his trained senses. A crushed beetle or caterpillar, the bark on a limb scuffed by a horny hand or foot, a bit of reddish brown hair caught by a twig, the scent spoor of both the ape and the girl which still hung, even though faintly, in the quiet air of the forest.

In a little natural clearing in the forest Tarzan overtook his quarry. Oju had been aware that he was being followed, and now he elected to stand and fight, if fighting were to be necessary, in this open space. He still clung to his prize, and it happened that he was holding Corrie in such a position that she could not see Tarzan.

She knew that Oju was facing an enemy, for he was growling savagely. And she heard his opponent growl in reply, but this sounded more like the growl of a lion. Of course there were no lions in Sumatra, but the voice was not the voice of a tiger. She wondered what manner of beast it might be.

The voice was coming closer. Suddenly the orangutan dropped her and lumbered forward. Corrie raised herself on her hands and looked back. And at that instant Tarzan closed with Oju. Corrie leaped to her feet and drew her pistol. But she dared not fire for fear of hitting Tarzan. The two were locked in an embrace of death. Oju was attempting to close his powerful jaws on the man's throat, and the man held the yellow fangs away with one mighty arm. Both were growling, but lower now. Corrie was suddenly conscious of the feeling that she was watching two beasts fighting to the death—and for her.

Tarzan was holding Oju's jaws from his throat with his right arm. His left was pinned to his side by one of the ape's. Tarzan was straining to release himself from this hold. Inch by inch he was dragging his left arm free. Inch by inch Oju was forcing his fangs closer and closer to the man's throat.

Corrie was horrified. She circled the struggling combatants, trying to get a shot at the orangutan; but they were

121

moving too rapidly. She might as easily have hit Tarzan as his opponent.

The two were still on their feet, pulling and straining. Suddenly Tarzan locked one leg around those of the ape and surged heavily against him. Oju fell backward, Tarzan on top of him. In trying to save himself, the ape had released his hold on the man's left arm. Then Corrie saw a knife flash, saw it driven into the ape's breast, heard his screams of pain and rage. Again and again the knife was driven home. The screaming waned, the great body quivered and lay still. Oju was dead.

Tarzan rose and placed a foot upon the body of his foe. He raised his face toward the heavens—and then, suddenly, he smiled. The victory cry of the bull ape died in his throat. Why he did not voice it, he himself did not know.

Corrie felt very limp. Her legs refused to hold her, and she sat down. She just looked at Tarzan and shook her head. "All in?" he asked. Corrie nodded. "Well, your troubles are over for today at least, I hope. Jerry, van der Bos, and the sergeants are coming along the trail. We'd better get over there and meet them." He swung her across his shoulder and swung back along the leafy way that the ape had brought her, but how different were her feelings now!

When they reached the trail, Tarzan examined it and found that the others had not yet passed; so they sat down beside it and waited. They did not talk. The man realized that the girl had undergone terrific shock, and so he left her alone and did not question her. He wanted her to rest.

But finally Corrie broke the silence herself. "I am an awful fool," she said. "I have had to exert all the will power I possess to keep from crying. I thought death was so near, and then you came. It was just as though you had materialized out of thin air. I suppose that it was the reaction that nearly broke me down. But how in the world did you know where I was? How could you have known what had happened to me?"

"Stories are not written in books alone," he said. "It was not difficult." Then he told her just how he had trailed her. "I had an encounter with that same ape a few days ago. I got the better of him then, but I refrained from killing him. I wish now that I had not. His name was Oju."

"You never said anything about that," she said.

"It was of no importance."

"You are a very strange man."

"I am more beast than man, Corrie."

She knitted her brows and shook her head. "You are very far from being a beast."

"You mean that for a compliment. That is because you don't know the beasts very well. They have many fine qualities that men would do well to emulate. They have no vices. It was left for man to have those as well as many disagreeable and criminal characteristics that the beasts do not have. When I said that I was more beast than man, I didn't mean that I possessed all their noble qualities. I simply meant that I thought and reacted more like a beast than a man. I have the psychology of a wild beast."

"Well, you may be right; but if I were going out to dinner, I'd rather go with a man than a tiger."

Tarzan smiled. "That is one of the nice things about being a beast. You don't have to go to dinners and listen to speeches and be bored to death."

Corrie laughed. "But one of your fellow beasts may leap on you and take you for his dinner."

"Or a nice man may come along and shoot you, just for fun."

"You win," said Corrie.

"The others are coming," said Tarzan.

"How do you know?"

"Usha tells me."

"Usha? Who is Usha?"

"The wind. It carries to both my ears and my nostrils evidence that men are coming along the trail. Each race has its distinctive body odor; so I know these are white men."

A moment later, Rosetti came into view around a curve in the trail. When he saw Tarzan and Corrie he voiced a whoop of pleasure and shouted the word back to those behind him. Soon the others joined them. It was a happy reunion.

"Just like old home week," observed Bubonovitch.

"It seems as though you had been gone for weeks, Corrie," said Jerry.

"I went a long way into the Valley of the Shadow," said Corrie. "I thought that I should never see any of you again in this world. Then Tarzan came."

Tak van der Bos came and kissed her. "If my hair hasn't turned white since you disappeared, then worry doesn't turn hair white. Don't you ever get out of our sight again, darling."

Jerry wished that he didn't like van der Bos. He would greatly have enjoyed hating him. Then he thought: *You are an idiot, Lucas. You haven't a ghost of a show anyway, and those two were made for each other. They are both swell.* So Jerry lagged along behind and left them together as they resumed the march toward the village.

Tarzan had gone ahead to act as point. The others listened as Corrie recounted her adventures, telling of Amat's treachery, of Sarina's unexpected help, of her horrifying experience with Oju, and of her rescue by Tarzan.

"He is magnificent," she said. "In battle he is terrifying. He seems to become a wild beast, with the strength and agility of a tiger guided by the intelligence of a man. He growls like a beast. I was almost afraid of him. But when the fight was over and he smiled he was all human again."

"He has added one more debt which we owe him and can never repay," said Jerry.

"Dat guy's sure some guy," said Rosetti, "even if he is a Britisher. I bet he didn't have nuttin' to do wit dat Geo'ge Toid."

"That's a safe bet, Shrimp," said Bubonovitch. "You can also lay 100 to 1 that he didn't run around with Caligula either."

Tak van der Bos found these Americans amusing. He liked them, but often he could not make head nor tail of what they were talking about.

"Who was Geo'ge Toid?" he asked.

"He is dat king of England wot Mayor Thompson said he would poke in de snoot if he ever came to Chicago," explained Rosetti.

"You mean George Third?"

"Dat's who I said—Geo'ge Toid."

"Oh," said van der Bos. Bubonovitch was watching him, and noticed that he did not smile. He liked him for that. Bubonovitch could rib Shrimp, but he wouldn't stand for any foreigner ribbing him.

"This lame brain," he said, jerking a thumb in Rosetti's direction, "doesn't know that the War of the Revolution is over."

"You disliked Englishmen because of what George Third did?" Tak asked Shrimp.

124

"You said it."

"Maybe you won't think so badly of Englishmen if you'll just remember that George Third was not an Englishman."

"Wot?"

"He was a German."

"No kiddin'?"

"No kidding. Many of the Englishmen of his day didn't like him any more than you do."

"So de guy was a Heinie! Dat explains everyt'ing." Shrimp was satisfied now. He could like Tarzan and not be ashamed of it.

Presently they caught up with Tarzan. He was talking to two bearded white men. They were sentries posted by the guerrillas who had occupied the village. The two other trails were similarly guarded.

Within a few minutes the returning party had entered the kampong; and as they did so, Amat departed into the forest on the opposite side of the village. He had caught a glimpse of Rosetti.

20

CAPT. VAN PRINS and Lieut. de Lettenhove, as well as several others of the guerrilla force, knew both Corrie and Tak, whom they had believed to be dead. They gathered around them, laughing and talking, congratulating them and exchanging snatches of their various experiences during the more than two years since they had seen one another. Corrie and Tak asked of news of old friends. Some were known to be dead, others had been prisoners of the Japs when last heard of. They spoke in their own tongue.

Jerry, feeling very much an outsider, sought Bubonovitch and Rosetti. They sat together beneath a tree and cleaned their rifles and pistols, for since they had captured the equipment of the Japs they had all that was necessary to keep their weapons cleaned and oiled, an endless procedure in the humid equatorial atmosphere of the Sumatran mountains.

Presently van Prins and de Lettenhove joined them to discuss plans for the future. Corrie and Tak were sitting together in the shade of another tree at a little distance. Corrie had noticed that Jerry had been avoiding her of late; so she did not suggest joining the conference. She wondered if she had done anything to offend him, or if he were just tired of her company. She was piqued, and so she redoubled her attentions to Tak van der Bos. Jerry was keenly aware of this and was miserable. He took no part in the discussion that was going on. Both Bubonovitch and Rosetti noticed this and wondered at the change that had come over him.

The conference resulted in a decision that the two parties would join forces for the time being at least, but it was not thought wise to remain where they were. When the detail that was to have been relieved did not return to the base, there would be an investigation, unquestionably in force; and the Dutchmen did not wish to risk a major engagement. They had other plans for harassing the enemy.

It was therefore decided to move to an easily defended position of which they knew. This would mean backtracking for Tarzan and the Americans, but van Prins assured them that in the end it would improve their chances of reaching the southwest coast.

"From where I plan on making camp," he explained, "there is a comparatively easy route over the summit. You can then move down the east side of the mountains where, I am informed, there are comparatively few Japs in the higher reaches, while on this side there are many. I will furnish you with a map and mark out a route that will bring you back to the west side at a point where I think you will find it much easier to reach the coast, if you decide to persist in what I believe a very foolhardy venture."

"What do you think about it, Jerry?" asked Tarzan.

Jerry, awakened from a day dream, looked up blankly. "Think about what?" he demanded.

Tarzan looked at him in surprise. Then he repeated the plan. "Whatever suits the rest of you suits me," said Jerry indifferently.

Bubonovitch and Rosetti looked at one another. "Wot the hell's happened to the 'old man'?" whispered the latter.

Bubonovitch shrugged and looked in the direction of Corrie and van der Bos. *"Cherchez la femme,"* he said.

"Talk American," said Rosetti.

"I think the captain is going to be a misogynist again pretty soon," said Bubonovitch.

"I getcha. I guess maybe as how I'll be one of dem t'ings again myself. Trouble is a dame's middle name—trouble, trouble, nuttin' but trouble."

"When do you plan on leaving?" Tarzan asked van Prins.

"I think we can remain here safely today and tomorrow. The Japs won't really commence to worry about that detail for several days, and then it will take them another day to reach this village. We can leave here day after tomorrow, early in the morning. That will give my men time to fix up their foot gear. I can't call the things we are wearing shoes. The chief here has plenty of material, and some of the women are helping us make sandals. We were just about barefoot when we got here. Even if the Japs do come, we shall be ready for them. Some of my men are cutting a trail from the village paralleling the main trail toward the Jap base. I'm having them run it out about five hundred yards. If the Japs come, we'll have a surprise for them."

The conference broke up. Van Prins went out into the forest to see how his men were getting ahead with the trail. The other Dutchmen went to work on their sandals or cleaned their weapons. Corrie had been surreptitiously watching Jerry. She noticed how glum he looked and that he only spoke when directly addressed, and then curtly. Suddenly she thought that he might be ill. She had been angry with him, but that thought destroyed her anger and filled her with compassion. She walked over to where he was now sitting alone, reassembling the Jap pistol that he had stripped and cleaned. She sat down beside him.

"What's the matter, Jerry?" she asked. "You're not ill, are you?"

"No," he said. He had worked himself into such a state of utter misery that he couldn't even be civil.

Corrie looked at him in surprise and hurt. He did not see the expression on her face; because he pretended to be engrossed with the pistol. He knew that he was being sophomoric and he hated himself. *What the hell is the matter with me?* he thought. Corrie arose slowly and walked away. Jerry thought about committing suicide. He was being an ass, and he knew it. But Jerry was very young and very much in love. He slammed the last piece of the pistol into place viciously and stood up.

Corrie was walking toward the little house she occupied with the native girl, Lara. Jerry walked quickly after her. He wanted to tell her how sorry he was. As she reached the foot of the ladder leading up into the house, he called to her: "Corrie!" She did not pause nor look back. She climbed the ladder and disappeared through the doorway.

He knew that she had heard him. He also knew that Tarzan and Bubonovitch and Rosetti had witnessed the whole thing. But worst of all, so had Tak van der Bos. Jerry could feel his face burning. He stood there for a moment, not knowing what to do. *The hell with all women,* he thought. He had faced death many times, but to face his friends now was worse. It required all his will power to turn around and walk back to them.

No one said anything as he sat down among them. They appeared wholly occupied by whatever they were doing. Tarzan broke the silence. "I am going out to see if I can bring in some fresh meat," he said. "Anyone want to come with me?" It was the first time he had ever asked anyone to hunt with him. They all knew that he meant Jerry; so no one spoke, waiting for Jerry.

"Yes, I'd like to, if no one else wants to," he said.

"Come along," said Tarzan.

They picked up rifles and went out into the forest.

Bubonovitch and Rosetti were sitting a little apart from the Dutchmen. "That was swell of Tarzan," said the former. "I sure felt sorry for Jerry. I wonder what's got into Corrie."

"Oh, hell; they're all alike," said Rosetti.

Bubonovitch shook his head. "It wasn't like Corrie—she's different. Jerry must have said something. He's been as grouchy as a bear with a sore head."

"It's dat Dutchman," said Rosetti. "He and Corrie are just like dat." He crossed a middle finger over an index finger. "An' I t'ought all de time she was fallin' for de Cap'n. I told you w'en we foist picked up dat dame dat it meant trouble."

"You sort of fell for her yourself, Shrimp."

"I liked her all right. Maybe she ain't done nuttin'. Maybe de Cap'n's de wrong guy. Dey don't have to do nuttin'. Just bein' a dame spells trouble. Geeze! I t'ink w'en I gets back to Chi I'll join a convent."

Bubonovitch grinned. "That would be just the place for you, Shrimp—a nice convent without any women. If you

128

can't find one in Chicago, you might try Hollywood. Anything that's screwy, Hollywood's got."

Shrimp knew that Bubonovitch was ribbing him, but he didn't know just how. "Yes, sir! I t'ink I'll be a monk."

"The correlative wisecrack is too obvious."

"Talk American, Perfessor."

Tarzan and Jerry were gone a little more than an hour. They returned to the village with the carcass of a deer. Tarzan had shot it. Jerry was glad that he had not had to. Of course it was all right to kill for food, but still he didn't like to kill deer. He didn't mind killing Japs. That was different. The way he felt this afternoon, he would have enjoyed killing almost anything. But he was still glad that he hadn't killed the deer.

That evening, Corrie ate apart with the Dutchmen. She shouldn't have done it, and she knew that she shouldn't. She should have carried on just as though nothing had happened. Afterward she wished that she had, for she realized that now she had definitely acknowledged the rift. It would be difficult to close it again. It would probably widen. She was most unhappy; because she loved those men with whom she had been through so much—to whom she owed so much. She was sorry now that she hadn't waited when Jerry had called to her.

She made up her mind to swallow her pride and go over to them; but when she did so, Jerry got up and walked away. So she passed them and went to her house. There she threw herself down on her sleeping mats and cried. For the first time in years, she cried.

The day was drawing to a close and Amat was very tired when he reached the Jap base. He bowed low to the sentry who halted him, and in the few Japanese words he had learned he tried to explain that he had important news for the commanding officer.

The sentry called a non-commissioned officer of the guard who happened to have learned a smattering of the native dialect; and to him Amat repeated what he had told the sentry, almost forgetting to bow. So he bowed twice.

The sergeant took him to the adjutant, to whom Amat bowed three times. When the sergeant had reported, the adjutant questioned Amat, and what Amat told him excited him greatly. He lost no time in conducting Amat to the commanding officer, a Col. Kanji Tajiri, to whom Amat bowed four times.

When the colonel learned that some forty of his men had been killed, he was furious. Amat also told him just how many white men there were in the party in his village. He told about the sentries out on the trails. He told about the white girl. He told everything.

Tajiri gave orders that Amat should be fed and given a place to sleep. He also directed that two full companies should march at dawn to attack the village and destroy the white men. He himself would go in command, and they would take Amat along. If Amat had known this, he would not have slept so easily as he did.

21

AT breakfast the following morning, the cleavage was again definitely apparent. The Dutch prepared and ate their breakfast a little apart from the Americans and Tarzan. The Englishman knew that it was all very wrong and very stupid and that if the condition persisted it would affect the morale of the entire company. At the same time, however, he could not but be amused; for it was so obvious that the two principals who were responsible were very much in love with each other. They were probably the only ones who did not realize this. He knew that they must be in love; because it is only people who are very much in love who treat each other so damnably.

After they had eaten, Tarzan and the Americans went into the forest to inspect the trail the Dutchmen had cut. They found that it gave excellent concealment from the main trail, but Tarzan thought that the sentry post was not far enough in advance of the trail's outer end.

Capt. van Prins had posted four men on this post with orders to hold up the Japs as long as possible should they come, falling back slowly to give the main force of the guerrillas time to come from the village and prepare the ambush.

"I think he should have had one man very much farther

in advance," Tarzan said to Jerry, "and at least half his force posted constantly in this paralleling trail. He is not prepared for a surprise, and he is not giving the Japs credit for the cunning they possess."

"They'll have a man way out in front," said Jerry. "He'll be well camouflaged, and he'll sneak through the jungle like a snake. He'll see the guys on this post and then go back and report. Pretty soon some more will sneak up and toss a few grenades. That'll be the end of the sentries, and the Japs will rush the village before van Prins can get his men out here to ambush them."

"Let's go back and talk with him," suggested Tarzan.

Shortly after breakfast, Lara had sought out Corrie. "I have just discovered," she said, "that Amat did not return to the village last night. He left yesterday. I know him. He is a bad man. I am sure that he went to the big Japanese camp and reported everything that has happened here."

Corrie was repeating this to van Prins when Tarzan and Jerry returned. The Dutchman called them over; and as they came, Corrie walked away. Van Prins told them of Lara's warning, and Tarzan suggested the plan that he and Jerry had discussed.

"I think I'll put most of my force out there," said van Prins. "I'll just leave a welcoming committee here in case some of them break through to the village."

"It might be a good idea to withdraw your sentries entirely," suggested Jerry. "Then the Japs will walk right into the ambush without any warning."

"I don't know about that," said van Prins. "I'd like a little advance information myself, or we might be the ones who would be surprised."

Tarzan didn't agree with him, but he said, "I'll get advance information to you much sooner than your sentries could. I'll go out four or five miles, and when the Japs show up I'll be back with the word long before they reach your ambush."

"But suppose they see you?"

"They won't."

"You seem pretty sure of yourself, Sir," said the Dutchman, smiling.

"I am."

"I'll tell you what we'll do," said van Prins. "Just to make assurance doubly sure, I'll leave my sentries out. I'll tell them that when you come back, you'll order them in. How's that?"

"Fine," said Tarzan. I'll go along out now, and you can get your men camouflaged and posted for the ambush. O.K.?"

"O.K.," said van Prins.

Tarzan swung into a tree and was gone. The Dutchman shook his head. "If I had a battalion like him, I could pretty near chase the Japs off this island."

Jerry, Bubonovitch, and Rosetti, loaded down with ammunition and hand grenades, preceded the guerrillas into the ambush. They went to the far end of the paralleling trail and prepared to make themselves comfortable and also inconspicuous. With leaves and vines they camouflaged their heads and shoulders until they became a part of the surrounding jungle. Even had there not been several feet of shrubbery intervening between them and the main trail, an enemy would have had to be right on top of them before he could have discovered them.

The guerrillas were soon stationed and busy camouflaging themselves. Capt. van Prins walked back and forth along the main trail checking on the effectiveness of each man's camouflage. Finally he gave his orders.

"Don't fire until I fire, unless you are discovered; then start firing. A couple of men at the head of the line can use grenades if they can throw them far enough so as not to endanger our own people. The same goes for a couple at the opposite end, in case some of the Japs get past us. Try to get the Japs directly in front of you. If everything works out as I hope, each one of you will have Japs in front of him when I give the signal to commence firing. Any questions?"

"If they retreat, shall we follow them?" asked one of the men.

"No. We might run into an ambush ourselves. All I want to do is give them a little punishment and put the fear of God in them for Dutchmen." He came and took up a position about the center of the line.

Jerry presently discovered that van der Bos was next to him in line. Tak had had a little talk with Corrie shortly before. "What's the matter between you and Jerry?" he had asked.

"I didn't know there was anything the matter."

"Oh, yes you do. What's wrong with him?"

"I'm not interested in what's wrong with him. I'm not

132

interested in him at all. He's a boor, and I'm not interested in boors."

But Tak knew that she was interested, and he suddenly conceived an idea of what the trouble was. It came to him in a flash and made him voice a little whistle of amazement.

"What are you whistling about?" Corrie had asked.

"I whistle in amazement that there are so many damn fools in the world."

"Meaning me?"

"Meaning you and Jerry and myself."

"Whistle if you like, but mind your own business."

Tak chucked her under the chin and grinned; then he went out with van Prins into the forest.

Jerry was not particularly pleased to have van der Bos next to him. Of all the people he could think of van der Bos was the one he was least desirous of being chummy with. He hoped the fellow wouldn't try to start a conversation.

"Well, I guess we're in for a long wait," said van der Bos.

Jerry grunted.

"And no smoking," added van der Bos.

Jerry grunted again.

As Jerry was not looking at him, van der Bos allowed himself the luxury of a grin. "Corrie wanted to come out and get into the fight," he said; "but van Prins and I turned thumbs down on that idea."

"Quite right," said Jerry.

"Corrie's a great little girl," continued van der Bos. "We've known each other all our lives. She and my wife have been chums ever since either of them can remember. Corrie's exactly like a sister to us."

There was a silence. Van der Bos was enjoying himself greatly. Jerry was not. Finally he said, "I didn't know you were married."

"That only just occurred to me a few minutes ago," said van der Bos.

Jerry held out his hand. "Thanks," he said. "I am a goddam fool."

"Quite right," said van der Bos.

"Did your wife get away?"

"Yes. We tried to get old van der Meer to send Corrie

and her mother out, too; but the stubborn old fool wouldn't. God! and what a price he paid. That man's stubbornness was notorious all over the island. He gloried in it. Aside from that, he was a very fine person."

"Do you suppose that Corrie has inherited any of her father's stubbornness?" asked Jerry, fearfully.

"I shouldn't be surprised." Van der Bos was having the time of his life. He liked this American, but he felt that he had a little punishment coming to him.

Bubonovitch and Rosetti noticed with growing wonder the cordiality that existed between Jerry and van der Bos. As the day wore on, they also noticed that "the old man" was becoming more and more like his former self.

They commented on this. "He's gettin' almost human again," whispered Rosetti. "Whatever was eatin' him must o' quit."

"Probably died of indigestion," said Bubonovitch. "We've known 'the old man' a long while, but we've never seen him like he's been the last day or so."

"We never seen him wit a dame around. I'm tellin' you—"

"You needn't tell me. I know it all by heart. Dames are bad medicine. They spell nothing but trouble. You give me a pain in the neck. The trouble with you is that you never knew a decent girl. At least not till you met Corrie. And you haven't met my wife. You'd sing a different tune if you fell in love with some girl. And when you do, I'll bet you fall heavy. Your kind always does."

"Not a chance. I wouldn't have Dorothy Lamour if she got down on her knees and asked me."

"She won't," said Bubonovitch.

This edifying conversation was interrupted by the return of Tarzan. He sought out van Prins. "Your little brown cousins are coming," he said. "They are about two miles away. There are two full companies, I should judge. They have light machine guns and those dinky little mortars they use. A colonel is in command. They have a point of three men out only about a hundred yards. Your sentries are coming in."

"You have certainly done a swell job, Sir," said van Prins. "I can't thank you enough." He turned to the men nearest him. "Pass the word along that there is to be no more talking. The enemy will be along in thirty-five or forty minutes."

He turned back to Tarzan. "Pardon me, Sir," he said; "but they are not brown. The bastards are yellow."

Groen de Lettenhove had been left in command of the guerrillas who had been ordered to remain in the village. He was trying to persuade Corrie to find a place of safety against the possibility that some of the enemy might break through into the village.

"You may need every rifle you can get," she countered; "and furthermore, I haven't settled my account with the Japs."

"But you might get killed or wounded, Corrie."

"So might you and your men. Maybe we'd all better go and hide."

"You're hopeless," he said. "I might have known better than argue with a woman."

"Don't think of me as a woman. I'm another rifle, and I'm a veteran. I'm also a darned good shot."

Their conversation was interrupted by a burst of rifle fire from the forest.

22

JERRY was the first to see the approaching Japs, as he happened to be in a position that gave him a view of about a hundred feet of the trail just where it curved to the right toward the village directly in front of him. It was the three man point. They were advancing cautiously, watching the trail ahead of them. They were evidently so sure that their attack would be a surprise that they did not even consider the possibility of an ambush. They paid no attention to the jungle on either side of the trail. They passed the men lying in wait for the main body and stopped at the edge of the forest. The village lay below them. It appeared deserted. The guerrillas, concealed in and behind houses, saw them and waited.

Presently, Jerry saw the main body approaching. The colonel marched at the head of the column with drawn samurai sword. Behind him slogged Amat, and behind Amat a soldier walked with the tip of his bayonet aimed at a Sumatran kidney. Evidently, Amat had attempted to desert somewhere along the route. He did not appear happy. Shrimp saw him pass, and mentally cautioned his trigger finger to behave.

The trail was crowded with the men of the first company. They had closed up into a compact mass when the head of the column was halted behind the point at the edge of the forest. Then van Prins fired, and instantly a withering volley was poured into the ranks of the surprised enemy. Jerry hurled three grenades in quick succession down the back trail into the second company.

The Japs fired wildly into the jungle; then some who had not been hit turned and broke in retreat. A few leaped into the undergrowth with fixed bayonets in an effort to get into close quarters with the white men. Shrimp was enjoying a field day. He picked off Japs as fast as he could fire, until his rifle got so hot that it jammed.

Among those in the mad rush to escape were the colonel and Amat. Miraculously they had so far escaped unscathed. The colonel was shrieking in Japanese, which Amat could not understand; but he had glanced behind him, and was aware that the colonel had lethal designs upon him. As he fled, Amat screamed. He would have been deeply hurt had he known that the colonel was accusing him of having traitorously led them into ambush, and that it was for this reason that he wished to kill Amat.

Rosetti saw them just before they came abreast of him. "Nothing doing, yellow belly," he yelled. "That guy is my meat. They don't nobody else kill him if I can help it." Then he shot the colonel with his pistol. He took another shot at Amat and missed. "Doggone!" said Rosetti, as the terrified native dove into the underbrush farther along the trail.

Wholly disorganized, the remainder of the Jap force fled back into the forest, leaving their dead and wounded. Van Prins detailed a number of men to act as rear guard, others to collect the enemy's weapons and ammunition, and the remainder to carry the Jap wounded and their own into the village.

A moment later, a wounded Jap shot the Dutchman who was trying to help him. Shortly thereafter there were no wounded Japs.

Bubonovitch and Rosetti, who had jumped out into the trail to fire on the fleeing enemy, were helping gather up the abandoned Jap weapons and ammunition. Suddenly, Rosetti stopped and looked around. "Where's the Cap'n?" he asked.

Jerry was nowhere in sight. The two men forced their way back into the underbrush where they had last seen him. They found him there, lying on his back, his shirt, over his left breast, blood soaked. Both men dropped to their knees beside him.

"He ain't dead," said Rosetti. "He's breathing."

"He mustn't die," said Bubonovitch.

"You said a mouthful, soldier," said Rosetti.

Very tenderly, they picked him up and started back toward the village. The Dutchmen were carrying in three of their own dead and five wounded.

Tarzan saw the two sergeants carrying Jerry. He came and looked at the unconscious man. "Bad?" he asked.

"I'm afraid so, Sir," said Bubonovitch. They passed on, leaving Tarzan behind.

As the men entered the village with their pathetic burdens, those who had been left behind came to meet them. The dead were laid in a row and covered with sleeping mats. The wounded were placed in the shade of trees. Among the guerrillas was a doctor. He had no medicines, no sulfanilamide, no anesthetics. He just did the best he could, and Corrie helped him. At the edge of the jungle, men were already digging the graves for the three dead. Native women were boiling water in which to sterilize bandages.

Bubonovitch and Rosetti were sitting beside Jerry when the doctor and Corrie finally reached him. When Corrie saw who it was, she went white and caught her breath in a sudden gasp. Both Bubonovitch and Rosetti were watching her. Her reaction told them more than any words could have; because words are sometimes spoken to deceive.

With the help of the two sergeants and Corrie, each trying to do something for the man they all loved, the doctor removed Jerry's shirt and examined the wound carefully.

"Is it very bad?" asked Corrie.

"I don't think so," replied the doctor. "It certainly missed his heart, and I'm sure it missed his lungs, also. He hasn't brought up any blood, has he, sergeant?"

"No," said Bubonovitch.

"He's suffering mostly from shock and partly from loss of

137

blood. I think he's going to be all right. Help me turn him over—very gently, now."

There was a small round hole in Jerry's back just to the right of his left shoulder blade. It had not bled much.

"He must have been born under a lucky star," said the doctor. "We won't have to probe, and that's a good thing; because I have no instruments. The bullet bored straight through, clean as a whistle." He washed the wounds with sterile water, and bandaged them loosely. "That's all I can do," he said. "One of you stay with him. When he comes to, keep him quiet."

"I'll stay," said Corrie.

"You men can help me over here, if you will," said the doctor.

"If you need us, Miss, just holler," said Rosetti.

Corrie sat beside the wounded man and bathed his face with cool water. She didn't know what else to do, but she knew she wanted to do something for him. Whatever mild rancor she had thought that she felt toward him had been expunged by the sight of his blood and his helplessness.

Presently he sighed and opened his eyes. He blinked them a few times, an expression of incredulity in them, as he saw the girl's face close above his. Then he smiled; and reaching up, he pressed her hand.

"You're going to be all right, Jerry," she said.

"I am all right—now," he said.

He had held her hand for but a second. Now she took his and stroked it. They just smiled at each other. All was right with the world.

Capt. van Prins was having litters built for the wounded. He came over to see Jerry. "How you feeling?" he asked.

"Fine."

"Good. I've decided to move out of here just as soon as possible. The Japs are almost sure to sneak back on us to-night, and this is no place to defend successfully. I know a place that is. We can make it in two marches. As soon as the litters are finished and our dead buried, we'll move out of here. I'm going to burn the village as a lesson to the natives. These people have been collaborating with the enemy. They must be punished."

"Oh, no!" cried Corrie. "That would be most unfair. You would be punishing the innocent with the guilty. Take Lara, for instance. She has helped us twice. She has told me that there are only two people here who wanted to help the Japs—the chief and Amat. It would be cruel to burn down the homes of those who are loyal. Remember—if it had not been for Lara, the Japs might have taken us by surprise."

"I guess that you are right, Corrie," said van Prins. "Anyway, you've given me a better idea."

He walked away, and ten minutes later the chief was taken to one side of the village and shot by a firing squad.

The guerrillas gathered around the graves of their dead. The doctor said a short prayer, three volleys were fired, and the graves were filled. The wounded were lifted onto the litters, the rear guard marched into the village, the little company was ready to move.

Jerry objected to being carried, insisting that he could walk. Bubonovitch, Rosetti, and Corrie were trying to dissuade him when the doctor walked up. "What's going on here?" he asked. They told him. "You stay on that litter young man," he said to Jerry, and to Bubonovitch and Rosetti, "If he tries to get off of it, tie him down."

Jerry grinned. "I'll be good, Doc," he said, "but I hate to have four men carrying me when I can walk just as well as not."

Following the shooting of the chief, the natives were afraid. They did not know how many more might be shot. Lara came to Corrie just as van Prins came along. He recognized the girl.

"You can tell your people," he said, "that largely because of you and the help you gave us we did not burn the village as we intended. We punished only the chief. He had been helping our enemies. When we come back, if Amat is here we will punish him also. The rest of you need never fear us if you do not help the enemy. We know that you have to treat them well, or be mistreated. We understand that, but do not help them any more than is absolutely necessary." He took a quick look around the kampong. "Where is Tarzan?" he asked.

"That's right," said Bubonovitch. "Where is he?"

"Geeze," said Rosetti. "He never come back to the village after the scrap. But he wasn't wounded. He was all right when we seen him last, just before we brung the Cap'n out."

"Don't worry about him," said Bubonovitch. "He can take care of himself and all the rest of us into the bargain."

"I can leave some men here to tell him where we are going to camp," said van Prins.

"You don't even have to do that," said Bubonovitch. "He'll find us. Lara can tell him which way we went out. He'll track us better than a bloodhound."

"All right," said van Prins, "let's get going."

When Tarzan had looked at the wounded American, the latter had seemed in a very bad way. Tarzan was sure the wound was fatal. His anger against the Japs flared, for he liked this young flier. Unnoticed by the others, he swung into the trees and was off on the trail of the enemy.

He caught up with them at a point where a captain and two lieutenants had rallied them—the only surviving officers of the two companies. High in the trees above them, a grim figure looked down upon them. It fitted an arrow to its bow. The twang of the bow string was drowned by the jabbering of the monkey-men, the shouted commands of their officers. The captain lurched forward upon his face, a bamboo shaft through his heart. As he fell upon it, the arrow was driven through his body, so that it protruded from his back.

For a moment the Japs were stunned to silence; then the shouting commenced again, as they fired into the jungle in all directions with rifles and machine guns. Seventy-five feet above their bullets, Tarzan watched them, another bolt already to be shot.

This time he picked out one of the lieutenants. As he loosed the missile, he moved quietly to another position several hundred feet away. As their second officer fell, struck down mysteriously, the Japs commenced to show signs of panic. Now they fired wildly into the underbrush and into the trees.

When the last officer went down the Japs began to run along the trail in the direction of their main camp. They had had enough. But Tarzan had not. He followed them until all his arrows were gone, each one imbedded in the body of a Jap. The screaming wounded were tearing arrows from backs and bellies. The silent dead were left behind for the tigers and the wild dogs.

Tarzan unslung the rifle from across his back and emptied a clip into the broken ranks of the fleeing enemy; then he turned and swung back in the direction of the village. His American friend had been avenged.

140

He did not follow the trail. He did not even travel in the direction of the village for long. He ranged deep into the primeval forest, viewing ancient things that perhaps no other human eye had ever looked upon—patriarchs of the forest, moss covered and hoary with age, clothed in giant creepers, vines, and huge air plants, garlanded with orchids.

As the wind changed and a vagrant breeze blew into his face, he caught the scent of man. And presently he saw a little trail, such as men make. Dropping lower, he saw a snare, such as primitive hunters set for small game. He had come into the forest to be alone and get away from men. He was not antisocial; but occasionally he longed for solitude, or the restful companionship of beasts. Even the jabbering, scolding monkeys were often a welcome relief, for they were amusing. Few men were.

There were many monkeys here. They ran away from him at first, but when he spoke to them in their own language, they took courage and came closer. He even coaxed one little fellow to come and perch on his hand. It reminded him of little Nkima, boastful, belligerent, diminutive, arrant little coward, which loved Tarzan and which Tarzan loved. Africa! How far, far away it seemed.

He talked to the little monkey as he had talked to Nkima, and presently the little fellow's courage increased, and he leaped to Tarzan's shoulder. Like Nkima, he seemed to sense safety there; and there he rode as Tarzan swung through the trees.

The man's curiosity had been aroused by the strange scent spoor, and so he followed it. It led him to a small lake in the waters of which, along the shore, were a number of rude shelters built of branches and leaves upon platforms that were supported a few feet above the water by crude piling that had been driven into the mud of the lake's bottom.

The shelters were open on all sides. Their occupants were a people below average height, their skins a rich olive brown, their hair jet black. They were naked savages whom civilization had never touched. Fortunate people, thought Tarzan. Several men and women were in the water fishing with nets. The men carried bows and arrows.

The little monkey said that they were bad gomangani. "So manu," he said—*eat monkey*. Then he commenced to scream at them and scold, feeling secure in doing so by

141

virtue of distance and the presence of his big new friend. Tarzan smiled, it reminded him so much of Nkima.

The monkey made so much noise that some of the natives looked up. Tarzan made the universal sign of peace that has been debauched and befouled by a schizophrenic in a greasy raincoat, but the natives threatened him with their arrows. They jabbered and gesticulated at him, doubtless warning him away. The Lord of the Jungle was in full sympathy with them and admired their good judgment. Were they always successful in keeping white men at a distance they would continue to enjoy the peace and security of their idyllic existence.

He watched them for a few minutes, and then turned back into the forest to wander aimlessly, enjoying this brief interlude in the grim business of war. Keta, the little monkey, rode sometimes on the man's shoulder. Sometimes he swung through the trees with him. He seemed to have attached himself permanently to the big tarmangani.

23

S/SGT. TONY ROSETTI squatted on the sentry platform on the trail outside the former camp of the outlaws where the guerrillas were now bivouacked for a day to let their wounded rest.

His tour of duty was about completed, and he was waiting for his relief when he saw a figure approaching him along the trail. It was a slender, boyish figure; but even in the dim, cathedral light of the forest afternoon the sergeant realized that, notwithstanding the trousers, the rifle, the pistol, the parang, and the ammunition belt, it was no boy.

When the woman caught sight of Rosetti, she stopped. "Halt!" commanded Rosetti, bringing his rifle to the ready.

"I am already halted," said the woman in good English.

"Who are you and where do you think you're goin' wit all dat armor?"

"You must be the cute little sergeant Corrie van der Meer told me about—the one who hates women and speaks funny English."

"I don't speak English. I speak American. And wot's funny about it? And who are you?"

"I am Sarina. I am looking for Corrie van der Meer."

"Advance," said Rosetti. Then he dropped down off the platform into the trail. He stood there with a finger on the trigger of his rifle and the point of his bayonet belly high. The woman came and stopped a few feet from him.

"I wish that you would aim that thing some other way," she said.

"Nuttin' doin', sister. You belong to dat outlaw gang. How do I know you ain't just a front an' de rest of dem is trailin' behind you? If dey are, youse is goin' to get shot, sister."

"I'm alone," said Sarina.

"Maybe you are, an' maybe you ain't. Drop dat gun an' stick up your mitts. I'm goin' to frisk you."

"Speak English, if you can," said Sarina. "I don't understand American. What are mitts, and what is frisk?"

"Put up your hands, an' I'll show you what friskin' is. An' make it snappy, sister." Sarina hesitated. "I ain't goin' to bite you," said Rosetti; "but I ain't goin' to take no chances, neither. W'en you've sloughed dat arsenal, I'll take you into camp as soon as my relief shows up."

Sarina laid her rifle down and raised her hands. Shrimp made her face the other way; then, from behind, he took her pistol and parang. "Okay," he said. "You can put 'em down now." He put her weapons in a pile behind him. "Now you know wot frisk means," he said.

Sarina sat down beside the trail. "You are a good soldier," she said. "I like good soldiers. And you *are* cute."

Rosetti grinned. "You ain't so bad yourself, sister." Even a misogynist may have an eye for beauty. "How come you're wanderin' around in de woods alone?—if you are alone."

"I *am* alone. I quit those people. I want to be with Corrie van der Meer. She should have a woman with her. A woman gets very tired of seeing only men all the time. I shall look after her. She *is* here, isn't she?"

"Yep, she's in camp; but she don't need no dame to look after her. She's got four men dat have made a pretty good job of it so far."

"I know," said Sarina. "She has told me, but she will be glad to have a woman with her." After a silence, she said, "Do you suppose that they will let me stay?"

143

"If Corrie says so, dey will. If you are really de dame dat broke her outta dat camp, we'll all be strong for you."

"American is a strange language, but I think I know what you were trying to say: If I am really the woman who helped Corrie escape from Hooft, you will like me. Is that it?"

"Ain't dat wot I said?"

A man coming along the trail from the direction of the camp interrupted their conversation. He was a Dutchman coming to relieve Rosetti. He did not speak English. His expression showed his surprise when he saw Sarina, and he questioned Rosetti in Dutch.

"No soap, Dutchie," said the American.

"He did not ask for soap," explained Sarina. "He asked about me."

"You savvy his lingo?" asked Shrimp.

Sarina shook her head. "Please try to speak English," she said. "I cannot understand you. What is 'savvy his lingo'?"

"Do you talk Dutch?"

"Oh, yes."

"Den wot did he say?"

"He asked about me."

"Well tell him, and also tell him to bring in your armor w'en he comes off. I can't pack dat mess an' guard a prisoner all at de same time."

Sarina smiled and translated. The man answered her in Dutch and nodded to Rosetti. "Get goin'," said the sergeant to Sarina. He followed her along the trail into camp, and took her to Jerry, who was lying on a litter beneath a tree.

"Sergeant Rosetti reportin' wit a prisoner, sir," he said.

Corrie, who was sitting beside Jerry, looked up; and when she recognized Sarina, she sprang to her feet. "Sarina!" she cried. "What in the world are you doing here?"

"I came to be with you. Tell them to let me stay." She spoke in Dutch, and Corrie translated to Jerry.

"As far as I am concerned she can stay if you want her to," said Jerry; "but I suppose that Capt. van Prins will have to decide. Take your prisoner and report to Capt. van Prins, sergeant."

Rosetti, who recognized no higher authority than that of Jerry, showed his disgust; but he obeyed. "Come along, sister," he said to Sarina.

"All right, brother," she replied; "but you don't have to keep that bayonet in my back all the time. I know you are a good soldier, but you don't have to overdo it." Corrie looked at her in surprise. This was the first intimation she had had that Sarina spoke English. And good English, too, she thought. She wondered where Sarina had learned it.

"Okay, sweetheart," said Rosetti. "I guess you won't try to make no break now."

"I'll come along," said Corrie. "If I vouch for you, I am sure Capt. van Prins will let you remain with us."

They found the captain, and he listened intently to all that Sarina and Corrie had to say. Then he asked, "Why did you choose to join that outlaw band and stay with it?"

"It was either them or the Japs," said Sarina. "I have always intended to leave them and join a guerrilla company when I could find one. This is the first opportunity I have had."

"If Miss van der Meer vouches for you and Capt. Lucas has no objection, you may remain."

"Then that settles it," said Corrie. "Thanks, Kervyn."

Rosetti no longer had a prisoner, but he walked back with Corrie and Sarina to where Jerry lay. He pretended that he came to inquire about Jerry's wound, but he sat down and remained after Jerry had assured him that he was all right.

At a little distance from them, Bubonovitch was cleaning his rifle. He thought that Rosetti would soon join him, and then he could ask about the woman Shrimp had brought in. But Shrimp did not join him. He remained with Jerry and the two women. It was most unlike Shrimp, to choose the society of ladies when he could avoid it. Bubonovitch was puzzled; so he went over and joined the party.

Sarina was telling about her encounter with Rosetti. "He told me to stick up my mitts, and said he was going to frisk me. American is a very funny language."

Jerry was laughing. "Rosetti doesn't speak American—just Chicagoese."

"Where in the world did you learn to speak English, Sarina?" asked Corrie.

"In a Catholic missionary school in the Gilberts. My father always took my mother and me on all his cruises. Except for the two years I spent at the mission at Tarawa, I lived my entire life on board his schooner until I was twenty-nine. My mother died when I was still a little girl, but my father kept me with him. He was a very wicked man, but he was always kind to us. We cruised all over the South Seas, and about every two years we made the Gilberts, trading at different islands along the way, with piracy and murder as a side line.

"Father wanted me to have an education; so, when I was twelve, he left me at that mission school until his next trip two years later. I learned a great deal there. From my father, I learned Dutch. I think he was a well educated man. He had a library of very good books on his ship. He never told me anything about his past—not even his true name. Everybody called him Big Jon. He taught me navigation. From the time I was fourteen I was his first mate. It was not a nice job for a girl, as father's crews were usually made up of the lowest types of criminals. No one else would sail with him. I got a smattering of Japanese and Chinese from various crew members. We shipped all nationalities. Oftentimes father Shanghaied them. When father was drunk, I captained the ship. It was a tough job, and I had to be tough. I carried on with the help of a couple of pistols. I was never without them."

Rosetti never took his eyes from Sarina. He seemed hypnotized by her. Bubonovitch watched him with something akin to amazement. However, he had to admit that Sarina was not hard on the eyes.

"Where is your father now?" asked Jerry.

"Probably in Hell. One of his murders finally caught up with him, and he was hanged. It was after he was arrested that Mr. and Mrs. van der Meer were so kind to me."

The gathering broke up a moment later, when the doctor came to check on Jerry. Corrie and Sarina went to the shelter occupied by the former, and Bubonovitch and Rosetti went and sat down in front of theirs.

"Wot a dame!" exclaimed Rosetti.

"Who? Corrie?"

Shrimp shot a quick glance at Bubonovitch and caught the tail end of a fleeting smile. He guessed he was being ribbed.

"No," he said. "I was referrin' to Eleanor."

"Did you by any chance notice that pistol packin' mamma with Corrie?" asked Bubonovitch. "Now there is a cute little piece of femininity after my own heart. I sure fell for her."

"You got a wife an' a kid," Shrimp reminded him.

"My affection is merely platonic. I shouldn't care to have a lady pirate take me too seriously. I suppose that if any of her gentlemen friends annoyed her, she made them walk the plank."

"Just think of dat little kid alone on a ship wit a lot of pirates an' her ol' man drunk!"

"I sort of got the impression that the little lady can take care of herself. Just take a slant at her background. You remember Corrie told us one of her grandfathers was a head hunter and the other was a cannibal, and now it develops that her father was a pirate and a murderer. And just to make the whole picture perfect Sārina was doing life in the clink for a little murder of her own."

"Just the same she's awful pretty," said Rosetti.

"Migawd!" exclaimed Bubonovitch. *"Et tu, Brute!"*

"I don't know wot you're talkin' about; but if you're crackin' wise about dat little dame—don't."

"I was not cracking wise. I wouldn't think of offending your sensibilities for the world, Shrimp. I was merely recalling a statement you made quite recently. Let's see—how did it go? 'I wouldn't have Dorothy Lamour if she got down on her knees and asked me!' "

"Well, I wouldn't. I wouldn't have none of 'em. But can't a guy say a dame's pretty widout you soundin' off?"

"Shrimpy, I saw you looking at her—goggle-eyed. I know the symptoms. You've gone plain ga-ga."

"You're nuts."

24

THEY broke camp the following morning and moved slowly, the wounded men still litter borne. Where the trail was wide enough, Corrie walked beside Jerry's litter. Sarina was behind her, and Rosetti walked with Sarina. Bubonovitch and several Dutchmen formed a rear guard. As none of the latter spoke English and Bubonovitch spoke no Dutch, the American had opportunity for meditation. Among other things, he meditated on the remarkable effect that some women had on some men. Reefers or snow made men goofy. Corrie and Sarina seemed to have a similar effect on Jerry and Rosetti. In Jerry's case it was not so remarkable. But Shrimp! Shrimp was a confirmed woman hater, yet all of a sudden he had gone overboard for a brown skinned Eurasian murderess old enough to be his mother.

Bubonovitch had to admit that Sarina was plenty good-looking. That was the hell of it. He was mighty fond of Rosetti, and so he hoped that the little sergeant didn't go too far. He didn't know much about women, and Sarina didn't seem exactly the safe type to learn from. Bubonovitch recalled a verse from Kipling;

She knifed me one night 'cause I wished she was white, An' I learned about women from 'er.

Bubonovitch sighed. After all, he thought, maybe Shrimp wasn't altogether wrong when he said, "Dey don't have to do nuttin'. Just bein' a dame spells trouble."

He abandoned this line of thought as unprofitable, and commenced to wonder about Tarzan. Jerry was wondering about him, too; and he voiced his misgivings to Corrie. "I'm commencing to worry about Tarzan," he said. "He's been gone two days now, and shortly after he disappeared some of the men thought they heard firing far off in the forest from the direction in which the Japs retreated."

"But what in he world would he be doing back there?" objected Corrie.

"He is not like other men; so it would be useless for one of us to try to imagine what might impel him to the commission of any act. At times, as you well know, he acts like a wild beast. So there must be stimuli which cause him to think and react like a wild beast. You know how he feels about taking life, yet you heard him say that it was his duty to kill Japs."

"And you think he may have followed them in order to kill some more of them?" suggested Corrie.

"Yes, and maybe got killed himself."

"Oh, no! That is too terrible, even to think."

"I know, but it is possible. And if he doesn't show up, we'll have to carry on without him. Cripes! I haven't half realized how dependent we have been on him. We'd certainly have been on short rations most of the time if he hadn't been along to hunt for us."

"I should long since have quit needing rations but for him," said Corrie. "I still see that tiger sometimes in my dreams. And Oju—ugh!"

They were silent for a while. Jerry lay with his eyes half closed. He was rolling his head slightly from side to side. "Feeling all right?" Corrie asked.

"Yes—fine. I wonder how much farther it is to camp."

"I think Kervyn plans on camping for the night about where the outlaws were camping when I escaped," said Corrie. "That is not far." She noticed that Jerry's face was very red, and placed a hand on his forehead. She dropped back and whispered to Sarina, and word was passed down the line for the doctor. Then she returned to the side of Jerry's litter.

The American was muttering incoherently. She spoke to him, but he did not reply. He was turning restlessly, and she had to restrain him to prevent his rolling off the litter. She was terribly frightened.

She did not speak when Dr. Reyd came up to the other side of the litter. Jerry's condition was too obvious to require explanation. Practically the only tool of his profession that Dr. Reyd had salvaged was a clinical thermometer. When he read it two minutes later, he shook his head.

"Bad?" asked Corrie.

"Not too good. But I don't understand it. I expected him to run a little fever the night he was wounded, but he didn't. I thought he was pretty safe by now."

"Will he—? Will he—?"

The doctor looked across the litter at her and smiled. "Let's not worry until we have to," he said. "Millions of people have survived much worse wounds and higher temperatures."

"But can't you *do* something for him?"

Reyd shrugged. "I have nothing with which to do. Perhaps it is just as well. He is young, strong, in good condition, and physically as near perfect as a man can be. Nature is a damn good doctor, Corrie."

"But you'll stay here with him, won't you, Doctor?"

"Certainly. And don't you worry."

Jerry mumbled, "Three Zeros at two o'clock," and sat up.

Corrie and the doctor forced him back gently. Jerry opened his eyes and looked at Corrie. He smiled and said,

149

"Mabel." After that he lay quietly for a while. Rosetti had come up and was walking beside the litter. He had seen that perhaps Corrie and the doctor might need help. His eyes reflected worry and fear.

Jerry said, "Lucas to Melrose! Lucas to Melrose!"

Rosetti choked back a sob. Melrose had been the tail gunner who had been killed—and Jerry was talking to him! The implication terrified Rosetti, but he kept his head. "Melrose to Lucas," he said. "All quiet on de western front, Cap'n."

Jerry relaxed, and said, "Roger."

Corrie patted Rosetti's shoulder. "You're sweet," she said. Shrimp flushed. "Who is Melrose?" Corrie asked.

"Our tail gunner. He was killed before the Lovely Lady crashed. An' he was talkin' to him! Geeze!"

Jerry turned and twisted. It was all that three of them could do to keep him on the litter. "I guess we'll have to tie him down," said the doctor.

Rosetti shook his head. "Get Bubonovitch up here, an' me and him'll take care of him. The Cap'n wouldn't want to be tied down."

Word was passed back down the column for Bubonovitch. Jerry was trying to get off the litter when he arrived. It took the combined strength of four to force him back. Bubonovitch was swearing softly under his breath. "The goddam Japs. The yellow bastards." He turned on Rosetti. "Why in hell didn't you send for me before?" he demanded. "Why didn't somebody tell me he was like this?"

"Keep your shirt on, Bum," said Rosetti. "I sends for you as soon as he needs you."

"He hasn't been this way long," Corrie told Bubonovitch.

"I'm sorry," said the latter. "I was frightened when I saw him this way. You see, we're sort of fond of the guy."

Tears almost came to Corrie's eyes. "I guess we all are," she said.

"Is he very bad, Doctor?" asked Bubonovitch.

"He is running quite a fever," replied Reyd; "but it isn't high enough to be dangerous—yet."

They had come out of the forest into the valley where they were to camp. Now, out of the narrow trail, Sarina had come up beside the litter. When Jerry yelled, "Cripes! I can't get her nose up. You fellows jump! Make it snappy!" and tried to jump off the litter, she helped hold him down.

Corrie stroked his forehead and said, soothingly, "Everything's all right, Jerry. Just lie still and try to rest."

He reached up and took her hand. "Mabel," he said and sighed. Then he fell asleep. Rosetti and Bubonovitch tried not to look at Corrie.

Reyd sighed, too. "That's the best medicine he could have," he said.

A half hour later, van Prins called a halt; and they made camp beneath some trees beside the little stream that ran through the valley.

Jerry slept through the remainder of the afternoon and all the following night. Corrie and Sarina slept on one side of the litter, Bubonovitch and Rosetti on the other. They took turns remaining awake to watch over their patient.

When it was Corrie's turn to remain awake, she kept thinking of Mabel. She had never heard the name of that girl in Oklahoma City who had married the 4-F, but she knew now that her name was Mabel. So he still loved her! Corrie tried not to care. Wasn't Mabel lost to him? She was married. Then she thought that maybe it was some other girl named Mabel, and maybe this other girl wasn't married. She wanted to ask Bubonovitch what the name of the girl in Oklahoma City was, but her pride wouldn't let her.

When Jerry awoke he lay for several seconds looking up at the leafy canopy above him, trying to coax his memory to reveal its secrets. Slowly he recalled that the last thing he had been conscious of was being very uncomfortable on a litter that was being borne along a narrow forest trail. Now the litter had come to rest and he was very comfortable. Quite near him he heard the purling laughter of the little river rippling among the boulders as it hurried gaily on to keep its assignation with the sea.

Jerry looked toward it and saw Bubonovitch and Rosetti kneeling on its grassy bank washing their hands and faces. He smiled happily as he thought how fortunate he had been in the comrades the war had given him. He fought away the sadness for those he would never see again. A fellow mustn't brood about things like that, those inescapable concomitants of war.

Turning his head away from the river, he looked for Corrie. She was sitting close beside his litter, cross-legged, elbows on knees, her face buried in her opened palms. Her hair was gold again; but she still wore it bobbed, being, as she was, a very practical little person. That, too, was why she continued to wear pants.

Jerry looked at her fondly, thinking what a cute boy she looked. And also thinking, thank God she's not. He knew she wasn't; because he wouldn't have wanted to take a boy in his arms and kiss him. And that was exactly what he wanted to do with Corrie that very moment, but he didn't have the nerve. Coward! he thought.

"Corrie," he said, very softly.

She opened her eyes and raised her head. "Oh, Jerry!"

He reached over and took one of her hands. She placed her other hand on his forehead. "Oh, Jerry! Jerry! Your fever is all gone. How do you feel?"

"As though I could eat a cow, hoofs, horns, and hide."

Corrie choked back a sob. This sudden relief from fear and strain broke down the barriers of emotional restraint that had been her spiritual shield and buckler for so long. Corrie scrambled to her feet and ran away. She took refuge behind a tree and leaned against it and cried. She couldn't recall when she had been so happy.

"Wot," Rosetti asked Bubonovitch, "was de name of dat dame in Oklahoma City wot gave de Cap'n de brush-off?"

"I don't know," said Bubonovitch.

"I wonder was it Mabel," wondered Rosetti.

"Could be."

Jerry looked after Corrie, with knitted brows. Now what the hell? he thought. Sarina, having attached herself to Corrie and the Americans, was preparing their breakfast nearby. Dr. Reyd, making the round of his patients, came to Jerry. "How goes it this morning?"

"Feeling great," Jerry told him. "Won't have to be carried any longer."

"Maybe that's what you think," said Reyd, grinning. "But you're wrong."

Captain van Prins and Tak van der Bos came over. "Think you can stand another day of it?" the former asked Jerry.

"Sure I can."

"Good! I want to start as soon as possible. This place is too exposed."

"You had us worrying yesterday, Jerry," said van der Bos.

"I had a good doctor," said Jerry.

"If I'd had you back in civilian life," said Reyd, "I'd have given you a pill yesterday; and this morning I'd have told you how near death's door you were yesterday."

Corrie came out from behind her tree and joined them. Jerry saw that her eyes were red, and knew why she had run away. "Just getting up, lazy?" Tak asked her.

"I've been out looking for a cow," said Corrie.

"A cow! Why?"

"Jerry wanted one for breakfast."

"So he'll eat rice," said van Prins, grinning.

"When I get off your lovely island," said Jerry, "and anyone says rice to me, he'd better smile."

The others went on about their duties, leaving Corrie alone with Jerry. "I must have passed out cold yesterday," he said. "Can't remember a thing after about a couple of hours on the trail."

"You were a very sick man—just burning up with fever. You kept trying to jump off the litter. It took four of us to hold you down. The doctor wanted to tie you to the litter, but that sweet little sergeant wouldn't hear of it. He said, 'De Cap'n wouldn't want to be tied down'; so he and Bubonovitch and the doctor and Sarina and I walked beside the litter."

"Shrimp's a good little guy," said Jerry.

"Those boys are very fond of you, Jerry."

"That works both ways," said Jerry. "Members of a combat crew have to like one another. You don't trust a guy you don't like, and we got enough worries when we're flying a mission without having to worry about some fellow we can't trust. I'm sorry I was such a nuisance yesterday."

"You weren't a nuisance. We were just frightened; because we thought you were so terribly sick. And your being delirious made it seem much worse than it really was." She paused a moment, and then she said, "Who is Mabel?"

"Mabel? What do you know about Mabel?"

"Nothing. But you kept asking for her."

Jerry laughed. "That's what Dad called Mother. It isn't her name, but he started calling her Mabel even before they were married. He got the name from a series of 'Dere Mabel' letters that were popular during World War I; and we kids thought it was funny to call her Mabel, too."

"We were all wondering who Mabel was," said Corrie, lamely.

"I suppose it had Shrimp and Bubonovitch and Sarina and the doctor terribly worried," said Jerry.

"That is not funny, and you are not nice," said Corrie.

25

AT the head of the valley, where the stream was born in a
little spring that gurgled from beneath a limestone cliff,
there were many caves, easily defendable. Here van
Prins decided to make a more or less premanent camp and
await the coming of Allied forces under MacArthur, for
since the Americans had come he had learned for the first
time that MacArthur was really drawing nearer week by
week. When the Allies established a beachhead, he and other
guerrilla leaders would come down out of the mountains
and harass the enemy's rear and communications. In the
meantime about all that they could accomplish was an occasional sally against a Jap outpost.

From this camp the Americans planned to cross over to
the other side of the mountains, as soon as Jerry was fully
recovered, and follow a trail along the eastern side of the
range to the point where they would recross to the west and
try to make their way to the coast. Tak van der Bos was going
with them; because it was thought that his knowledge of
Sumatra and the location of Jap positions might prove of
value to the Allied forces. "In the very doubtful eventuality
that you ever reach them," said van Prins.

He had little hope for the success of what he considered
a mad venture, and he tried to persuade Corrie not to take
the risk. "We can hide you here in the mountains indefi-
nitely," he told her, "and you will be safe among your own
people."

Jerry wasn't so sure that she would be safe. If the Japs
ever made a serious effort to liquidate the guerrillas, using
both infantry and planes, Corrie would be anything but
safe. Yet he did not urge her to come with him. He would
have felt much more assured of the chances for the success
of their venture if Tarzan had not been lost to them.

Tak ven der Bos agreed with van Prins. "I really think
you'd be safer here, Corrie," he told her. "And I think that
we four men would stand a better chance of getting away if
—if—"

"If you weren't burdened with a couple of women. Why don't you say it, Tak?"

"I didn't know just how to say it inoffensively, Corrie; but that's what I meant."

"Sarina and I will not be a burden. We'll be two more rifles. We have proved that we can hold our own on the trail with any of you men. I think you will admit that Sarina would prove an even more ferocious fighter than any of you, and I have already shown that I won't scream and faint when the shooting starts. Besides all that, Sarina believes that she knows exactly where she can locate a boat for us and get it provisioned by friendly natives. And another thing to consider: Sarina has sailed these seas all her life. She not only knows them, but she is an experienced navigator. I think that we can be a lot of help to you. As far as the danger is concerned, it's six of one and half a dozen of the other. The Japs may get us if we try to get away, or they may get us if we stay. Sarina and I want to go with you men; but if Jerry says no, that will settle it."

Bubonovitch and Rosetti were interested listeners to the discussion. Jerry turned to them. "What do you fellows think?" he asked. "Would you want Corrie and Sarina to come with us, or would you rather they didn't?"

"Well, it's like this," said Bubonovitch. "If we had two men who were as good soldiers as they are, there wouldn't be any question. It's just that a man hesitates to place a woman in danger if he can avoid it."

"That's the hell of it," said Jerry. He looked at Rosetti, questioningly, Rosetti the confirmed woman hater.

"I say let's all go, or all stay. Let's stick togedder."

"Corrie and Sarina know what dangers and hardships may be involved," said Bubonovitch. "Let them decide. I can't see that any of us has any right to do their thinking for them."

"Good for you, sergeant," said Corrie. "Sarina and I have already decided."

Captain van Prins shrugged. "I think you are crazy," he said; "but I admire your courage, and I wish you luck."

"Look!" exclaimed Rosetti, pointing. "Everyt'ing's goin' to be hotsy-totsy now."

Everyone looked in the direction that Rosetti was pointing. Coming toward them was the familiar, bronzed figure that the Americans and Corrie had so grown to lean upon; and upon one of its shoulders squatted a little monkey; across the other was the carcass of a deer.

Tarzan dropped the deer at the edge of camp and walked toward the group gathered around Jerry's litter. Keta encircled Tarzan's neck with both arms, screaming at the strange tarmangani, hurling jungle invective at them. Little Keta was terrified.

"They are friends, Keta," said Tarzan in their common language. "Do not be afraid."

"Keta not afraid," shrilled the monkey. "Keta bite tarmangani."

Tarzan was welcomed with enthusiasm. He went at once to Jerry and stood looking down at him, smiling. "So they didn't get you," he said.

"Just nicked me," said Jerry.

"The last time I saw you, I thought you were dead."

"We have been afraid that you were dead. Did you get into some trouble?"

"Yes," replied Tarzan, "but it wasn't my trouble; it was the Japs'. I followed them. No matter what they may do to you in the future, you are already avenged."

Jerry grinned. "I wish I had been there to see."

"It was not pretty," said Tarzan: "Soulless creatures in a panic of terror—living robots helpless without their masters. I was careful to pick those off first." He smiled at the recollection.

"You must have followed them a long way," suggested van Prins.

"No; but after I finished with them I wandered deep into the forest. I am always curious about a country with which I am not familiar. However, I did not learn much of value. Late yesterday afternoon I located an enemy battery of big guns; and this morning, another. If you have a map, I can mark their positions fairly closely.

"The first day, I found an isolated village of natives. It was built in the shallow waters near the shore of a lake in a great primeval forest which appeared to me impenetrable. The people were fishing with nets. They threatened me with bows and arrows after I gave them the peace sign."

"I think I know the village," said van Prins. "Fliers have seen it; but as far as is known, no other civilized men have seen it and lived. One or two have tried to reach it. Maybe they did, but they never came back. The inhabitants of that village are thought to be the remnants of an aboriginal people from whom the Battaks descended—true savages and cannibals. Until recently the modern Battaks were cannibals—what one might call beneficent cannibals. They ate their old people in the belief that thus they would confer immortality upon them, for they would continue to live in the persons of those who devoured them. Also, the devourer would acquire the strengths and virtues of the devoured. For this latter reason, they also ate their enemies—partly cooked and with a dash of lemon."

"These lake dwellers," said van der Bos, "are also supposed to have discovered the secret of perpetual youth."

"That, of course, is all tommy-rot," said Dr. Reyd.

"Perhaps not," said Tarzan.

Reyd looked at him in surprise. "You don't mean to tell me that you believe any such silly nonsense as that, do you?" he demanded.

Tarzan smiled and nodded. "Naturally, I believe in those things which I have myself seen or experienced; and I have twice seen absolute proof that perpetual youth can be achieved. Also, I learned long ago not to deny the possibility of anything emanating from the superstitions of religions of primitive peoples. I have seen strange things in the depths of Darkest Africa." He ceased speaking, evidently having no intention to elaborate. His eyes, wandering over the faces of his listeners, fixed on Sarina. "What is that woman doing here?" he asked. "She belongs to Hooft and his gang of outlaws."

Corrie and Rosetti both tried to explain simultaneously, the latter fairly leaping to Sarina's defense. When he had heard the story, Tarzan was satisfied. "If Sergeant Rosetti is satisfied to have *any* woman around, she must be beyond criticism."

Rosetti flushed uncomfortably, but he said, "Sarina's okay, Colonel."

Dr. Reyd cleared his throat. "What you said about the verity of the superstitions and religions of primitive peoples and that perpetual youth might be achieved, interests me. Would you mind being more explicit?"

Tarzan sat down cross-legged beside Jerry. "On numerous occasions, I have known witch doctors to kill people at great distances from them; and some times after a lapse of years. I do not know how they do it. I merely know that they do do it. Perhaps they plant the idea in the mind of their victim

157

and he induces death by autosuggestion. Most of their mumbo jumbo is pure charlatanism. Occasionally it appears as an exact science."

"We are easily fooled, though," said Jerry. "Take some of these fellows who have made a hobby of so-called parlor magic. They admit that they are tricking you; but if you were an ignorant savage and they told you it was true magic, you'd believe them. I had a friend in Honolulu when I was stationed at Hickam, who was as good as any professional I have ever seen. Paint Colonel Kendall J. Fielder black, dress him up in a breechclout and a feather headdress, give him some odds and ends of bones and pieces of wood and a zebra's tale, and turn him loose in Africa; and he'd have all the other witch doctors green with envy.

"And what he could do with cards! I used to play bridge against him, and he always won. Of course his game was on the level, but he had two strikes on you before you started— just like Tarzan's witch doctors had on *their* victims. You just autosuggested yourself to defeat. It was humiliating, too," added Jerry, "because I am a very much better bridge player than he."

"Of course anyone can learn that kind of magic," said Reyd, "but how about perpetual youth? You have really seen instances of this, Colonel?"

"When I was a young man," said Tarzan, "I saved a black from a man-eating lion. He was very grateful, and wished to repay me in some way. He offered me perpetual youth. I told him that I didn't think such a thing was possible. He asked me how old I thought he was, and I said that he appeared to be in his twenties. He told me that he was a witch doctor. All the witch doctors I had ever seen were much older men than he; so I rather discounted that statement as well as his claim to being able to confer perpetual youth on me.

"He took me to his village, where I met his chief. He asked the chief how long he had known him. 'All my life,' replied the chief, who was a very old man. The chief told me that no one knew how old the witch doctor was; but that he must be very old, as he had known Tippoo Tib's grandfather. Tippoo Tib was born, probably, in the 1840's, or, possibly, the 1830's; so his grandfather may have been born as long ago as the eighteenth century.

"I was quite young and, like most young men, adventurous. I would try anything; so I let the witch doctor go to

158

work on me. Before he was through with me, I understood why he was not conferring perpetual youth wholesale. It required a full month of concocting vile brews, observing solemn rituals, and the transfusion of a couple of quarts of the witch doctor's blood into my veins. Long before it was over, I regretted that I had let myself in for it; because I didn't take any stock in his claims." Tarzan ceased speaking as though he had finished his story.

"And you were quite right," said Dr. Reyd.

"You think I will age, then?"

"Most certainly," said the doctor.

"How old do you think I am now?" asked Tarzan.

"In your twenties."

Tarzan smiled. "That which I have told you of occurred many years ago."

Dr. Reyd shook his head. "It is very strange," he said. It was evident that he was not convinced.

"I never gave a thought to your age, Colonel," said Jerry; "but I remember now that my father said that he read about you when he was a boy. And I was brought up on you. You influenced my life more than anyone else."

"I give up," said Dr. Reyd. "But you said that you had known of two instances in which perpetual youth was achieved. What was the other one. You've certainly aroused my interest."

"A tribe of white fanatics in a remote part of Africa compounded a hellish thing that achieved perpetual youth. I mean the way that they obtained one of the principal ingredients was hellish. They kidnaped young girls, killed them, and removed certain glands.

"In the course of tracing a couple of girls they had stolen, I found their village. To make a long story short, my companions and I succeeded in rescuing the girls and obtaining a supply of their compound.* Those who have taken it, including a little monkey, have shown no signs of aging since."

"Amazing!" said Dr. Reyd. "Do you expect to live forever?"

"I don't know what to expect."

"Maybe," suggested Bubonovitch, "you'll just fall to pieces all at once, like the One Hoss Shay."

"Would you want to live forever?" asked van der Bos.

"Of course—if I never had to suffer the infirmities of old age."

* See Tarzan's Quest.

"But all your friends would be gone."

"One misses the old friends, but one constantly makes new ones. But really my chances of living forever are very slight. Any day, I may stop a bullet; or a tiger may get me, or a python. If I live to get back to my Africa, I may find a lion waiting for me, or a buffalo. Death has many tricks up his sleeve beside old age. One may outplay him for a while, but he always wins in the end."

26

THE little band that was to make the attempt to reach Australia, comprising, as it did, Americans, Dutch, an Englishman, and an Eurasian, had been dubbed The Foreign Legion by the guerrillas. Jerry amplified the basis for this designation by calling attention to the fact that Bubonovitch was Russian, Rosetti Italian, and he himself part Cherokee Indian.

"If poor old Sing Tai were with us," said Corrie, "the four principal Allied Nations would be represented."

"If Italy hadn't surrendered," said Bubonovitch, "we'd have had to liquidate Shrimp. He's the only Axis partner in our midst."

"I ain't a Eye-talian," said Rosetti, "but I'd rather be a Eye-talian than a lousy Russian Communist." Bubonovitch grinned, and winked at Corrie.

Captain van Prins, who was sitting a little apart with Tarzan, said in a low tone, "It's too bad that there's hard feelings between those two. It may cause a lot of trouble before you're through."

Tarzan looked at him in surprise. "I guess you don't know Americans very well, Captain. Either one of those boys would willingly risk his life for the other."

"Then why do they try to insult each other?" demanded van Prins. "This is not the first time I have heard them."

Tarzan shrugged. "If I were an American, perhaps I could tell you."

Where the guerrillas had made their camp, the valley narrowed and ended in a box canyon the limestone walls of which were pitted with several large caves on each side. Rifles and machine guns firing from the mouths of these caves could develop a deadly cross fire that might render the position impregnable. Another advantage lay in the ability to conceal all evidence of the presence of men which the caves offered. Occasionally, a Jap plane flew over. At the first sound of its motors, the company vanished into the caves.

A sentry, posted on a cliff above the camp, had a full view down the valley as far as binoculars would reach. Should he discover even a single human being approaching, his signal would similarly empty the floor of the canyon.

In this camp, for the first time, The Foreign Legion felt reasonably secure. It was a relief from the constant nervous strain they had been undergoing, and they relaxed and rested while waiting for Jerry's wound to heal and for him to regain his strength.

Tarzan was often away on reconnaissance missions or hunting. It was he who kept the camp supplied with fresh meat, as he could kill quietly, which was most desirable. A rifle shot might attract the attention of an enemy patrol.

Occasionally, Tarzan was away for several days at a time. On one such mission he found the camp of the outlaws far down the valley. It was located not far from the kampong where Captain Tokujo Matsuo and Lieutenant Hideo Sokabe still held forth, and it was evident that the outlaws were openly collaborating with the Japs.

The outlaws had set up a still and were making schnapps, with which they carried on a brisk trade with the enemy. Tarzan saw much drunkenness in both camps. One observable result of this was a relaxation of discipline and alertness in the enemy camp. There were no sentries out on the trails leading to the village. A single soldier was on guard beside a small barbed wire enclosure. Inside this, beneath a flimsy shelter, Tarzan could see two figures, but he could not make out who nor what they were. They were evidently prisoners, but whether natives or Japs he could not tell. They did not interest him.

As Tarzan turned to leave the village and return to the camp of the guerrillas, a radio blared from one of the houses. He paused a moment to listen; but the voice spoke in Japanese, which he could not understand, and he continued on his way.

However, Lieutenant Hideo Sokabe understood it, and he

did not like what he heard. Captain Tokujo Matsuo understood it and was pleased. He was not a little drunk on schnapps, as was Sokabe also. The schnapps heightened the acclaim with which Matsuo received the broadcast from Tokyo. He was quite noisy about it.

"So your honorable uncle has been kicked out," he exulted. "You may now write to your honorable uncle, General Hideki Tojo, every day; but I shall remain a captain—until I am promoted. Now the situation is reversed. The 'Singing Frog' is now Premier. He is not my uncle, but he is my friend. I served under him in the Kwantung army in Manchuria."

"So did a million other peasants," said Sokabe.

Thus was the bad blood between the two officers made worse, which was not well for the morale and discipline of their command.

Corrie had often expressed concern over the fate of Sing Tai whom they had left in hiding in the village of Tiang Umar; so Tarzan decided to visit this village before returning to the camp of the guerrillas. This necessitated a considerable detour, but only rarely did either time or distance cause the Lord of the Jungle any concern. One of the features of civilization to which he could never accustom himself was the slavish subservience of civilized man to the demands of time. Sometimes his lack of conformity with established custom proved embarrassing to others, but never to Tarzan. He ate when he was hungry, slept when he was sleepy. He started on journeys when the spirit or necessity moved him, without concerning himself about the time which might be involved.

He moved leisurely now. He made a kill, and after eating, laid up for the night. It was midmorning when he approached the kampong of Tiang Umar. Motivated by the inherent caution and suspicion of the wild beast, Tarzan moved silently through the trees which encircled the kampong, to assure himself that no enemy lurked there. He saw the natives carrying on their normal, peaceful activities. Presently he recognized Alam, and a moment later he dropped to the ground and walked into the village.

As soon as the natives recognized him, they greeted him cordially and gathered around him, asking questions in a language he could not understand. He asked if anyone in the village spoke Dutch; and an old man replied in that language, saying that he did.

Through the interpreter Alam inquired about Corrie, and showed his pleasure when told that she was safe. Then Tarzan asked what had become of Sing Tai, and was told that he was still in the village but never ventured out in the daytime, which was well, as twice Jap scouting parties had come to the kampong without warning.

Tarzan was taken to the Chinese. He found him entirely recovered from his wound and in good physical condition. His first question was of Corrie, and when he was assured that she was all right and among friends he beamed with pleasure.

"Do you want to stay here, Sing Tai," Tarzan asked, "or do you want to come with us? We are going to try to escape from the island."

"I come with you," replied Sing Tai.

"Very well," said Tarzan. "We'll start now."

*　　*　　*

The Foreign Legion was becoming restless. Jerry had entirely recovered, had regained his strength, and was anxious to move on. He only awaited the return of Tarzan, who had been away for several days.

"Wish he would show up," he said to Corrie. "I know he can take care of himself, but something *could* happen to him." Several of the party were gathered beneath the concealing branches of a tree. They had been stripping, oiling, and reassembling their weapons. The stripping and reassembling they did with their eyes closed. It was a game that relieved the monotony of this ceaseless attention to weapons in the humid atmosphere of these equatorial mountains. Occasionally they timed one another; and, much to the chagrin of the men, it was discovered that Corrie and Sarina were the most adept.

Sarina replaced the bolt in her rifle, aimed at the sky, and squeezed the trigger. She leaned the piece against the tree, and looked long and searchingly down the valley. "Tony has been gone a long time," she said. "If he does not come soon, I shall go and look for him."

"Where did he go?" asked Jerry.

"Hunting."

"The orders are no hunting," said Jerry. "Rosetti knows that. We can't take the chance of attracting the attention of the Japs with rifle fire."

"Tony took his bow and arrows for hunting," Sarina explained. "He will not fire his rifle except in self defense."

"He couldn't hit anything smaller than an elephant with that archery set of his," said Bubonovitch.

"How long has he been gone?" asked Jerry.

"Too long," said Sarina; "three or four hours at least."

"I'll go look for him," said Bubonovitch. He picked up his rifle and stood up.

Just then the sentry on the cliff called down: "A man coming. Looks like Sergeant Rosetti. Yes, it is Sergeant Rosetti."

"Is he carrying an elephant?" Bubonovitch shouted.

The sentry laughed. "He is carrying something, but I do not think it is an elephant."

They all looked down the valley, and presently they could see a man approaching. He was still a long way off. Only the sentry with binoculars could have recognized him. After a while Rosetti walked into camp. He was carrying a hare.

"Here's your supper," he said, tossing the hare to the ground. "I missed three deer, and then I gets this little squirt."

"Was he asleep at the time, or did somebody hold him for you?" asked Bubonovitch.

"He was runnin' like a bat outta hell," said Rosetti, grinning. "He runs into a tree an' knocks hisself cold."

"Nice work, Hiawatha," said Bubonovitch.

"Anyway, I tried," said Rosetti. "I didn't sit around on my big, fat fanny waitin' for some udder guy to bring home de bacon."

"That is right, Sergeant Bum," said Sarina.

"Always the perfect little gentleman, I will not contradict a lady," said Bubonovitch. "Now the question is, who is going to prepare the feast? There are only fifty of us to eat it. What is left, we can send to the starving Armenians."

"De starvin' Armenians don't get none of dis rabbit. Neither do you. It's all for Sarina and Corrie."

"Two people coming up the valley!" called down the sentry. "Can't make them out yet. Something peculiar about them." Every eye was strained down the valley, every ear waiting to hear the next report from the sentry. After a few moments it came: "Each of them is carrying some sort of load. One of them is naked."

"Must be Tarzan," said Jerry.

It was Tarzan. With him was Sing Tai. When they reached camp, each of them dropped the carcass of a deer to the ground. Corrie was delighted to see Sing Tai and to learn that he had completely recovered from his wound. And Jerry was relieved and delighted to see Tarzan.

"I'm sure glad you're back," he said. "We're all ready to shove off, and have only been waiting for you."

"I think we have another job to do before we can start," said Tarzan. "I located Hooft's gang far down the valley, not far from the village where we got Corrie away from the Japs. The Japs are still there, and while I was scouting the place I saw two prisoners behind barbed wire. I couldn't make out what they were, but on the way back here from Tiang Umar's kampong Sing Tai told me that some Japs had passed through the kampong a few days ago with two American prisoners. The Japs told the natives that they were fliers whose plane had been shot down some time ago."

"Douglas and Davis!" exclaimed Bubonovitch.

"Must be," agreed Jerry. "They are the only two unaccounted for."

Bubonovitch buckled on his ammunition belt and picked up his rifle. "Let's go, Captain," he said.

Tarzan glanced at the sun. "If we travel fast," he said, "we can make it while it is still dark; but we should take only men who can travel fast."

"How many?" asked van Prins.

"Twenty should be enough. If everything goes all right, I can do it alone. If everything doesn't go all right, twenty men plus the element of surprise should make everything all right."

"I'll come along with enough of my men to make the twenty," said van Prins.

All the members of The Foreign Legion were preparing to go, but Tarzan said no to Corrie and Sarina. They started to argue the matter, but Tarzan was adamant. "You'd be an added responsibility for us," he said. "We'd have to be thinking of your safety when our minds should be on nothing but our mission."

"The Colonel is right," said Jerry.

"I suppose he is," admitted Corrie.

"That's the good soldier," said Tak.

"There is another who should not go," said Doctor Reyd. Everybody looked at Jerry. "Captain Lucas has been a very ill man. If he goes on a long forced march now, he'll be in no condition to undertake the trying marches to the south which you are contemplating."

165

Jerry glanced questioningly at Tarzan. "I wish you wouldn't insist, Jerry," said the Englishman.

Jerry unbuckled his ammunition belt and laid it at the foot of the tree. He grinned ruefully. "If Corrie and Sarina can be good soldiers, I guess I can, too; but I sure hate to miss out on this."

Ten minutes later twenty men started down the valley at a brisk pace that was almost a dogtrot. Tarzan, at the head of the column with van Prins, explained his plan to the Dutchman.

*　　*　　*

Captain Tokujo Matsuo and Lieutenant Hideo Sokabe had been drinking all night—drinking and quarreling. There had been much drinking among their men, too. The native men of the kampong had taken their women into the forest to escape the brutal advances of the drunken soldiers. But now, shortly before dawn, the camp had quieted, except for the quarreling of the two officers; for the others lay for the most part in a drunken stupor.

The single guard before the prison pen had just come on duty. He had slept off some of the effects of the schnapps he had drunk, but he was still far from sober. He resented having been awakened; so he vented some of his anger on the two prisoners, awakening them to revile and threaten them. Having been born and educated in Honolulu, he spoke English. He was an adept in invective in two languages. He loosed a flow of profanity and obscenity upon the two men within the barbed wire enclosure.

Staff Sergeant Carter Douglas of Van Nuys, California, stirred on his filthy sleeping mat, and raised himself on one elbow. "Aroha, sweetheart!" he called to the guard. This plunged the Jap into inarticulate rage.

"What's eatin' the guy?" demanded Staff Sergeant Bill Davis of Waco, Texas.

"I think he doesn't like us," said Douglas. "Before you woke up he said he would kill us right now except that his honorable captain wanted to lop our beans off himself in the morning."

"Maybe he's just handin' us a line to scare us," suggested Davis.

"Could be," said Douglas. "The guy's spiflicated. That stuff

166

they drink must be potent as hell. It sounded like everybody in camp was drunk."

"Remember that butterfly brandy they tried to sell us in Noumea at eighty-five smackers a bottle? Three drinks, and a private would spit in a captain's face. Maybe that's what they're drinking."

"If this guy had got a little drunker," said Douglas, "we could have made our get away tonight."

"If we could get out of here, we could rush him."

"But we can't get out of here."

"Hell's bells! I don't want to have my head lopped off. What a hell of a birthday present."

"What do you mean, birthday present?"

"If I haven't lost track, tomorrow should be my birthday," said Davis. "I'll be twenty-five tomorrow."

"You didn't expect to live forever, did you? I don't know what you old guys expect."

"How old are you, Doug?"

"Twenty."

"Gawd! They dragged you right out of the cradle. Oh, hell!" he said after a moment's pause. "We're just tryin' to kid ourselves that we ain't scared. I'm good and goddam scared."

"I'm scairt as hell," admitted Davis.

"What you talk about in there?" demanded the guard. "Shut up!"

"Shut up yourself, Tojo," said Douglas; "you're drunk."

"Now, for that, I kill you," yelled the Jap. "I tell the captain you try to escape." He raised his rifle and aimed into the darkness of the shelter that housed the two prisoners.

Silently, in the shadows of the native houses, a figure moved toward him. It approached from behind him.

Matsuo and Sokabe were screaming insults at one another in their quarters at the far end of the kampong. Suddenly, the former drew his pistol and fired at Sokabe. He missed, and the lieutenant returned the fire. They were too drunk to hit one another except by accident, but they kept blazing away.

Almost simultaneously with Matsuo's first shot, the guard fired into the shelter that housed the two Americans. Before he could fire a second shot, an arm encircled his head and drew it back, and a knife almost severed it from his body.

"Were you hit, Bill?" ask Douglas.

"No. He missed us a mile. What's going on out there? Somebody jumped him."

Aroused by the firing in their officers' quarters, dopey, drunken soldiers were staggering toward the far end of the village, thinking the camp had been attacked. Some of them ran so close past Tarzan that he could almost have reached out and touched them. He crouched beside the dead guard, waiting. He was as ignorant of the cause of the fusillade as the Japs. Van Prins and his party were at the opposite end of the kampong; so he knew that it could not be they firing.

When he thought the last Jap had passed him, he called to the prisoners in a low tone. "Are you Douglas and Davis?"

"We sure are."

"Where's the gate?"

"Right in front of you, but it's padlocked."

Van Prins, hearing the firing, thought that it was directed at Tarzan; so he brought his men into the village at a run. They spread out, dodging from house to house.

Tarzan stepped to the gate. Its posts were the trunks of small saplings. Douglas and Davis had come from the shelter and were standing close inside the gate.

Tarzan took hold of the posts, one with each hand. "Each of you fellows push on a post," he said, "and I'll pull." As he spoke, he surged back with all his weight and strength; and the posts snapped off before the prisoners could lend a hand. The wire was pulled down to the ground with the posts, and Douglas and Davis walked out to freedom over it.

Tarzan had heard the men coming in from van Prin's position, and guessed it was they. He called to van Prins, and the latter answered. "The prisoners are with me," said Tarzan. "You'd better assemble your men so that we can get out of here." Then he took the rifle and ammunition from the dead Jap and handed them to Davis.

As the party moved out of the village, they could hear the Japs jabbering and shouting at the far end. They did not know the cause of the diversion that had aided them so materially in the rescue of the two men without having suffered any casualties, and many of them regretted leaving without having fired a shot.

Bubonovitch and Rosetti fairly swarmed over their two

buddies, asking and answering innumerable questions. One of Davis's first questions was about Tarzan. "Who was that naked guy that got us out?" he asked.

"Don't you remember the English dook that come aboard just before we shoved off?" asked Rosetti. "Well, that's him; and he's one swell guy. An' who do you t'ink he is?"

"You just told us—the RAF colonel."

"He's Tarzan of the Apes."

"Who you think you're kiddin'?"

"On the level," said Bubonovitch. "He's Tarzan all right."

"The old man ain't here," said Douglas. "He wasn't—?"

"No. He's O.K. He got wounded, and they wouldn't let him come along; but he's all right."

The four talked almost constantly all the way back to the guerrilla camp. They had fought together on many missions. They were linked by ties more binding than blood. There existed between them something that cannot be expressed in words, nor would they have thought of trying to. Perhaps Rosetti came nearest it when he slapped Davis on the back and said, "You old sonofabitch!"

27

Two days later, The Foreign Legion, now numbering ten, said goodby to the guerrillas and started on their long march toward a hazy destination. Douglas and Davis took their places in the little company with the easy adaptability of the American soldier. Douglas called it the League of Nations.

At first the two newcomers had been skeptical of the ability of the two women to endure the hardships and the dangers of the almost trackless mountain wilderness that the necessity of avoiding contact with the enemy forced them to traverse. But they soon discovered that they were doing pretty well themselves if they kept up with Corrie and Sarina. There were other surprises, too.

"What's happened to Shrimp?" Davis asked Bubonovitch. "I thought he didn't have time for any fem, but he's always hangin' around that brown gal. Not that I blame him any. She could park her shoes in my locker any time."

"I fear," said Bubonovitch, "that Staff Sergeant Rosetti has fallen with a dull and sickening thud. At first he was coy about it, but now he is absolutely without shame. He drools."

"And the old man," said Davis. "He used to be what you called a misnogomist."

"That isn't exactly what I called it," said Bubonovitch, "but you have the general idea. Maybe he used to be, but he isn't any more."

"Sort of silly," remarked Carter Douglas. "What do old men know about love?"

"You'd be surprised, little one," said Bubonovitch.

The going was cruel. With parangs, they hacked their way through virgin jungle. Deep gorges and mountain torrents blocked their advance with discouraging frequency. Often, the walls of the former dropped sheer for hundreds of feet, offering no hand nor toe hold, necessitating long detours. Scarcely a day passed without rain, blinding, torrential downpours. They marched and slept in wet, soggy clothing. Their shoes and sandals rotted.

Tarzan hunted for them, and those who had not already done so learned to eat their meat raw. He scouted ahead, picking the best routes, alert for enemy outposts or patrols. By night, they slept very close together, a guard constantly posted against the sudden, stealthy attack of tigers. Sometimes muscles flagged, but morale never.

Little Keta did all the scolding and complaining. When Tarzan had gone to the rescue of Davis and Douglas, Keta had been left behind tied to a tree. He had been very indignant about this and had bitten three Dutchmen who had tried to make friends with him. Since then he had usually been left severely alone, consorting only with Tarzan. The only exception was Rosetti. He voluntarily made friends with the little sergeant, often curling up in his arms when the company was not on the march.

"He probably recognizes Shrimp as a kindred spirit," said Bubonovitch, "if not a near relative."

"He t'inks you're one of dem big apes we seen dat he's a-scairt of."

"You refer, I presume, to *Pongo pygmaeus*," said Bubonovitch.

Shrimp registered disgust. "I wisht I was a poet. I'd write a pome."

"About me, darling?"

"You said a mouthful. I got a word wot you rhyme with."

They had stopped for the night earlier than usual because Tarzan had found a large dry cave that would accommodate them all. It had probably been occupied many times before, as there were charred pieces of wood near the entrance and a supply of dry wood stored within it. They had a fire, and they were sitting close to it, absorbing its welcome warmth and drying as much of their clothing as the presence of mixed company permitted them to remove. Which was considerable, as the silly interdictions of false modesty had largely been scrapped long since. They were a company of "fighting men."

Jerry, Bubonovitch, and Rosetti were looking at the rough map that van Prins had drawn for them. "Here's where we crossed over to the east side of the range," said Jerry, pointing, "—just below Alahanpandjang."

"Geeze, wot a moniker fer a burg! Or is it a burg?"

"It's just a dot on a map to me," admitted Jerry.

"Lookit," continued Rosetti. "Here it says dat to where we cross back again to de udder side it is 170 kilometers. Wot's dat in United States?"

"Oh-h, about one hundred and five or six miles. That's in an air line."

"What do you think we're averaging, Jerry?" asked Bubonovitch.

"I doubt if we're making five miles a day in an air line."

"Today," said Bubonovitch, "I doubt that we made five miles on any kind of a line—unless it was up and down."

"Geeze!" said Rosetti. "De Lovely Lady would have got us dere in maybe twenty-twenty-five minutes. Sloggin' along like dog-faces it probably take us a mont'."

"Maybe more," said Jerry.

"Wot t'ell!" said Rosetti. "We're lucky to be alive."

"And the scenery is magnificent," said Bubonovitch. "When we can see it through this soup, it looks mighty nice and peaceful down there."

"It sure does," agreed Rosetti. "It doesn't seem like dere could be a war in pretty country like dat. I don't suppose dey ever had no wars here before."

"That's about all they ever did have until within the

171

last hundred years," said Tak van der Bos. "During all historic times, and probably during all pre-historic times back to the days of *Pithecanthropus erectus* and *Homo Modjokertensis,* all the islands of the East Indies have been almost constantly overrun by warring men—the tribal chiefs, the petty princes, the little kings, the sultans. The Hindus came from India, the Chinese came, the Portuguese, the Spaniards from the Philippines, the English, the Dutch, and now the Japs. They all brought fleets and soldiers and war. In the thirteenth century, Kubla Khan sent a fleet of a thousand ships bearing 200,000 soldiers to punish a king of Java who had arrested the ambassadors of the Great Khan and sent them back to China with mutilated faces.

"We Dutch were often guilty of perpetrating cruelties and atrocities upon the Indonesians; but neither we, nor all the others who came before us, devasted the land and enslaved and massacred its people with the cruel ruthlessness of their own sultans. These drunken, rapacious, licentious creatures massacred their own subjects if it satisfied some capricious whim. They took to themselves the loveliest women, the fairest virgins. One of them had fourteen thousand women in his harem."

"Geeze!" exclaimed Rosetti.

Tak grinned and continued. "And if they were still in power, they would still be doing the same things. Under us Dutch, the Indonesians have known the first freedom from slavery, the first peace, the first prosperity that they have ever known. Give them independence after the Japs are thrown out and in another generation they'll be back where we found them."

"Haven't all peoples a right to independence?" asked Bubonovitch.

"Get a soap box, communist," jeered Rosetti.

"Only those people who have won the right to independence deserve it," said van der Bos. "The first recorded contact with Sumatra was during the reign of Wang Mang, a Chinese emperor of the Han dynasty, just prior to A.D. 23. Indonesian civilization was ancient then. If, with all that background of ancient culture plus the nearly two thousand years before the Dutch completed the conquest of the islands, the people were still held in slavery by tyrant rulers; then they do not deserve what you call independence. Under the Dutch they have every liberty. What more can they ask?"

172

"Just to keep the record straight," said Bubonovitch, with a grin, "I'd like to state that I am not a Communist. I am a good anti-New Deal Republican. But here is my point: I thought that freedom was one of the things we were fighting for."

"Hell," said Jerry. "I don't think any of us know what we are fighting for except to kill Japs, get the war over, and get home. After we have done that, the goddam politicians will mess things all up again."

"And the saber rattlers will start preparing for World War III," said van der Bos.

"I don't think they will rattle their sabers very loudly for a while," said Corrie.

"Just about in time to catch our children in the next war," said Jerry.

There was an embarrassed silence. Jerry suddenly realized the interpretation that might be placed on his innocent remark, and flushed. So did Corrie. Everybody was looking at them, which made it worse.

Finally, van der Bos could no longer restrain his laughter; and they all joined him—even Corrie and Jerry. Sing Tai, who had been busy over a cooking fire, further relieved the tension by repeating a time honored phrase that he had been taught by Rosetti: "Come and get it!"

Wild pig, grouse, fruits, and nuts formed the menu for the meal.

"We sure live high," said Davis.

"De Drake Hotel ain't got nuttin' on us," agreed Rosetti.

"We have the choice of an enormous market, and without ration coupons," said Tarzan.

"And no coin on de line," said Rosetti. "Geeze! dis is de life."

"You gone batty?" inquired Bubonovitch.

"Come back here after the war, sergeant," said van der Bos, "and I'll show you a very different Sumatra."

Bubonovitch shook his head. "If I ever get back to Brooklyn," he said, "I'm going to stay there."

"And me for Texas," said Davis.

"Is Texas a nice state?" asked Corrie.

"Finest state in the Union," Davis assured her.

"But Jerry told me that Oklahoma was the finest state."

"That little Indian reservation?" demanded Davis. "Say! Texas is almost four times as big. She grows more cotton then any other state in the Union. She's first in cattle, sheep, mules. She's got the biggest ranch in the world."

"And the biggest liars," said Douglas. "Now if you really want to know which is the finest state in the Union, I'll tell you. It's California. You just come to the good old San Fernando Valley after the war and you'll never want to live anywhere else."

"We haven't heard from New York State," said Jerry, grinning.

"New Yorkers don't have to boast," said Bubonovitch. "They are not plagued by any inferiority feeling."

"That's going to be a hard one to top," said van der Bos.

"How about your state, Tony?" asked Sarina.

Rosetti thought for a moment. "Well," he said, "Illinois had Public Enemy Number One."

"Every American," said Tarzan, "lives in the finest town in the finest county in the finest state in the finest country in the world—and each one of them believes it. And that is what makes America a great country and is going to keep her so."

"You can say that again," said Davis.

"I have noticed the same thing in your Army," continued the Englishman. "Every soldier is serving in 'the best damned outfit in this man's Army,' and he's willing to fight you about it. That feeling makes for a great Army."

"Well," said Jerry, "we haven't done so bad for a nation of jitterbugging playboys. I guess we surprised the world."

"You certainly have surprised Hitler and Tojo. If you hadn't come in, first with materiel and then with men, the war would be over by now, and Hitler and Tojo would have won it. The World owes you an enormous debt."

"I wonder if it will pay it," said Jerry.

"Probably not," said Tarzan.

28

CORRIE was sitting with her back against the wall of the cave. Jerry came and sat down beside her. Sarina and Rosetti had wandered out of the cave together, arm in arm.

"Shrimp has become absolutely shameless," said Jerry. "Do you know, he really hated women. I think you are the first one he ever tolerated. He is very fond of you now."

"You weren't particularly keen about us yourself," Corrie reminded him.

"Well, you see, I'd never known a Dutch girl."

"That was nice. You're improving. But don't tell me that the finest State in the Union hasn't the finest girls in the world."

"There is only one 'finest girl in the world,' and she is not from Oklahoma."

Corrie laughed. "I know what you're doing?"

"What?"

"You're handing me a line. Isn't that what you Americans call it?"

"I'm not handing you a line, Corrie. You know how I feel about you."

"I'm not a mind reader."

"You're the most wonderful thing that has ever come into my life."

"Now don't tell me that you're making love to me!"

"That is the general idea that I have in mind," said Jerry, "but I guess I'm not so hot at it." He was looking into her eyes. Their misty depths reflected the firelight, but deep below the surface there burned another light, such a light as he had never seen in a woman's eyes before. "God! but you're wonderful," he said.

Corrie smiled. "That's what you said before, but that time you called me a thing. They tell me you're a great pilot, Captain."

He knew she was making fun of him; but he didn't care —he could still see that light in her eyes. "I'm not a great pilot. I'm a great coward. I'm so scared of you that I can't say three little words." Corrie laughed, and she didn't try to help him. "Listen!" he blurted. "How do you think you'll like living in Oklahoma?"

"I shall like it very much," she said.

"Darling!" said Jerry. "I've got to kiss you. I've got to kiss you right now—if it weren't for all these people in here."

"We could go outside," said Corrie.

Sergeant Rosetti held Sarina in his arms. His mouth covered hers. Her arms about his neck pressed him to her fiercely. Corrie and Jerry, coming from the firelight into the night, nearly bumped into them. Then they walked on to a distance.

"I suppose sergeants aren't supposed to be able to teach their captains anything," said Corrie; "but then Sergeant Rosetti is a most unusual sergeant." She was panting a little a moment later when she gently pushed him away. "You misogynists!" she gasped.

Sergeant Bubonovitch was sitting by the fire just inside the mouth of the cave. He had seen Shrimp and Sarina go out arm in arm; then Corrie and Jerry had gone out into the darkness. "I gotta have love," said Bubonovitch, trying to make friends with little Keta. Little Keta bit him. "Nobody loves me," said the sergeant, sorrowfully.

Day after day The Foreign Legion fought with nature for every hard won mile. Often some of them were so exhausted by the time they made camp at the end of a day that they fell asleep without eating. They were too tired even to talk much. But there was no complaining. Corrie and Sarina held their own with the men, who were very proud of them.

"They're lucky they haven't much to carry," remarked Bubonovitch. "Add them together and they wouldn't weigh any more than I do. Maybe they could throw in Shrimp, too. After the war I think I'll hire the three of them and start a flea circus."

"Yeah? Wot you ought to have did," said Shrimp, "is went in de Navy. Den you'd a had a battlewagon to haul you around, you big cow."

"What you should have done; not 'Wot you ought to have did,'" corrected Sarina, who had been laboring to bring Shrimp's English more into line with that which the Catholic sisters had taught her, to the secret amusement of the rest of the company.

Bubonovitch had once said to Jerry: "The granddaughter of a Borneo head hunter teaching an American English! I have seen everything now."

Sarina made no effort to spare Shrimp's feelings. She corrected him in front of everybody, and often in the middle of a sentence. And Shrimp never objected. He just grinned and started over. And he was improving. He had almost stopped saying dis and dat, but did and done still troubled him. Douglas said: "Ain't love wonderful!"

They were nearing Mt. Masoerai, slightly short of which they were to recross the range and start down toward the sea. It had already been a month since they had left the camp of

176

the guerrillas, and they had had only hardships with which to contend. Never had any of them been in great danger, nor had they seen a human being other than themselves. And then, out of a clear sky, disaster struck. Tarzan was captured by the Japs.

They were following a well marked game trail, Tarzan moving through the trees a short distance ahead of them, as usual. Suddenly he came upon a patrol of Japs. They had stopped in the trail to rest. Tarzan moved closer to determine the strength of the detachment. He still had ample time to return and warn his companions and dispose them for whatever might eventuate. Little Keta rode upon his shoulder. Tarzan cautioned him to silence.

The man's attention was riveted upon the Japs. He was unaware of the menace hanging just above him. But Keta saw it and commenced to scream. The Japs looked up. The coils of a huge python encircled the body of the man, galvanizing him to action. His knife flashed. The wounded snake writhed frantically in pain and rage, loosing its hold upon the branch that had supported it, and the two fell into the trail at the feet of the Japs. Keta fled.

The Japs fell upon the snake with bayonets and swords, killing it quickly. And Tarzan was at their mercy. There were too many of them. A dozen bayonets were hovering but inches above his body as he lay in the trail upon his back, helpless.

They took his bow and arrows and knife from him. An officer stepped close and kicked him in the side. "Get up!" he said, in English. He had been a truck gardener in Culver City. He was short and bandy legged. He had buck teeth, and he wore horn rimmed glasses. He might have stepped out of a Lichty cartoon. His men had nicknamed him "Whale" on account of his size. He stood a full five feet six in his sandals.

"Who are you?" demanded the officer.

"Col. John Clayton, Royal Air Force."

"You're an American," said the Jap. Tarzan did not reply. "What are you doing here?" was the next question.

"I have told you all that I am required to tell you, and all that I intend telling you."

"We'll see about that." He turned to a sergeant and gave instructions in Japanese. The sergeant formed the detachment, half in front of and half behind the prisoner, then they started along the trail in the same direction that the Foreign

Legion was travelling. Tarzan saw from indications along the trail that they were retracing their steps from the point at which they had halted. He assumed that whatever their mission had been, they had completed it and were returning to camp.

Little Keta fled through the trees until he sighted the Foreign Legion; then he dropped down and leaped to Shrimp's shoulder. He threw both arms about the man's neck and screamed and jabbered in his ear.

"Something must have happened to Tarzan," said Jerry. "Keta is trying to tell us. He wouldn't leave Tarzan if things were all right with him."

"May I go along the trail and take a look, Cap?" asked Rosetti. "I can travel faster'n the rest of you."

"Yes. Get going. We'll follow."

Shrimp moved at an easy trot. Keta seemed satisfied now; so the man was sure that Jerry had been right. Tarzan was in trouble. Soon Shrimp heard voices ahead and the clank of accouterments. The Japs, apprehending no danger, marched carelessly. Shrimp came closer; and presently, towering above the little pseudo men, he saw the head and shoulders of Tarzan. Tarzan a prisoner of the Japs! It was incredible. Shrimp's heart sank—the heart which, not so long ago, had been filled with hatred of Englishmen.

The news that Rosetti brought back to the others appalled them all. The loss of the Lord of the Jungle would be a sore blow to the little company, but they thought first of Tarzan's safety rather than their own. He had inspired within the breasts of all not only respect and admiration, but real affection as well. That was because, as Shrimp had once confided to Bubonovitch, "De guy's regular."

"How many Japs were there, Rosetti?" asked Jerry.

"About twenty. They's nine of us, Cap'n, which is more than enough."

"You can say that again," said Bubonovitch. "Let's go get him."

"We can't attack them from the rear on this narrow trail without endangering Tarzan. We'll have to trail them until we find a better place to attack," said Jerry.

The trail broke from the forest at the rim of a narrow canyon. Below him, Tarzan saw what was evidently a temporary camp. Half a dozen Jap soldiers guarded some equipment and a few pack animals. The equipment was scat-

178

tered about in a disorderly manner. Some of it, probably perishable provisions, was covered with tarpaulin. There were no shelters. From the appearance of the camp, Tarzan concluded that the officer was inefficient. The less efficient, the easier he would be to escape from.

2nd Lieut. Kenzo Kaneko snapped instructions at a sergeant, and the sergeant bound the prisoner's wrists behind his back. Though the lieutenant may have been inefficient, the sergeant was not. He bound Tarzan's wrists so securely and with so many strands that not even the muscles of the Lord of the Jungle could have freed him.

The sergeant similarly bound the captive's ankles. This done, he pushed and tripped him; so that Tarzan fell to the ground heavily. A horse was brought and the packsaddle adjusted. A line was made fast to the saddle, the other end was then attached to Tarzan's feet. Lieut. Kaneko came and stood over him. He smiled benignly.

"I should hate to have the horse whipped into a run," he said. "It would hurt me, but it would hurt you more."

The horse had been bridled, and a soldier carrying a whip had mounted it. The other soldiers stood about, grinning. They were about to witness an exhibition that would appeal to their sadistic natures.

"If you will answer my questions," continued Kaneko, "the horse will not be whipped, the line will be detached. How many are in your party and where are they?"

Tarzan remained silent. Kaneko no longer smiled. His features became convulsed with rage, or maybe he was only simulating rage in order to frighten his victim. He stepped closer and kicked Tarzan in the side.

"You refuse to answer?" he demanded.

Tarzan returned the Jap's stare. His face registered no emotion, not even the contempt he felt for this grotesque caricature of man. Kaneko's eyes fell beneath those of his prisoner. Something in those eyes frightened him, and that really filled him with genuine rage.

He snapped a command at the man on the horse. The fellow leaned forward and raised his whip. A rifle cracked. The horse reared and toppled backward. Another shot. 2nd Lieut. Kenzo Kaneko screamed and sprawled upon his face. Then came a fusillade of shots. Soldiers fell in rapid succession. Those who could, fled down the valley in utter demoralization as nine riflemen leaped down the steep trail into the camp.

A wounded Jap rose on an elbow and fired at them. Corrie shot him. Then Rosetti and Sarina were among them with bayonet and parang, and there were no more wounded Japs.

Jerry cut Tarzan's bonds. "You arrived just about on time," said Tarzan.

"Just like the cavalry in a horse opera," said Bubonovitch.

"What do you think we'd better do now?" Jerry asked Tarzan.

"We must try to finish off the rest of them. This is evidently just a detachment from a larger force. If any of these fellows get back to that force, we'll be hunted down."

"Have you any idea how many there were?"

"About twenty-five or twenty-six. How many have we killed?"

"Sixteen," said Rosetti. "I just counted 'em."

Tarzan picked up a rifle and took a belt of ammunition from one of the dead Japs. "We'll go back up to the rim of the valley. I'll go ahead through the trees and try to head them off. The rest of you work down along the rim until you can fire down on them."

A half mile below the camp Tarzan overhauled the survivors. There were ten of them. A sergeant had gathered them together, and was evidently exhorting them to return to the fight. As they turned back, none too enthusiastically, Tarzan fired and brought down the sergeant. A private started to run down the valley. Tarzan fired again, and the man dropped. Now, the others realized that the shots had come from farther down the valley. They sought cover from that direction. Tarzan held his fire so as not to reveal his position.

The Foreign Legion, hearing the two shots, knew that Tarzan had contacted the enemy. They pushed forward through the trees at the rim of the valley. Jerry was in the lead. Presently he saw a Jap who had taken cover behind a fallen tree. Then he saw another and another. He pointed them out, and the firing commenced. Tarzan also started firing again.

The Japs, cut off in both directions in the narrow valley, without a leader, lacking sufficient intelligence or initiative to act otherwise, blew themselves up with their own grenades.

"They're damned accommodating," said Douglas.

"Nice little guys," said Davis; "trying to save us ammunition."

"I'm goin' down to help 'em out," said Rosetti, "if any of 'em are left alive." He slid and rolled down the steep cliffside, and Sarina was right behind him.

"There," said Bubonovitch, "is the ideal helpmeet."

29

Six weeks later the Foreign Legion came down to the coast below Moekemoeko. It had been a strenuous six weeks beset by many hazards. Jap positions in increasing numbers had necessitated many long detours. Only the keen sensibility of the Lord of the Jungle, ranging well ahead of the little company, had saved them from disaster on numerous occasions.

There was a Jap anti-aircraft battery about a kilometer up the coast from where they lay concealed. Between them and the battery was a native village. It was in this village that Sarina expected to find friends who could furnish them a boat and provisions.

"If I had a sarong," she said, "I could walk right into the village in daytime, even if Japs were there; but this outfit might arouse suspicion. I'll have to take a chance, and sneak in after dark."

"Perhaps I can get you a sarong," said Tarzan.

"You will go into the village?" asked Sarina.

"Tonight," replied Tarzan.

"You will probably find sarongs that were washed today and hung out to dry."

After dark Tarzan left them. He moved silently through the stagnant air of the humid, equatorial night. In the camp that he had left that was not a camp but a hiding place, the others spoke in whispers. They were oppressed by the heat and the humidity and the constant sense of lurking danger. When they had been in the mountains they had thought their lot rather miserable. Now they recalled with regret the relative coolness of the higher altitudes.

"I have been in the hills for so long," said Corrie, "that I had almost forgotten how frightful the coast climate can be."

"It is rather rotten," agreed van der Bos.

"Dutchmen must be gluttons for punishment," said Bubonovitch, "to colonize a Turkish bath."

"No," said van der Bos; "we are gluttons for profit. This is a very rich part of the world."

"You can have it," said Rosetti. "I don't want no part of it."

"We wish that the rest of the world felt the same way," said van der Bos.

Tarzan swung into a tree that overlooked the village. A full moon lighted the open spaces. The ornate, native houses cast dense shadows. Natives squatted in the moonlight, smoking and gossiping. Three sarongs hung limp in the dead air from a pole across which they had been thrown to dry. Tarzan settled himself to wait until the people had gone into their houses for the night.

After a while a man entered the kampong from the west. In the bright moonlight, Tarzan could see him plainly. He was a Jap officer, the commanding officer of the anti-aircraft battery a short distance away. When the natives saw him they arose and bowed. He approached them with an arrogant swagger, speaking a few words to a young woman. She arose meekly and followed him into the house that he had commandeered for his own use.

When his back was turned the natives made faces at him, and obscene gestures. Tarzan was content. What he had seen assured him that the natives would be friendly to any enemy of the Japs. After a while the natives went into their houses and silence descended upon the kampong.

Tarzan dropped to the ground and moved into the shadow of a building. He stole silently to a point as near to the sarongs as he could get without coming out into the moonlight. He stood there for a moment listening; then he stepped quickly across the moon drenched space and seized a sarong.

Returning, he had almost reached the shadow when a woman stepped from behind the corner of a building. They met face to face in the moonlight. The woman, startled, opened her mouth to scream. Tarzan seized her and clapped a hand over her parted lips. Then he dragged her into the shadow.

"Quiet!" he commanded in Dutch, "and I will not harm you." He hoped that she understood Dutch. She did.

"Who are you?" she asked.

"A friend," he replied.

"Friends do not steal from us," she said.

"I am only borrowing this sarong. It will be returned. You will not tell the Jap about this? He is my enemy, too."

"I will not tell him. We tell them nothing."

"Good," said Tarzan. "The sarong will be returned tomorrow."

He wheeled and was lost in the shadows. The woman shook her head, and climbed the ladder that gave entrance to her house. She told her family of the adventure that had befallen her.

"You will never see the sarong again," said one.

"For the sarong, I do not care," she replied. "It did not belong to me. But I should like to see the wild man again. He was very beautiful."

The following morning, Sarina entered the village. The first woman she met recognized her, and soon she was surrounded by old friends. She warned them away for fear that there might be Japs in the village who would recognize from their greetings that she must be a newcomer and therefore some one to be investigated. Sarina did not wish to be investigated by any Japs. The villagers understood, and returned to their normal activities. Then Sarina sought out Alauddin Shah, the village chief. He seemed glad to see her, and asked her many questions, most of which she avoided answering until she could determine what his relations were with the Japs.

She soon learned that he hated them. Alauddin Shah was a proud old man, a hereditary chief. The Japs had slapped and kicked him and forced him to bow low even to their enlisted men. Satisfied, Sarina told her story, explained what she and her companions needed, and solicited his aid.

"It will be a hazardous journey," he said. "There are many enemy ships in these waters, and it is a long way to Australia. But if you and your friends wish to risk it, I will help you. There is a large proa hidden in the river a few kilometers down the coast from the village. We will provision it for you, but it will take time. We are not regularly watched; because we have given the Japs no trouble, but they are in and out of the kampong almost every day. One officer sleeps here every night. Everything that we do must be done with the utmost caution."

"If you will leave provisions every day in a house near the edge of the kampong, we will come at night and take them to the proa," Sarina told him. "Thus you can escape blame if we are discovered. You can be very much surprised when you discover that some one has come into the village at night and stolen food."

Alauddin Shah smiled. "You are a true daughter of Big Jon," he said.

* * * * * * *

A month passed, a month of narrow escapes from detection, a month of harrowed nerves; but at last the proa was provisioned. And now they waited for a moonless night and a favorable wind. Barbed wire and obstructions at the mouth of the stream had been left in place until the proa was ready. Now they had to be removed—a dangerous job in waters infested with crocodiles. But at last even that was accomplished.

At last it came—N-Night they called it. The tide was right. There was no moon. There was a brisk off-shore wind. Slowly they poled the proa down to the sea. The great lateen sail was hoisted. Close in the lee of the shore it caught little wind, but farther out it bellied to a strong breeze, and the proa gained speed.

While moonless, the night was clear. They set a course due south, the Southern Cross their lodestar. They had fashioned a crude log and log line, and while the knots were running they tried to estimate their speed. Sarina guessed twelve knots. She was not far off.

"If this wind holds," she said, "we'll be well off the southern tip of Nassau Island before 2:00 o'clock tomorrow morning. Then we'll take a southwesterly course. I want to get out of the coastal waters of Sumatra and Java before we swing to the southeast toward Australia. This way we'll give Engano a wide berth. Then there'll be only the Cocos Islands to worry about, as far as land is concerned. I don't know if the Japs have anything on Cocos."

"Are they the same as the Keeling Islands?" asked Jerry.

"Yes, but my father always called them the Cocos Islands because he said Keeling was 'a damned Englishman.'" She laughed, and so did Tarzan.

"Nobody loves an Englishman," he said. "But I'm not so sure that Keeling was an Englishman."

"There's a light at 2:00 o'clock," said Davis.

"Probably on Nassau," said Sarina. "Let's hope so, for if it isn't, it's a ship's light; and we don't want any business with ships."

"I don't think their ships would be showing any lights," said Jerry. "There are too many Allied subs in these waters."

Morning found them in an empty ocean—just a vast, round cauldron of tumbling gray water. The wind had freshened, and great seas were running. S/Sgt. Rosetti was sick. Between spasms he remarked, "I got a half-wit cousin. He joined the Navy." After a while he said, "It won't be long now. This crate won't stand much more, and it can't come too soon to suit me. This is the first time in my life I ever wanted to die." Then he leaned over the rail and heaved again.

"Cheer up, Shrimp," said Bubonovitch. "It won't be long now before we go ashore on Australia—maybe only a month or so."

"Geeze!" groaned Rosetti.

"You will get over being sick pretty soon, Tony," said Sarina.

"Some admirals always get sick when they first go to sea after shore duty," said Tarzan.

"I don't want to be an admiral. I joins up for air, and what do I get? For couple or three months I been a doughboy; now I'm a gob. Geeze!" He leaned over the rail again.

"Poor Tony," said Sarina.

The long days passed. The wind veered into the southeast. The southeast trade wind that would blow for ten months had started. Sarina took long tacks, first to starboard and then to port. It was slow going, but their luck had held. They were well past the Keeling Islands now, and no sign of enemy shipping.

Douglas, who had been standing his trick as lookout, had come aft. "It's an awful lot of water," he said. "Flying it, it seems terrible big—the Pacific, I mean; but down here on the surface it seems like there isn't anything in the world but water; and this is only the Indian Ocean, which ain't a drop in the bucket alongside the Pacific. It makes you feel pretty small and insignificant."

"There's sure a lot of water in the world," agreed van der Bos.

"Three quarters of the whole surface of the Earth is water," said Corrie.

"And the Pacific has a greater area than all the land surfaces of the Earth combined," said Jerry.

"If I owned it," said Rosetti, "I'd trade the whole damn works for any old street corner in Chi."

"What I don't like about it," said Douglas, "is the total absence of scenery. Now, in California——"

"He's off again," said Bubonovitch.

"But he's got something just the same," said Davis. "Gawd! how I'd like to see a cow—just one measly little cow deep in the heart of Texas."

"I'll settle for land, any old land, right now," said Rosetti. "Even Brooklyn would look good. I might even settle down there. I'm fed up on travellin'."

"Travel is broadening, Shrimp," said Bubonovitch. "Just look what it's done for you. You like a Britisher, you love a dame, and you have learned to speak fairly intelligible English, thanks to Sarina."

"I ain't getting broadened much lately," objected Rosetti. "We ain't seen nothing but water for weeks. I'd like to see something else."

"Smoke at eleven o'clock!" called Jerry, who had gone forward as lookout. Sarina smiled. The airmen's method of indicating direction always amused her, but she had to admit that it was practical.

Everybody looked in the direction indicated where a black smudge was showing just above the horizon.

"Maybe you're going to see something beside water now, Shrimp," said Davis. "Your wish was granted in a hurry."

"That must be a ship," called Jerry, "and I think we'd better hightail it out of here."

"Toward five o'clock?" asked Sarina.

"Keerect," said Jerry, "and pronto."

They came about and sailed before the wind in a northwesterly direction, every eye on that ominous black smudge. "It might be British," said Corrie, hopefully.

"It might be," agreed Tak, "but we can't take any chances. It might just as well be Jap."

For what seemed a long time there was no noticeable change in the appearance of the thing they watched so fearfully; then Tarzan's keen eyes discerned the superstructure of a ship rising above the horizon. He watched closely for a few minutes. "It is going to cut right across our course," he said. "It will pass astern, but they're bound to sight us."

"If it's Jap," said Sarina, "it's bound for Sumatra or Java. Our only chance is to hold this course and pray—pray for wind and more wind. If it's one of those little Jap merchant ships, we can outrun it if the wind picks up. Or if we can just hold our lead until after dark, we can get away."

The proa seemed never to have moved more slowly. Straining eyes watched the menace grow larger, as the hull of a ship climbed over the rim of the world. "It's like a bad dream," said Corrie, "where something horrible is chasing you, and you can't move. And the wind is dying."

"You guys ain't prayin' hard enough," said Rosetti.

"All I can remember," said Davis, "is 'now I lay me down to sleep,' and I can't remember all of that."

A sudden gust of wind bellied the great sail, and the speed of the proa increased noticeably. "Somebody hit the jack pot," said Douglas.

But the strange ship continued to gain on them. "She's changed course," said Tarzan. "She's heading for us." A moment later he said, "I can see her colors now. She's a Jap all right."

"I should have gone to church like Mom always wanted me to," said Davis. "I might have learned some good prayers. But if I can't pray so good," he said a moment later, "I sure can shoot good." He picked up his rifle and slipped a clip into the magazine.

"We can all shoot good," said Jerry, "but we can't sink a ship with what we got to shoot with."

"That's a small, armed merchantman," said Tarzan. "She probably carries 20 mm anti-aircraft guns and .30 caliber machine guns."

"I guess we're out gunned," said Bubonovitch, with a wry grin.

"The effective range of the 20s is only about 1200 yards," said Jerry. "These pop guns will do better than that. We ought to be able to get a few Nips before they finish us off—

187

that is if you folks want to fight." He looked around at them. "We can surrender, or we can fight. What do you say?"

"I say fight," said Rosetti.

"Think it over carefully," admonished Jerry. "If we put up a fight, we shall all be killed."

"I don't intend to let those yellow sonsabitches knock me around again," said Bubonovitch. "If the rest of you don't want to fight, I won't either; but I won't be taken alive."

"Neither shall I," said Corrie. "How do you feel about it, Jerry?"

"Fight, of course." He looked at Tarzan. "And you, Colonel?"

Tarzan smiled at him. "What do you think, Captain?"

"Does anyone object to fighting rather than surrendering?" No one did. "Then we'd better check our rifles and load 'em. And may I say in conclusion, it's been nice knowing you."

"That sounds terribly final," said Corrie, "even if you did mean it for a joke."

"I'm afraid it is—final and no joke."

The merchantman was closing up on them rapidly now, for after that one fitful gust the wind had slackened to a breeze that didn't even fill the great triangular sail of the proa.

"We've been mighty lucky for a long time," said Tak. "According to the law of chance, it should be about time for our luck to run out."

There was a red flash aboard the Jap, followed by a puff of smoke. A moment later a shell burst far short of them.

"Lady Luck is getting ready to hit the breeze," said Rosetti.

30

"BEAUTIFUL gunnery!" said Bubonovitch. "The poor sap doesn't even know the range of his gun."

"Itchy fingers probably," said Douglas.

"I doubt that the little admirals put their top gunnery officers aboard little merchantmen," said Jerry; "so maybe our luck is holding."

The proa was barely making headway now, a̶ ̶ ̶ ̶
fell on long swells. The forefoot of the onco̶ ̶ ̶
plowed through the deep blue of the ocean, turning u̶ ̶ ̶
water, as the mold board of a plow turns up the rich lo̶ ̶ ̶
a field.

Again the Jap fired. This shell fell wide, but not so short.
Jerry and Corrie were sitting close together, one of his hands
covering one of hers. "I guess van Prins was right," said
Jerry. "He said we were crazy. I shouldn't have brought you
along, darling."

"I wouldn't have it otherwise," said Corrie. "We've had this
much time together, that we wouldn't have had if I hadn't
come with you. I've never had a chance to say 'for better or
for worse,' but it has been in my heart always."

He leaned closer to her. "Do you, Corrie, take this man
to be your wedded husband?"

"I do," said Corrie, very softly. "Do you, Jerry, take this
woman to be your wedded wife, to cherish and protect until
death do you part?"

"I do," said Jerry, a little huskily. He slipped the class
ring from his finger and on to Corrie's ring finger. "With
this ring I do thee wed, and with all my worldly goods en-
dow." Then he kissed her.

"I think," said Corrie, "that as far as the service is concerned our memories were a little lame; but we had the
general idea at least. And I feel very much married, sweetheart."

A near miss deluged them with water. They did not seem
to notice it.

"My wife," said Jerry. "So young, so beautiful."

" 'Wife!'," repeated Corrie.

"The guy's gettin' closer," said Rosetti.

The fin of a shark cut the water between the proa and the
Jap. Little Keta watched it, fortunately unaware of what it
might portend. Tarzan raised the sights on his rifle and fired
at the figures lining the rail of the Jap. The others followed
his example, and presently ten rifles were blazing away. If
they accomplished nothing else, they emptied the rail of
sightseers and caused much confusion aboard the merchantman. Yes, they accomplished one more thing: They spurred
the anti-aircraft gunners into frenzied activity. Shell bursts
dotted the ocean.

...eir ammo holds out," said Rosetti, "they got to hit , just accidentally. Geeze! what lousy shootin'!"

At last it came, as they knew it must—a direct hit. Jerry saw half of Sing Tai's body hurled fifty feet into the air. Tak van der Bos's right leg was torn off. The entire company was thrown into the ocean; then the Jap moved in and commenced to machine gun them as they swam about or clung to pieces of the wreckage. The aim of the gunners was execrable, but again they knew that this was the end of the Foreign Legion—that eventually some of those hundreds of whining bullets would find them all.

Bubonovitch and Douglas were holding up van der Bos, who had fainted. Jerry was trying to keep between Corrie and the machine guns. Suddenly something commenced to drag van der Bos down. One of Bubonovitch's feet struck a solid body moving beneath. "Migawd!" he yelled. "A shark's got Tak." Bullets were ricocheting off the water all around them.

Tarzan, who had been thrown some distance by the shell burst, was swimming toward Bubonovitch and Douglas when he heard the former's warning. Diving quickly beneath the surface, he drew his knife. A few swift, strong strokes brought him close to the shark. A mighty surge of his knife arm ripped open the belly of the huge fish, disemboweling it. It released its hold on van der Bos and turned on Tarzan, but the man eluded its jaws and struck again and again with his knife.

The water was red with blood as another shark darted in and attacked its fellow. The first shark swam sluggishly away while the other bit and tore at it. For the moment the survivors were freed from one menace, but the bullets still pinged close.

With Tarzan's help, Bubonovitch and Douglas got van der Bos to a large piece of wreckage—one of the outrigger floats. Tarzan tore a strip from what remained of van der Bos's trousers, and while he and Douglas held the man on the float, Bubonovitch applied a tourniquet. Tak still breathed, but fortunately he was unconscious.

Bubonovitch shook his head. "He ain't got a chance," he said. "But then, neither have we."

"The sharks are going to have plenty good feeding today," said Douglas.

They were all looking at the Jap ship. Again the rail was

lined with bandy legged little men. Some of them were firing pistols at the people in the water. Keta, perched on a piece of wreckage, scolded and threatened.

There was a terrific detonation. A great fan shaped burst of flame shot hundreds of feet into the air from amidships of the merchantman, and a pillar of smoke rose hundreds of feet higher. A second explosion followed and the ship broke in two, the bow hurled almost clear of the water. The two halves sunk almost immediately, leaving a few scorched and screaming creatures struggling in burning oil.

For a few moments the survivors of the proa looked on in stunned silence, which was broken by Rosetti. "I knew She'd hear me," he said. "She ain't ever failed me yet."

"She'll have to pull a real miracle yet to get us out of the middle of the Indian Ocean before we drown or the sharks get us," said Jerry.

"Pray like hell, Shrimp," said Bubonovitch.

"Don't think I ain't, brother," said Rosetti.

"Look! Look!" shouted Corrie, pointing.

Three hundred yards beyond the burning oil a submarine was surfacing. The Union Jack was painted on the side of its conning tower.

"There's your miracle, Cap'n," said Rosetti. "She ain't ever failed me yet. I mean in a real pinch."

"What do you think of the British now, sergeant?" asked Tarzan, smiling.

"I love 'em," said Rosetti.

The sub circled to windward of the burning oil and drew alongside the wreckage of the proa. The hatch spewed men to haul the castaways aboard. Tarzan and Bubonovitch passed van der Bos up first. He died as they laid him gently on the deck.

Corrie and Sarina followed, and then the men. Lt. Cmdr. Bolton, skipper of the sub, was full of amazement and questions. Corrie knelt beside van der Bos's body, trying to hold back the teers. Jerry joined her.

"Poor Tak," she said.

They did not take him below. He was buried at sea, Bolton reading the burial service. Then they all went below for dry clothing and hot coffee, and presently the sorrow and depression seemed less, for they were all young and they had all seen much of death.

When Bolton heard their story, he said, "Well, you have

191

certainly played in luck from the start; but my happening to be right where I was when you needed me is little short of a miracle."

"It hasn't been luck, sir," said Rosetti. "It's been Holy Mary, Mother of Jesus from start to finish, including the miracle."

"I can well believe it," said Bolton, "for none of you has any business being alive now, by all the laws of chance. Nothing but divine intervention could have preserved you. It even arranged that I saved my last two fish for that Jap. You really should all be dead."

"Mary certainly helped in a pinch," said Jerry, "but if Tarzan hadn't been on the job all the time, pinch hitting for her, we'd have been sunk months ago."

"Well," said Bolton, "I think you won't have to call on either Mary or Tarzan from now on. I'm ordered to Sydney, and it won't be so long now before you can sit down in Ushers Hotel with a steak and kidney pie in front of you."

"And drink warm beer," said Bubonovitch.

Later that evening Jerry and Rosetti approached Bolton. "Captain," said the former, "are you authorized to perform marriage ceremonies at sea?"

"I certainly am."

"Then you got two jobs right now, skipper," said Rosetti.